The Mysteries of Tomorrow
Volume 2:
The World of the Damned

BY THE SAME AUTHORS

Paul Féval, fils. *Felifax, The Tiger-Man*

The Mysteries of Tomorrow
Volume 2:
The World of the Damned

by

Paul Féval, *fils* & H.-J. Magog

Translated by

Brian Stableford

A Black Coat Press Book

Visit our website at www.blackcoatpress.com

ISBN 978-1-61227-948-0. First Printing. April 2020. Published by Black Coat Press, an imprint of Hollywood Comics.com, LLC, P.O. Box 17270, Encino, CA 91416.

The Story So Far

This five-volume saga (of which this is the second), purporting to chronicle the early years of the 21st century, takes place in a quasi-utopia-like Earth, where war no longer exists, poverty has been banished, men no longer consume meat, and, thanks to the genius of master scientist Oronius, humanity has mastered natural forces.

However, there exists a snake in this garden of Eden: Oronius' former colleague Otto Hentzen, a mad scientist who has allied himself with the beautiful, deadly enchantress Yogha. From their impregnable citadel located atop Mount Everest, they wish to crush the world and rule it.

In our first volume, *The Fiancés of the Year 2000*,[1] Hentzen challenges Oronius' power by creating an *überstorm* above Paris, but the master scientist easily thwarts his rival. Then the villains kidnap Cyprienne, Oronius' own daughter, and her maid Turlurette. Hentzen also sends one of Oronius' former disgruntled students, Jarrousse, to kill the master scientist, which he achieves by causing an explosion that destroys Oronius' Villa in Belleville (a suburb of Paris).

Meanwhile, Oronius' pupil, Jean Chapuis, ably assisted by his mechanic Victor Laridon, and their African manservant, Julep, has gone after the kidnappers. They invade Hentzen's citadel. After various exploits, Jean learns that Yogha is secretly in love with him. They eventually succeed in blowing the fortress– and the villains – up.

---

[1] ISBN 978-1-61227-945-9.

Chapter One
THE GULF

"A true mirror! If it were frozen, it would be a fine skating-rink. Too bad the weather isn't icy! But no!"

Leaning over the sea, pronouncing those words with a hint of regret, the individual translating his impressions of the voyage thus far in a loud voice mopped his brow,

The cosmopolitan group surrounding him nodded assent

A cosmopolitan group, we said. It was, in fact, composed of a young Chinese woman, a singular African and a gracious specimen of the white race.

The Chinese woman was named Mandarinette. We shall soon specify the bizarre circumstances in which she had been introduced into the society.

The African was called Julep; his body, once uniformly black, like that of an honest descendant of Ham, presented strange variations which made his skin a color chart of all hues. He owed that eccentric envelope not to superficial dyes but simply to experiments in skin discoloration carried out on him by his master, the greatest scientist of the epoch. Let us note in addition that Julep was as proud as can be of his polychromy.

The young white woman responded to the casual nickname of Turlurette. She had a piquant physiognomy, in the middle of which projected the amusingly turned-up little nose of an authentic Parisienne. By that token she proved herself to be a compatriot of the speaker who would have preferred the temperature to be a little less high.

In addition, as a promise of marriage had been made between Mademoiselle Turlurette and Monsieur Victor Laridon, the advocate of coolness, no one contested that the couple must be very well matched.

All of them, on that sultry May afternoon, were leaning over the side of the yacht *La Stella,* whose prow was cleaving through the mirror of the Indian Ocean at a rapid speed.

What was the vessel's destination? Why had equipment and provisions sufficient for a distant expedition been stowed in its holds? That was the secret of the owners of the yacht, two young people, also fiancés, who were on the bridge chatting in low voices not far from the group formed by the quartet that we have just described.

Next to them were agitating two delightful little papillon dogs, Pipigg and Kukuss.

To tell the truth, neither Cyprienne Oronius nor Jean Chapuis, her associate and fiancé, could have explained in a satisfactory fashion the mysterious conditions in which *La Stella* was navigating.

Every morning and every evening the route was indicated by them to the captain, but with regard to the next day's, they would only have been able to respond with sincerity that they had no knowledge of it. What, then, inspired them? By what means did that indication reach them? The ship's telegraphist swore to his great gods that it was not, at any rate, via the wireless. But, the crew being royally paid, no one worried or protested and the vessel pursued its route placidly, guided by the mysterious will.

What the young couple would have been able to respond to those astonished by that cruise, so contrary to custom, was that they were obeying an imperious sentiment. For them, the bizarre voyage that was drawing them toward the unknown was a duty.

We shall have occasion before long to clarify that mystery and to reveal the powerful reasons that had impelled the future household to embark with the unique escort of the mechanic Laridon, Master Julep and Cyprienne Oronius' two chambermaids. For the moment, let us only specify that the daughter of the greatest scientist of the twenty-first century—the illustrious Oronius, who had disappeared in a catastrophe that had nearly annihilated Paris and had turned the heights of

Belleville into the crater of a volcano—was a young woman of rare beauty.

That beauty, which had not yet attained its full bloom, made Cyprienne Oronius' nineteen years a veritable enchantment. Tall, slim and svelte, with serpentine contours that the light fabric of her fashionable tunic allowed to be divined, she combined all the elegances of a virgin and al the seductions of a woman. Above a high forehead, as that of a person given to study ought to be, was a rich efflorescence of golden threads, which streamed over the whiteness of her neck and her blonde shoulders. She had breeding, and eyes of an ultramarine blue, which knew how to smile and command, and must have cast trouble into the hearts of all those on which they fixed.

Jean Chapuis, her fiancé, a young engineer of great merit, was twenty-eight, also handsome, with an energetic and masculine beauty, truly worthy of being associated with Cyprienne. Besides which, in addition to the bonds of the heart, were those two elite individuals not attached to one another by an anguishing and tragic past? Had they not undergone, in the company of their faithful companions Laridon and the soubrette Turlurette, the most extraordinary adventures? Was not the presence in their company of the young Chinese woman Mandarinette a kind of living souvenir of that?

Days of living together had brought people closer and created indissoluble bonds by teaching them to know one another and esteem one another. Jean Chapuis and Cyprienne had been able to measure the devotion of Laridon and Turlurette, and they were not unaware that, in their example, Mandarinette rivaled Master Julep in zeal.

Laridon, in particular, claimed in all circumstances, in tirades somewhat excessively ornamented with argot, that he was ready to throw himself into fire for his employers. An empty boast? Well, no. Was he not in the process of proving that that was not a simple metaphor, since, for love of them, he was presently exposing himself to a tropical sun with which he was *fed up*, to use his own picturesque expression. Loquacity not being his least fault, he could not help cursing and evoking the coolness of skating-rinks.

Fundamentally, and in spite of the unknown toward which he knew he was being borne by the ship's course, he was not far from finding the crossing too calm and almost monotonous.

"Nix on adventures!" he sighed, leaning over the oil-smooth sea whose surface reflected his sympathetic features ironically. "I miss them. That's what comes of bad habits! We've seen so many that I can no longer tolerate homely life. You can laugh, dainty Turlurette, but that's the way it is. I'm intoxicated, as they say. I need my little dose of local upheaval… even of catastrophic novelties."

As his audience protested, sketching objections, he continued in a conciliatory tone: "In sum, anyway, something to shake things up and permit me to exhibit my modest talents. I like to earn the pills I swallow, I do!"

By the word "pills" the worthy mechanic meant the alimentary concentrates that had replaced for humans the indigestible nutriments of olden days.

It is always temeritous to challenge fate. Victor Laridon was about to make an immediate experiment.

The sea, so calm and thus far of a truly exemplary docility, suddenly became agitated, swelling and lifting the yacht to the summit of a gigantic mountain of water.

Turlurette and Mandarinette uttered cries of fright, and Julep's wide eyes started rolling fearfully, white in their dark orbits.

The intrepid Laridon welcomed that manifestation by clapping his hands. "Nice!" he cried. "Here comes a roller-coaster. We're going for a ride. Hold on tight, Turlurette!" And he put his arm round the young woman's waist, while the negro and the Chinese woman, obedient to a sudden inspiration, drew closer together.

At the same time, Cyprienne and Jean Chapuis exchanged glances.

"That phenomenon?" murmured the engineer.

"Can it be the expected summons?"

The young woman did not have time to say anymore. A formidable vortex suddenly and silently rose up from the ocean depths.

In itself and in that region, the phenomenon was not surprising, for the Indian Ocean, with its monsoons, accompanied by periodic cyclones and whirlwinds, has a very bad reputation; mariners distrust its treacheries, with good reason. But the brutal and entirely spontaneous fashion in which the sea had just become irritated and tossed the ship on its undulating surface was nevertheless disquieting, and presented a troubling, almost supernatural character.

Certainly, the engineer Jean Chapuis could not be unaware of the existence of submarine volcanoes, certain eruptions of which are no less terrible than those of their cousins on the surface; he also knew that the convulsions of the terrestrial crust, in certain parts covered by water, can give birth to frightful tidal waves. He had heard mention via Oronius of the one that had been provoked in the Sunda archipelago two centuries before by the terrible explosion of Krakatoa.

The one produced as the yacht was passing, however, surpassed in violence and rapidity all those of which human memory had been able to preserve the memory. At the same time as a column of water, caught by the tornado, rose up in a spiral all the way to the clouds, the basal layer of which was stretched by suction as if to join it, the Ocean seemed to open up. And it did in fact, open up, in the fashion of a gigantic whirlpool, hollowing out its funnel as he Red Sea had once hollowed out in order to permit the passage of the Hebrews.

The mass of water drawn back into high walls opened to such a depth that the rocky bed became perceptible.

"Land ho!" the joker Laridon tried to cry—but his voice caught in his throat. The situation immediately became grave enough to take away any desire to joke.

Balanced on the crest of the gigantic wave that had lifted it up, *La Stella* was suddenly projected down the liquid slope and slid toward the bottom of the gulf with a prodigious velocity, which cut off the respiration of the passengers clinging to the bulwarks and the rigging.

The fall was rapid and brief, scarcely lasting a few seconds. Everyone—owners, mariners, passengers and servants—hardly had time to exchange terrified glances. Then Cyprienne, very pale, felt her hands, disobedient to her will, become detached from the rail to which, instinctively, they had clung hard.

"Jean!" she screamed, bewildered by an inexpressible aguish.

The engineer's right arm was already around her waist. Was he trying to retain Cyprienne or did he want to follow her? Was he too yielding to the strange force that was snatching the young woman away from her support?

Together, the fiancés lost their balance, were thrown overboard, and disappeared into the turbulent water.

And it was at that moment that the prodigy was produced that marked the beginning of this unforgettable adventure.

Afterwards, Jean Chapuis, was unable to specify the fashion in which it happened; he saw nothing, or almost nothing, of the fall into the abyss; he scarcely retained the memory of a long slide along a wall of water, a vertiginous glissade that obliged him to close his eyes, like Cyprienne, only to open them again when the fall stopped and he felt firm ground beneath his feet.

Astonished to be still alive, he opened his eyes. Then he was able to observe, not without amazement, that he had arrived, safe and sound, at the bottom of the gulf, still holding tight against him the friend of his heart, similarly unhurt. He paraded a bewildered gaze around him, unable to understand how he could have survived that formidable fall, and why the gulf had not yet closed again to engulf them.

"It's a miracle, Jean," sighed Cyprienne's voice, close by.

"Name of a sugar-plum, talk about a toboggan ride!" riposted another voice, that one no more emotional than if it were a matter of a fairground attraction.

Mechanically, the engineer turned his head, and his amazement increased as he discovered his mechanic, Julep and the two soubrettes a few paces away, projected out of the ship like him and reposing, bewildered, on the damp sand of the sea-bed. Shaking himself like a barbet, Laridon had lost none of his verve.

The yacht, carried away by another current, had disappeared at the top of the liquid mountain; but it was to be presumed that it had not escaped unscathed from the adventure, and that it had been smashed or disemboweled, for a multitude of pieces of wreckage launched over the liquid slope, were reaching the bottom of the abyss in their turn.

The evidence of the catastrophe that must have annihilated their ship scarcely struck the escapees; the sentiment of the danger suspended over their heads took possession of all their faculties.

In fact, could they be under any illusion? Inexplicably opened, the damp gulf was about to close again. The ocean bed would be their tomb. It was only a question of seconds. No rescue was possible; no hope was permitted by the situation, which had no other issue but death.

Yes, it was death, terrifying death under the shroud of the ocean. Would it not have been better to have shared the fate of the crew of the yacht, who must at least have been spared the throes of agony?

The temporary escapees scarcely had the leisure to ask themselves that question. They did not even think of communicating their impressions to one another—but their gazes spoke for them. Horrified, they contemplated the strange décor that surrounded them: the ground that the unprecedented cataclysm revealed to their eyes.

How long did they stare at that hallucinatory spectacle? It was doubtless only a few seconds, for the liquid mass looming up like a rearing horse and oscillating, as if it were struggling against an invisible force opposed to its fall, could not leave the gulf whose secret it had betrayed open for long—but there are seconds that seem to last for centuries; the ones lived by the castaways on the ocean bed in that tragic circumstance were certainly among them. The thoughts must have been upset in their heads with a chaotic precipitation, which multiplied tenfold the consciousness of the immensity of the peril to which they seemed consecrated.

Fallen to the bottom of that well, which was about to be filled in by the mass of the momentarily-parted waters, how could they retain the hope of ever returning to the surface? How could they admit the possibility of being spared for a second time? Some miracles are not renewable, and it was surely one of those that had kept the alive in the course of the frightful descent.

Wanting to be united in death as they had wished to be for life, Jean and Cyprienne, clinging to one another, their fingers enlaced, awaited the fatal second.

But now, suddenly, they felt themselves seized and dragged away, while Laridon's voice resounded, troubling the solemn silence.

"Don't stay there, Boss! Nor you, Mamzelle Cyprienne! Necessary not to wait for the shower if one can do otherwise. Nothing says that the hour to kick the bucket is about to sound... there's a shelter! Look!"

And the astonishing Parisian, who prided himself on never having his eyes in his pocket, designated, a few paces away from the group, a hole in the rock, toward which his gaze had been invincibly attracted. Chance? The mysterious intervention of an occult protection? They would not take long to find out.

The hole gaping in the midst of a chaos of rock, probably upset by the seismic shock that had lifted up the submarine depths, appeared to plunge obliquely into the ground.

Jean Chapuis did not have time to smile at Laridon's naivety. Nor did he have time to say: "What's the point? Do you imagine that the closing ocean won't come to reoccupy that tiny space and drown us in the depths of your pretended refuge? There's no hiding-place from the death that is lying in wait for us."

No, he did not have time to express that thought. Suddenly sharing the mechanic's hope, Cyprienne shoved her fiancé into the opening; and they all followed, while Laridon repeated, with a slight tremor of emotion in his voice: "What are we risking? Necessary to try! If you knew, M'sieur Jean, what I seemed to see! It's enough to make me wonder whether I'm not in the process of going loopy!"

A terrible rumble covered his voice. Joining up and collapsing upon one another, the masses of water drawn up facing one another fell back into the well that they had hollowed out, and filled it in.

Having opened momentarily, the ocean closed again over its inviolable empire.

Chapter Two
AN ORDER FROM THE BEYOND

A few months earlier, the passengers of the yacht *La Stella* had been mixed up in an adventure no less extraordinary. For the sake of clarifying what is to follow, it is necessary for us to summarize it.

A rivalry of scientists had brought into conflict the illustrious Master Oronius, the glory of the twenty-first century and the father of the exquisite Cyprienne, and one of those evil geniuses who turn against humankind the marvelous intelligence with which Destiny has gratified them.

Otto Hantzen—that was the name of the baleful individual in question—thanks to the support of a Hindu princess, Yogha, something of a magicienne, because she was a pupil of the sacred sect of Yoghis, had been able to accumulate at an unknown point of the globe destructive forces that would permit them to annihilate or enslave his contemporaries. Inspired by his ally, Yogha, who was jealous of Cyprienne, Hantzen had abducted the latter while attacking Paris scientifically. At the same time, one of his spies, a man named Jarrousse, sent by him to discover the secret of Oronius' experiments, had come to grips with Bambo, a formidable ape, the Master's favorite, and had provoked an explosion by breaking, in the course of the struggle, a flask of nitrocolle, a new explosive of unsuspected power.

That explosion had transformed the heights of Belleville into an immense crater in which Oronius' Villa had been engulfed, with its owner, along with the two combatants, the man and the ape, the imprudent cause of the catastrophe.

The illustrious Master could therefore be presumed to be dead. By virtue of that fact, Hantzen, almost victorious after the first skirmish, was able to put into execution his project to destroy and reconstruct the word to his whim, since he did not have to fear his powerful rival any longer. He took prisoner in his flying machine, the *Spherus*, the daughter of Oronius, her maidservant Turlurette, the engineer Jean Chapuis and Cyprienne's two little dogs, Pipigg and Kukuss. But he had counted without the intelligent tenacity of the Parisian Victor Laridon and the irrational devotion of their African manservant Julep; manning the Halcyon-Car, they had contrived to pursue the *Spherus* all the way to Mont Everest, the highest peak in the world, in the flanks and on the summit of which Hantzen had installed his fortress in a metallic tower.

We shall not detail all the ruses employed by Laridon to penetrate that mysterious fortress. He had succeeded, and had been able to liberate successively all those dear to his heart, as well as Mandarinette, who had been unusually mingled with the lot of his friends.

Before fleeing Mount Everest, Jean Chapuis had blown up the metallic tower and its occupants. Delivered from Hantzen and Yogha, all aboard the Halcyon-Car, they had been able to resume the route to Paris.

In the course of that journey, when Cyprienne, learning of the death of her father, had begun to sob, a supernatural voice arriving as if via waves had cried: "*One only mourns the dead!*"

Was that an illusion of their overstretched minds? Perhaps. At any rate, Cyprienne had not been able to reconcile herself to the idea that stupid death had been able to triumph over the genius of Oronius. It seemed to her that the voice had been his, and that he had been able to escape the destructive power.

No, Oronius could not be dead!

In those conditions, and to respond to an old desire formulated by her father, she had asked her fiancé to postpone their marriage until the scientist's return.

His return from where? Since the Magical Villa had been engulfed in the Belleville volcano, and a skeleton discovered in the ashes had been given a national funeral! It was crazy! For what was Cyprienne hoping? What did she expect? She dared not specify it, and when the engineer interrogated her, tenderly and anxiously, she sighed without responding.

But one day, a stupefying rumor had spread through spiritist milieux, and had soon overflowed that circle. The news had reached the ears of Jean Chapuis and Cyprienne. A medium claimed to be in communication with the beyond. The particular character of the responses received made that communication rather troubling.

To the ordinary question, "Who are you?" the spirit had replied: "I am a dead man who is not dead."

"What do you desire?"

"To put humans on their guard against the scourge that is fermenting in the shadows."

"What is that scourge?"

"I cannot be more precise yet. Mistrust whatever might fall from the sky."

Then, pressed by questions, it had pronounced two names that seemed incomprehensible: Yogha and Hantzen.

When Cyprienne Oronius had cognizance of those sibylline responses, she gave evidence of an extraordinary emotion. Jean Chapuis could not help sharing her anguish.

"We need to see this medium," she said, feverishly. "I want to make contact with that spirit, for we alone can understand its words."

To that desire her fiancé could only acquiesce. They went to see the medium.

In the domicile of the latter, obedient to a kind of internal appeal, the young woman asked to be alone with the intermediary of the spirits.

The conversation was brief. When the young woman rejoined her fiancé a quarter of an hour later, she was frightfully pale.

"If you love me, my dear Jean, you will prepare everything in accordance with my indications for a voyage that we need to undertake without delay."

"You desire is an order, my dear Cyprienne. May I ask where we're going?"

She plunged her gaze into the engineer's eyes and uttered the enigmatic words: "To meet my father, whom I've just seen." Immediately collecting herself, she explained: "It was, you'll divine, a manifestation of the spiritist phenomenon known as a materialization. Mine presents the marvelous particularity that Oronius affirms that he isn't dead. In any case, I had already sensed that."

"You had already...?"

"Yes. Consult your memories. When that voice rocked our Halcyon, crying: '*One only mourns the dead.*'"

"Yes, that's true," Jean Chapuis exclaimed. "Where are we going, then?"

"I don't know. Although he thinks he has the ability to draw us to him, he doesn't have the possibility of revealing his retreat to us. Or perhaps he fears revealing it at the same time to enemies who, for the moment, are outside humanity."

"Is it a matter of Yogha and Hantzen?" asked the engineer, sharply.

"Shh!" said Cyprienne. "We ought not to pronounce any names. It's even necessary to abstain from thinking about it and questioning. Let's only obey the inspirations that will be transmitted to me mentally at the desired moments."

Those words left the young man facing a double problem. Did the Master he had believed to be dead still exist? In the improbable case that he might, was it possible to rejoin him in the place inaccessible to humans that Cyprienne's allusions enabled him to suspect?

The perspective opened up by a part of the strange communication was terrible. If it really was the voice of Oronius that had made itself heard via the intermediary of the medium, what meaning was it necessary to give to its warning? Fear Yogha and Hantzen, it had said.

Was Jean Chapuis mistaken, then, in thinking that he had rid the world of those two monsters?

Not being able to respond to such questions, he had resolved to follow point by point the suggestions of his fiancée. And it was thus that he had decided upon and undertaken the expedition of *La Stella*—the expedition that had just ended with their fall to the ocean bed, momentarily laid dry.

Chapter Three
IN THE SUBMARINE TOMB

As soon as they were in the submarine grotto, the escapees from *La Stella* expected with an understandable fear the avalanche of the returning water. Their fear was not justified yet. The liquid mountain did not penetrate after them into the gallery because, in its fall, it came to collide with a giant polyp whose branches, enormous but sensitive, had been tightly applied to the opening, obstructing it completely.

"Shall we take a look around?" proposed the Parisian, pointing at a low tunnel. "Let's go!"

A conscientious guide, the mechanic Laridon took the lead and started walking.

We are employing an inexact expression there, for the improvised guide could not precede his companions in the ordinary posture of walking. He advanced frankly on all fours, which permitted him to examine at closer range the terrain on which he was risking himself. To tell the truth, the tunnel of sorts that welcomed our troglodytes was not completely plunged in darkness. Doubtless for the first time in thousands of years, it had seen daylight again, and that light, penetrating through the unblocked opening in its armor of rocks, passed though the violet branches of polyps, dissipating the darkness slightly. During the first steps, they could see vaguely where they were.

Naturally, the entire company, including its minuscule dog-pack, was scarcely in a curious mood. It was not as tourists that they were penetrating that singular place. There was too much chance that it would be their tomb. Nevertheless, they all cast mechanical glances around them, which permitted them rapidly to distinguish a rather spacious cavern plunging obliquely into the ground; a rock-fall had blocked its entrance imperfectly.

That was all they could see, for the depths of the cavern were lost in almost complete darkness, which their gazes could not pierce. Furthermore, their volunteer guide did not give them the leisure to examine the place any longer. Fixing his searching gaze on one of the dark corners of the cavern, he precipitated himself into it like a man recognizing the right road. Did he know that one existed? In that case, how did he recognize it? But it was not a time for questions, and let us repeat, Laridon had the bump of action.

"This way, Mesdames, M'sieur!" he commanded, with a singular assurance.

They all followed without argument, sliding on the mechanic's heels into the orifice of the lateral tunnel.

A fortunate inspiration!

Scarcely had they taken refuge there that a formidable noise filled the cavern. The polyp-tree, perhaps weary of its sentry duty, had just folded up its curtain, letting through a gush of water, which precipitated through the opening, seeping before it and rolling in its waves the rocky boulders and all the debris that it encountered in its passage.

As Jean Chapuis had foreseen, in reoccupying the space momentarily deserted, the ocean also took possession of all the new fissures created by the submarine earthquake. Logically, it was necessary to suppose that the waters would also come to drown the tunnel into which Laridon had drawn the troupe. It was only a matter of seconds.

Involuntarily, Jean Chapuis shivered and clutched his companion more tightly. It was pointless to have played hide-and-seek with death. Inevitably, it would be able to seek them out and attain them in their refuge; it would have the last word.

Full of anguish, he awaited the roaring flood.

But the seconds went by, and then the minutes, without bringing the expected assault. In the grotto, the noise appeared to even out; it was not the tumult of a torrent or a cataract, bounding and foaming over the bed that it had chosen. Its course passed noisily beside the buried humans, sparing them.

There was only one possible explanation. The grotto did not end a few meters from its opening; it presented a fissure that plunged into the entrails of the earth: an issue that permitted the torrent to run through.

But that could only accord the condemned a temporary respite.

Thinking about the enormous mass of water that the ocean represents, Jean Chapuis was under no illusion. Whatever the dimensions of the fissure might be, the water would fill it. And when it reached the bottom, it would fatally flow into the lateral corridors that it seemed to be disdaining for the moment.

The young engineer uttered a profound sigh. He found the play of destiny cruel. Why prolong the agony for so long while forbidding them hope?

Nearby, Laridon was delivering himself to reflections far less pessimistic; for, having taken, from his pocket one of the photophores with a solarium base that had so advantageously replaced electric lamps, he directed its luminous beam toward the torrent. Then he smiled with satisfaction.

"Keep prancing, Cascade," he said, mocking the water. "One won't come to join you in your dancing; we're too serious, we sons of Pantruche."[2]

"Simpleton!" riposted Jean Chapuis, sadly. "Do you imagine that we're out of danger?"

"Of course, Boss. There's no lack of room in this bottle. Take a look at the staircase. If we can't reach the top floor, we'll go down to the cellar, that's all."

The engineer shrugged his shoulders.

"What advantage is there in that, since it can't take us anywhere? Do you know where we are, my poor Victor?"

The mechanic was not put off, and responded immediately, shouting because the cataract was making a deafening noise: "Wherever we are, we're here, aren't we? And we even

---

[2] A nickname of Pantin, a popular neighborhood of Paris.

find our feet dry after having nearly taken a cold bath. That privileged situation gives me confidence for the future."

Silently, Cyprienne approved with a nod of the head. It was obvious that she shared the brave mechanic's confidence entirely.

The latter had moved back toward the entrance to the grotto and was contemplating the waterfall. The light of the photophore illuminated confused forms: blocks of rock and various pieces of wreckage that the water was dragging with it.. The mechanic appeared to be examining them with evident interest. The sight certainly suggested satisfactory reflections to him. Master Laridon sometimes saw things distantly.

"Oho!" he muttered, with an enigmatic smile. "It's an express train, and non-stop. That could replace the luggage-wagon. I'll wager that it will get there before us." He made a little hand gesture. "*Bon voyage!* See you soon!"

The wit of the Parisian gamin! Always a flippant quip, even when circumstances do not seem to warrant one. What did Laridon mean? He certainly had an idea at the back of his mind, which he did not judge it appropriate to communicate to his dejected companions. The only ones who had conserved any appearance of hope and vigor were himself and Cyprienne.

But on what could such confidence repose? If they had been asked that question, it is probable that the young woman and the mechanic would have given contrasting answers. Cyprienne Oronius doubtless had reasons different from Laridon's for remaining calm in that frightful adventure.

For a few moments, the noise of the cataract had been joined by other noises even louder. One might have thought them the detonations of artillery or the explosion of mines; they shook the rocky mass in the bosom of which the buried had found refuge. It was as if a colossal battering ram were striking the walls at almost regular intervals.

Then something surprising happened. The noise and the volume of the torrent suddenly diminished; soon, there was no more than a trickle of water running and disappearing, as if the source from which it was coming had run dry.

Was such a hypothesis not implausible, when that source was nothing other than the inexhaustible ocean?

Jean Chapuis, bewildered, could not believe his eyes. He marched toward the entrance of the tunnel and darted an astonished gaze into the silent grotto. The obscurity there had become complete again; he needed to have recourse to the photophore.

"Light me up, Victor!"

The mechanic approached in his turn and inspected the entrance with his engineer

"Something has blocked bottleneck again," he observed. "Listen, M'sieur Jean; it's in the process of caulking the joints."

That was true. Drawn by the water, blocks of stone had accumulated in the corridor and had ended up obstructing the entrance completely. Under the pressure of the water, those blocks had agglomerated into a kind of masonry so compact that all infiltration had ceased. The danger of the inundation of the refuge was no longer redoubtable.

On the other hand, the unfortunates who were buried had to consider themselves as immured alive in a tomb. Ought they to rejoice in that unexpected salvation? No, undoubtedly, for it seemed to have reserved them for another kind of death, slower and no less atrocious. Thousands of cubic meters of salt water separated them at present from the open air and the surface of the waves.

No matter! Men of the temper of Jean Chapuis and Laridon could look that situation in the face.

They were alive. They were breathing. The mechanic was definitely right. In sum, it was to his inspiration that they all owed being still in this world, on the threshold of the other.

Jean Chapuis clapped him on the shoulder amicably. "Victor, my friend," he said, "You've had a famous idea, and I was wrong to make fun of it. Without the game of hide-and-seek that you've obliged us to engage in with the ocean, we'd have a terrible indigestion of salt water."

"Yes," translated the mechanic, "the lemonade was there to be taken." Then, more seriously, he added: "To be frank, perhaps I didn't have that idea on my own; it was whispered to me."

"Whispered?"

Cyprienne made a gesture. She seemed to understand.

"You had the impression of being drawn, didn't you?" she said, involuntarily. "What happened to us can't be imputed to hazard."

Jean Chapuis addressed a gaze of affectionate reproach to her. "Don't abandon yourself to irrational chimeras, Cyprienne," he objected. "I can't believe that we've been drawn into this tomb by a friendly volcano. In any case, this can't be a way susceptible of conducting us to the person who is summoning you. You ought to sense, as I do, how absurd that supposition is. If it's necessary to admit that our terrible submersion was provoked, I rather fear that it ought be attributed to the intervention of an enemy."

Cyprienne made no response to that objection. Her confidence was perhaps not dented, but she appeared to want to avoid debate.

"In any case," she said, "We haven't been separated; that's the main thing. We'll support together whatever happens to us. So what I think is that whatever it is and wherever it takes us, we ought to explore this abode into which destiny—in your opinion—has just thrown us."

"The situation doesn't appear to have any issue," murmured Jean Chapuis, anxiously. "In spite of everything, with reason, my dear Cyprienne, we ought to act as if it were possible to conserve some hope. Abandoning oneself is what cowards do; there are none of those here."

His gaze—which, in order not to worry his fiancée, he obliged to be firm, studied the faces of his companions.

Neither Turlurette nor Mandarinette had taken complete account of the adventure; they seemed quite bewildered.

Pipigg and Kukuss had found pebbles salted by the fall, and were occupied in licking them.

As for the worthy Julep, he was sitting on a shelf of rock with an expression so detached from things of this world that the engineer was astonished.

"What's the matter, Master Julep? He asked. "You don't appear to be keeping up, *mon brave*."

"No point in budging, M'sieur," replied the polychrome negro. "No more to do to reach Paradise."

"Why is that?"

"Julep is dead. Julep has arrived in the better world, M'sieur Laridon is here too, and Pipigg and Kukuss! Julep is finished, croaked, dead with all his friends."

That was said with such conviction that the listeners could not help bursting into laughter.

"If we were dead," observed Laridon, judiciously, "we'd no longer be subject to human necessities, my old friend. Now, my stomach is twingeing, and no mistake. I'm hungry, therefore I'm alive."

"Julep has also much appetite," admitted the negro, on reflection.

The mechanic searched his head and went on: "You can see clearly, impassioned fellow, that you have bulimia. However, my beloved man, in a sense, you might be right. Your hunger might be that of a recalcitrant corpse, for we must have kicked the bucket without perceiving it. That's the only possible explanation. It's only the dead to whom such an adventure can happen. We're in the land of the dead. The proof is that I've seen one of them."

Cyprienne Oronius gave signs of intense emotion. The others were merely bewildered.

"What are you singing?" exclaimed the engineer.

"The truth, M'sieur Jean. I haven't told you, first because I haven't had time, and then because I'm still pale green, the color of tobacco-juice. The thing happened just as we reached the bottom of the gulf, when my eyes, looking around instinctively, perceived the entrance to the submarine cavern. Well, word of Laridon, I distinguished a human silhouette… a head with extraordinary eyes, staring at us."

"Hallucination, Victor. You thought you saw it."

"I saw it, M'sieur Jean. Saw it, with my eyes."

"A human creature, you say? A living creature emerging from the entrails of the earth. You're crazy. It's impossible."

"Why not?" Cyprienne put in, softly, her eyes animated.

"Because there are limits that life can't cross," riposted the engineer, shaking his head. "Don't complicate our adventure by imagining the implausible. It's sufficiently extraordinary already. I explain it thus: a series of favorable hazards has enabled us to survive the loss of our ship and the fall that resulted. Let's hang on to that explanation. In full possession of our physical and intellectual faculties we reached the seabed, dislocated by an earthquake. Against all reasonable expectation, we found a refuge at the bottom of a crevice that the ocean itself took care of closing over us. The situation is perfectly clear, if not very cheerful. We're immured at the bottom of a cleft in the terrestrial crust, with the depth of the whole ocean over our heads. What are the dimensions of this cleft? Can we live here? And for how long? Those are the questions to examine, so we're going to proceed with that exploration right away."

"Let's go!" said Cyprienne, getting up with a haste they had not expected of her.

Laridon was bursting with enthusiasm. "Marvelous!" he repeated, to the less delighted Julep. "Oh, my Julep, what a tale I'll have to tell if I ever get back to Belleville! People who've been able to visit caves like this one aren't boring!"

His gesture indicated the galleries that plunged into the bowels of the earth. His eyes were shining.

"Who knows where they might lead? Who knows what we're going to discover?" The love of adventures was legible on the face of the intrepid fellow. His vivid imagination was working hard, and doubtless already inventing possibilities of subterranean existence ornamented with all the felicities of a paradise.

Jean Chapuis was not nourishing such illusions. For him, everything was summarized in the question of whether there was any chance of discovering anything in the fissure that might appease their hunger and thirst. And he could not help thinking that even if their lucky star favored them on that point, neither he nor his companions would be saved. At the most, the discovery of nutritive elements would permit them to vegetate miserably for some lapse of time, the length of which would depend on the resistance of their morale. But he thought that he did not have the right to depress his fiancée by letting her see his discouragement. He therefore headed toward the gallery through which the torrential waters had flowed.

"Forward ho!" he pronounced. "After all, the best thing we can do is to abandon ourselves to your inspiration, my dear Cyprienne."

Chapter Four
THE LUMINOUS STONE

For more than two hours they descended. Laridon, flanked by the two papillons. Cyprienne illuminated the march; Julep closed it and Jean Chapuis, in the middle, sustained the progress of the three women. No cellar staircase with shaky and worn steps ever offered a steeper or more uneasy slope. One might truly have thought that the strange explorers were descending into a well.

Knowing that he was followed, Laridon kept going forward. Leaping, tumbling, rolling or running, according to the declivity of the slope, he descended with a feverish haste and an inexplicable good humor, and the little quadrupeds ran out of breath yapping joyfully as they trotted at his sides.

Lassitude, however, began to make itself felt. Since their fall into the submarine volcanic maelstrom, they had been living on their taut nerves, unable to take any rest. Jean Chapuis ordered a halt. He judged the fatiguing gymnastics futile, and he was in no hurry personally to press on further forward.

Sustained by their unshakable confidence, Oronius' daughter and the enraged Parisian would have preferred to continue, but they took pity on the visible exhaustion of Turlurette and Mandarinette.

"So be it! Let's have a little rest," conceded the mechanic, collapsing on the ground. Who sleeps collects the crumbs, as the old proverb has it. We'll see whether it's true."

Then they heard him muttering in a low voice while he searched the darkness of the well with his gaze.

"All the same, I regret the comfortable Panas where three pills fabricated by alimentary chemistry are sufficient to take away hunger and thirst. And I could take a bath in radioactive currents to rid myself of fatigue. To think that we had everything in our luggage necessary to live in accordance with the principles of modern science! Where have our trunks gone?

Was he expecting a miracle? The apparition of a *djinn* bearing everything they lacked?

Alas, he was surrounded by darkness, for, in order to permit the young women the natural repose of sleep, for want of the restorative action of the currents mentioned by Laridon, Jean Chapuis had switched off the photophore.

Deprived of the conquests of twenty-first century science, it was necessary to revert to the usages of previous generations.

Laridon, the last representative, by virtue of atavism, of the obsolete syndicalism of bygone ages, took to his part in that new situation with difficulty. He seemed to be accusing some invisible creature of the disappointment he was experiencing, and he had a whim—an enormity!—to call a strike.

"True," he muttered bitterly. "There's no C.T.I. and C.G.T, underground.[3] If this is the way the tourists are treated down here, I won't send the lads!"

"Go to sleep!" whispered the engineer. "That'll be better. You're accumulating stupidities uselessly."

"Sleep? I must have lost the habit of it," retorted the mechanic. "Thanks to the radiation baths that have suppressed sand in the peepers, the camaros of today no longer know how to take forty winks. Every epoch has its mores. I'm modern, me."

He must, however, have rediscovered the usage of that method of repose, which he deemed obsolete, for they ceased to hear him.

For his part, along with Cyprienne, vanquished by fatigue, the young engineer had become drowsy. It was a sort of torpor that only left him a vague consciousness of his surroundings.

Then he had a strange dream; he was still lying on the ground; he felt that he had not budged, and would, in any case,

---

[3] French trade unions.

have been incapable of making the slightest movement. From the depths of the darkness, he saw a kind of luminous mist surge forth, the web of which advanced toward him, growing as it approached. The luminous sheet reached Jean, expelling the darkness around him. The ground on which he and his companions were lying was covered with a silvery carpet, which seemed to be produced by the play of a moonbeam.

The walls and the vault of the subterrain had also become visible, but the action of the luminous source did not extend beyond a circle with a radius of two or three meters.

Was the engineer dreaming or was he awake? He thought that his eyes were wide open and he kept them fixed on the luminous screen that had suddenly punctured the darkness. But, paralyzed by the sleep that still mastered his muscles, it was impossible for him to turn his head in order to see the source of the extraordinary phenomenon.

The hallucination was soon aggravated; it was no longer only a sheet of light at which the sleeper marveled; the vision was animated. A few paces away from him he saw a bizarre creature surge forth, whose silhouette was that of a frail human being of small stature: a species of homunculus, with singularly bright eyes in the middle of a spectral face.

Naked under a tunic made of vegetable fibers, which dissimulated nothing, the apparition glided without the slightest sound over the ground illuminated by the pale radiance, and bent down successively over the sleepers with a sort of fervor, simultaneously respectful and fearful.

That vision was so clear, its movements, although silent, had such an impression of life, that Jean Chapuis glimpsed confusedly the possibility that he was seeing something real.

The fingers of the crouching creature advanced toward the face of the sleeping Cyprienne; they were about to touch it. At that moment the fiancé experienced such a fright that he made a violent effort to wake up and to move.

Abruptly, the crouching homunculus leapt up and returned to the shadows.

At the same moment, Jean Chapuis raised himself up on his elbow, fully awake, and then leapt to his feet in his turn.

Although the apparition had vanished, the strange light subsisted.

Stupefied, the young engineer bent down and shook Laridon; the latter got up, muttering in a voice that the unaccustomed slumber had rendered thick.

"What? What? Oh, M'sieur Jean, I dreamed I was in a funk... that's rare."

"Get up," murmured Cyprienne's fiancé, in a low voice. "I too have just had a scare on perceiving something." He could not decide to say "someone," so abnormal did the fact seem to him.

He interrupted himself in order to launch himself outside the circle of light toward two brilliant dots whose fixity he had just sensed weighing upon him. They were like two phosphorescent eyes attached to him, watching him from the depths of the darkness.

As soon as his first steps in their direction the eyes were abruptly extinguished, but Jean Chapuis thought he distinguished a dark form fleeing at the end of the gallery. Then he stopped, fearing to bump his head on the asperities of the rock, and murmured, while rubbing his eyes: "Unimaginable! Is hunger troubling my brain? It would be insane to imagine living creatures buried in these submarine caverns. The doorway that gave us passage can only open once in every thousand years."

"What did you see, then, M'sieur Jean?" asked Laridon.

"I had the same hallucination that you had when we came in here," the engineer replied. "I seemed to distinguish near to us a human creature...or almost human. It could only be a phantasmagoria. And yet, the light that subsists..."

Only then did he notice the persistence of the luminous sheet. That, at least, was not an illusion. The creature leaning over Cyprienne might only have existed in his imagination. Awakened with a start, his mind still obsessed by a dream, he might have suggested the phosphorescent eyes and the flight of the silhouette into the darkness. The light, however, remained; it was necessary to find an explanation for that.

In his turn, Laridon observed the phenomenon and immediately rejoiced.

"Marvelous! There's the pallor that kills!" he exclaimed, considering the rock bathed in pale light. "It isn't kilometers wide, just a lance… but it's sufficient for us to see, and merely in seeing it I already feel warmed up. Word of honor! I'm visibly dryer, and you too, one would think. Where is that light coming from? Not the sky, that's for sure, since we're in the empire of the lobsters. Look, M'sieur Jean; it's flowing from this rock… here... flat on the ground..."

In fact, the luminous radiation appeared to be emanating from a fragment of mineral fallen in the middle of the corridor.

Jean Chapuis picked it up and examined it.

"It isn't solarium," he murmured. "It's even more marvelous, since this mineral seems to be endowed with radioactive luminous properties so powerful that the substance has no need to be isolated. It's radiant in its raw state. Properly speaking, it's a luminous stone. Perhaps it exists in large masses. If, for example, the walls of this gallery were composed of it, we'd be following a constellated path."

"That would be a nice thread. Unfortunately, it isn't the case. At the most, what we have there has the value of a night-light."

"Where can the stone have fallen from?" the young engineer asked himself, thoughtfully. "It's been detached from a larger block—the fracture is visible. I can't see any light in our surroundings revealing the presence of a quantity of this substance."

"You said it yourself, Boss. This little machine has been brought by the citizen just now. You know—the cavist."

"The homunculus?"

"Eh? What do you call him? Is that an insolence? No… at any rate, your *homuncule* had that stone. It must be like his lantern or his candle. That proves that underground, people are as civilized as up above. We make use of solarium… they have lunarium or something like."

"Pass for lunarium," smiled Jean Chapuis. "But I can't admit the reality of our vision. Can it be that the interior of the Earth is inhabited?"

"Why not?"

"Scientifically, one could admit it, on condition of eliminating the hypothesis of the central fire and the progressive elevation of temperature as one plunges into the ground. To certain conditions of life, anyway, beings correspond specially adapted to those conditions. But what we imagined we perceived resembled a human being; that's quite inadmissible; to believe in the existence of a human race acclimated to the great depths of the terrestrial crust would be pure folly."

"The luminous stone, however, didn't get there on its own, on its wheels or in its limousine, and you're not going to tell me that it might have been brought by a rat. Those dirty beasts wander around without lanterns."

"It might have been detached from a luminous rock that we didn't notice and rolled here following the slope of a tunnel."

"And this too, no doubt?"

Laridon had just discovered near to where they had picked up the luminous stone two little things, almost indistinct, which ignited gleams of covetousness in his eyes. sketching a joyful entrechat, he precipitated himself toward the place indicated by his gesture, bent down, and picked up the two objects, which he presented to the engineer, triumphantly.

"That'll inspire you, M'sieur Jean! That gift is tantamount telling you the date. We picked them up in the time of my great grandmother. It's a pancake, believe me! One of the pancakes that people ate in the last century, when humans still had quasi-savage tastes. Today, in view of the circumstance, I believe that one wouldn't trust it. It reeks of the old regime. And here's a garglette filled with a liquid that resembles water famously. The wherewithal to eat and drink, old style, I tell you. If you can demonstrate to me that this grows from the same rock and offers itself to illuminated passing tourists, I'll respond that we're in old Charles Perrault's Empire of Marvels!"

Jean Chapuis examined the provisions in his turn.

There was no doubt about it; it really was a cake kneaded from coarse flour, and the misshapen jug, produced by a rudimentary art and industry, contained drinkable water.

"Cyprienne! Cyprienne!" he called, accepting the miracle and yielding to the joy that was reborn in him.

In his eyes, as in those of the enthusiastic Laridon, that unexpected aid represented more than immediate salvation. It was not only a means of appeasing hunger and thirst, but a presage of a less somber future, the palpable testimony of a nearby protection, intelligent and clear-sighted, capable of understanding human needs and satisfying them.

In that mysterious protection it would be good to believe. Jean Chapuis' skepticism could not survive that manifestation. To understand it was unnecessary; he had only to share the naïve faith of Laridon and Julep.

"Cyprienne!" reiterated the engineer, in haste to share his joy and announce the god news. "Turlurette! Mandarinette! Wake up! Like the starving in the desert, we have received manna. This will relieve our distress. Look!"

Awoken with a start, the three young woman, soon followed by Julep, gathered around Jean Chapuis. He had broken up the pancake and he distributed the pieces. For his part, Laridon circulated the beverage.

Her thirst appeased, Oronius' daughter was brought up to date with the details of the opportune discovery. To the great surprise of her fiancé, she did not marvel as much as he would have thought natural. She seemed to find that unexpected help quite simple.

"This somber world is inhabited! There are living beings under the terrestrial crust!" repeated the engineer, emotionally. "Never have out geologists or anthropologist enabled us to know that interior humankind. Doubtless they're still unaware of it. However, one of those beings has come toward us and is watching over us."

"I think that it must be thus," affirmed Cyprienne. "Jean, I can no longer hide it from you; it's the will of my father that has drawn us into the depths of this abyss. We're going toward him. That's my profound, unshakable conviction."

"How is that possible, my dear Cyprienne? Let's admit for a moment that the genius of Oronius has survived. Is it in the bosom of the Earth that we might have a chance of discovering him? How and why would he not have emerged in order to come to us? Do you suppose, then, that he isn't free?"

"You're asking me too much, Jean. However, that really is what it's necessary to suppose. For a reason of which we don't have the secret, my father, a prisoner, cannot use the resources of his marvelous mind with a view to having room to maneuver. He has not even been able to inform us overtly of his fate or the place where he is. He has been content to attract us to him in order to obtain our entire assistance. That, I sense as if I know it. And I explain the mystery of such an attitude by the necessity in which my father finds himself of not revealing himself to his enemies—to that Yogha, and that Hantzen. Perhaps they too have not ceased to live and are lying in wait for him with the persistence you know. Do you understand me, Jean? My father would certainly have been able to transmit a message to us via cerebral waves, but those waves could be received by all brains endowed with the amplifier of the Aqueduct of Sylvius, and as you can't be unaware, Hantzen, being a former disciple of Oronius, must have received from him at one time the gift of the amplifier. I tell you, Jean, that we must be prudent ourselves and not think too much about my father. Let us allow ourselves to be drawn. We'll arrive at the goal, I'm convinced of it."

Silently, the fiancé acquiesced with a nod of the head. Such favorable premonitory symptoms were beginning to vanquish his incredulity.

"How I would like to talk to that creature you perceived," the young woman said, then. "Who can tell whether it isn't the person of which we're thinking who sent him to us?"

"Talking to it might be difficult," replied the engineer. "It's necessary for me to admit its existence, since it has given us palpable proofs of it, but from that to believing it capable of understanding and responding is a big step. In truth, I remain confounded by its presence in these depths and I can't explain how it came here, what it is doing here and in what manner it lives here."

"We're all right here," remarked Laridon.

"Undoubtedly. But without that presence anterior to ours, we'd be condemned to die here of hunger. I can, therefore, ask myself by what miracle a human creature—for I must believe until proven otherwise that it's a matter of a human creature—has been able to adapt to this frightful abode and subsist here."

"Why do you assume that it's frightful?" Cyprienne protested. "Perhaps we'll find a paradise at the bottom of the descent."

"I doubt it."

"I don't," the audacious Parisian dared to affirm. "Hasn't a good angel risen up to bring us something to scoff and swill?"

Jean Chapuis could not share such illusions. Evidently, the encounter with a living being, where it seemed that life could not exist, opened the field to all hypotheses, but to suppose the existence of a subterranean world unknown to human overturned all acquired ideas.

It was no more admissible, however, to suppose that the being he had glimpsed might be the only one if its species.

Sagely reserving his opinion, the young man ended up concluding: "Let's wait. We'll see."

And he emitted in his turn the hope that the providential creature might continue to provide for their needs and might end up allowing itself to be approached and domesticated.

That desire seemed unrealizable at first. Manifestly, the homunculus experienced the greatest reluctance to allowing itself to be perceived; it had been content to abandon in the path of the involuntary explorers the provisions that it destined for them. Why nourish them if it was afraid of them? That was an enigma.

After all, the fact was there, and patent. It continued its good offices with a remarkable punctuality, proof that it was not unaware of the quotidian demands of the stomach.

The descent continued, therefore, in excellent conditions.

However, because they were women—the twenty-first century having not brought any modification to the little foibles of the fair sex—Cyprienne and her two chambermaids felt the spur of curiosity more. In the course of one of the halts, while everyone else was asleep, united in a tacit conspiracy, they remained awake while simulating sleep, in the hope that the creature might approach and they would be able to contemplate it. Between their lowered eyelids their eyes searched the shadows, sometimes imagining that they distinguished a moving figure.

In the end, Cyprienne could not hold still; she got up quietly and moved to the limit of the circle of pale light with which they were surrounded by the luminous stone, preciously conserved as a beacon.

That was not yet sufficient.

In order to accustom her eyes to the darkness, the young woman decided to push on for a few more paces. Perhaps, in the shadows, the bizarre creature of the depths would be less skittish and would allow itself to approach her.

Cyprienne had no apprehension of the enigma of the darkness. The being that lent them its continual assistance could not do her any harm. And then, would not a single cry uttered by her be sufficient to awaken her companions and bring them running?

For all those reasons, the courageous young woman did not hesitate to penetrate further into the obscure gallery.

After a few paces, her foot collided with something soft. She bent down swiftly, felt the obstacle, and felt a frisson run through her whole body.

What she was touching was a body lying flat on the ground.

Her heart was beating rapidly. The body must be that of their enigmatic provider, for whom she was searching, probably asleep, taking advantage of the slumber of those whose march it was accompanying to obtain a reparative repose.

"Jean! Victor!" she called, in a voice vibrant with emotion. At the same time, her clenched hands maintained her prisoner immobile—who, woken up, was attempting to escape.

"Woof, woof!" said Pipigg and Kukuss, to affirm their presence. The valiant little animals had followed their mistress without being noticed by her.

Already, Turlurette and Mandarinette had run in answer to the appeal of Oronius' daughter. The arrival of the three men reinforced a circle from which the captive could no longer emerge.

Thanks to the luminous stone brought by the mechanic, they were all able to examine the singular little being that was struggling desperately in Cyprienne's slender and beautiful hands.

When the light reached it and it encountered the gazes of the six escapees from *La Stella* fixed upon it, it ceased agitating, fell to its knees and prostrated itself with its forehead on the ground, in an attitude of supplication and adoration.

It was a pale and paltry being; its face and hands had a livid transparency; its long and poorly-furnished hair was colorless, but its eyes were gleaming like carbuncles. Apart from those indications of physical degeneracy and those flaws, which could only be the characteristics of a race specially adapted to subterranean existence, it presented forms that were diminished but typical, proving that it belonged to the human species.

The fearful expression of its face indicated mildness. It would have been difficult to assign an age to it, for although its stature was that of an adolescent not yet fully developed, its features presented an aged aspect. In the same way, one could not say to which sex it belonged.

While they all examined it with a curiosity not exempt from sympathy, Laridon, more expansive and less ceremonious, seized it casually by the middle of the body, set it on its feet and shook its hand cordially.

"There, my lad!" he said, with a mocking affability. "You've given us enough *salamalecs*. Besides which, we're mates, since you share the bread of your hearth with Pantruchards. What's your name, old zig?"

It did not occur to him that it would be impossible for the singular little human of the obscure caverns to understand him. But as he formulated his question he placed his finger on his forehead, and the expression on his face was as legible as his mime; the subterranean being doubtless divined their meaning, for a monosyllable escaped its lips and it was certainly a response:

"Tai!"

Chapter Five
TAI, HUMAN OF THE UNDERWORLD

"Tai?" repeated Laridon. "Tai? Is that your name, my chick?"

The individual addressed sketched an affirmative sign while saying again, in a voice that was shrill to the point of hurting the ears: "Tai."

"There's no denying it, that's his name," concluded the mechanic. "It's not ordinary, but in this life everyone in the world can't call himself Gaillard or Foutriquet, can they? Well, Tai, my friend, since we've been introduced now, you'll travel with us, I think? Just when we have need of a guide, we've found you."

Tai's physiognomy was not devoid of intelligence; however, in spite of his application, they divined that he could not grasp the meaning of that amiable invitation. On the other hand, as the tone and the gestures denoted a real benevolence in his regard, he was no longer thinking of escaping. In any case, the unexpected explorers of the depths excited his curiosity to the highest degree. That was obvious; he had a sentiment of respectful and fearful wonderment in their regard.

Although he extended his hands toward the sextet with a sort of fervor, he dared not touch them, for their stature and, above all, their garments, inspired a sort of fetishism in him. In the matter of garments, he was not wearing any, but as we have said, the restricted stature of that being, which did not seem to be manifestly male or female, removed all inconvenience from his nudity.

Doubtless it was the first time that it had contemplated humans so different from himself. Their appearance must seem as marvelous to him as his own was to Cyprienne's companions.

Taking account of the sentiments that were agitating him, the young woman smiled and, placing one of her hands on his head, she stroked the colorless hair. By turns, Turlurette, Mandarinette and Jean Chapuis did the same. Julep addressed an amicable grimace to the new acquaintance, and Laridon repeated: "You're a mate, a friend, a pal."

Definitively reassured by those amicable manifestations, Tai smiled in his turn, with an expression of ecstasy; then, approaching each of them in turn, he prostrated himself and took a hand, which he kissed, before posing his head humbly thereon.

"That means that he accepts the proposed employment," assured the mechanic. "He's putting himself at our service. I'll take charge of training him and making a choice colt of him."

"Don't abuse his candor," recommended Cyprienne, threatening the facetious fellow with her finger.

"Me?" protested the latter, with the indignation of calumniated innocence. "I'll only give him good advice... and to begin with, you'll see whether I can make myself understood."

Picking up the fragment of luminous stone, he showed it to Tai, asking: "This comes from your home, eh? If one found a lot of that species, brother, the two of us could found a submarine bank."

Having listened to the question gravely without understanding it, Tai touched the stone; then, with the same hand, several times, he designated the direction of the descent and pronounced unintelligible syllables.

"He must be inviting us to follow him," suggested Cyprienne. "There's truly nothing but that to do." And, repeating Tai's gesture, she said: "Go! We'll accompany you."

Immediately, Tai set forth, carrying the luminous stone in two hands.

During the first quarter of an hour, he only advanced with circumspection, and turned round continually to make sure that he was being followed. At the second bend in the tunnel he stopped, crouched down in front of a hole in the rock, and took out provisions and another receptacle full of water; then he came to deposit them before his companions, renewing his respectful genuflections.

Neither the jokes of Laridon not the amicable caresses of Cyprienne, desirous of domesticating him completely, could succeed in making him abandon those exaggerated marks of respect.

"It's the local protocol; necessary to let it go," the mechanic thought he ought to explain. Nevertheless, he persuaded his new friend to take his share of the food and drink.

A few hours later, before a new hiding-place, the same ceremony recommenced.

"The fellow had definitely prepared his expedition and his relays," observed Jean Chapuis. "Whatever his objective was, he had abandoned provisions all along the route for the return journey."

It the mystery was no clearer, the future, by contrast, seemed brighter. The engineer ended up admitting the existence in the entrails of the Earth, if not of the marvelous world that his companions imagined, at least an embryo of organized life that offered them a chance of salvation. He said so, without absolute conviction

"When Cyprienne supposes that a fluid emanated from the mind of Oronius has attracted us and guided us into this maze, perhaps she's sensing the truth."

He therefore followed the human embryo eagerly, determined to push on to the end.

The strangest thing, in his estimation, was that they could find agreeably breathable air at such a depth, at a moderate temperature, thanks to which the march progressed, over smooth ground, without the accompaniment of the fatigues that they could not have failed to feel on the surface.

After the sixth stage—the only means at the disposal of the voyagers to measure time—the species of chimney through which they were descending gradually broadened out; the slope eased and they hazard the impression of progressing through an obscure and chaotic landscape, like the bed of a torrent descending the slopes of a mountain in order to end up in a valley; but the exiguity of the circle illuminated by the luminous stone did not permit them a sight of the ensemble, nor to verify their suppositions. The radiance of the singular pebble only made a hole of light in the midst of a mass of shadow, the opacity of which imprisoned the gaze of the subterranean explorers.

However, as Jean Chapuis could no longer see rock overhead or at his sides, and, no matter how far he deviated to the left or the right, he never encountered a wall, he deduced that they must have arrived in a grotto of gigantic proportions, or perhaps in the bosom of an enormous pocket existing within the terrestrial globe.

A further stage brought them into flat terrain; they sensed the declivity of the ground beneath their feet ceased. At the same time, at a distance which the continuous obscurity had previously hidden the existence, a bright patch became visible, like that perceived in the eastern sky shortly before dawn.

"Daylight!" exclaimed Laridon, in the fashion of a mariner announcing land.

Jean Chapuis shook his head. "No," he said, examining the distant light. "It's not daylight... or, at least, it must be daylight of a particular species, such as might be produced by the accumulation of an enormous quantity of that substance." He pointed at the fragment of luminous stone.

Tai, as always, paid a profound attention to the words, incomprehensible for him. Having surprised that gesture, his face became animated. he uttered an inarticulate cry and nodded his head several times, gesticulating. His hand went from the stone to the illuminated horizon.

It was impossible to mistake the significance of the two gestures, which were punctuated by a series of bizarre onomatopoeias, doubtless belonging to Tai's mother tongue. The whole clearly meant: "That's it... you've got it. The light over there is produced by an accumulation of this stone, which also come from the place to which I'm taking you."

Jean Chapuis understood that too. "You see," he said. "Tai is confirming my hypothesis. If life has been able to develop in this sad abode, it must be localized near that light source.

Laridon seemed very excited; he looked successively at the illuminated horizon and the mass of shadow that still surrounded it. Given his enthusiastic temperament, he should have precipitated himself forward or demanded an immediate departure, but he did nothing.

"It's the commencement of marvels," he declared, serenely. "It will be light tomorrow, as they say on earth. For the moment. M'sieur Jean, I'll ask for a little siesta. It's necessary to gather strength for the final stage."

That proposition was too reasonable not to be welcomed without argument. A quarter of an hour later they were all reposing around the fragment of luminous stone that had come from the mysterious abode that was about to be revealed to them.

Cyprienne's beautiful face was illuminated by the hope radiant in her gaze. She was doubtless approaching the moment when the mystery that she had not feared to confront would deliver its secret to her.

My father has survived! Tomorrow, I shall have proof of it, and an explanation, she thought, excitedly. *From the depths of this darkness, which ought to have filled me with horror and fear, his thought has never ceased to summon me and accompany me.*

Her exultation kept her awake for a long time, and when somnolence finally took possession of her, an exclamation on the part of Tai extracted her from it, awakening her companions at the same time.

They opened their eyes and perceived the subterranean being who was agitating before them, showing them alternately the luminous stone, diminished by a third, and the place where Victor Laridon had gone to sleep.

The location was empty. The sympathetic mechanic had disappeared, and Julep with him.

Chapter Six
IN THE SUBTERRANEAN SKY

Jean Chapuis' initial surprise was succeeded by a sharp anxiety. That disappearance also caused too great a chagrin to the sensitive Turlurette not to move them.

It was obvious, however, that without an apparent cause, perhaps yielding to a simple caprice, the ardent Laridon had departed in exploration, taking his inseparable companion with him. There was no doubt to formulate regarding the premeditation of that stupid recklessness, because in order not to deprive the troupe of its luminary, he had limited himself to a discreet borrowing. But the fact that he had forearmed himself with a source of light proved that he did not have the intention of limiting his exploration to the immediate vicinity of the camp.

Where had the imprudent Laridon gone? Was there not a risk that he might go astray, along with the docile Julep? Both ought to have already regained the bivouac of the stage, for the clandestine departure, effected while their companions were asleep, proved that they had expected to return before the general awakening.

As anxious as one another, and striving to console Turlurette, who was weeping copiously, the two fiancés interrogated the darkness. It was in vain; the opaque shadow in which they were still plunged did not allow them to divine the direction taken by the imprudent couple.

Jean Chapuis attempted a few appeals, but obtained no response. His perplexity increased. What should he do? To continue the journey toward the goal marked by the luminous mountain was to abandon the two brave fellows to their fate and risk never seeing them again. It was also to prolong cruelly the anguishing expectation of Oronius' daughter, who thought that she would find in the strange world the answer to the questions she was asking herself on the subject of her father. But then, it seemed just as impractical to set out in search of the strays; it would be setting forth at hazard.

While Jean Chapuis was meditating thus, a noise coming from the distant obscurity made them tremble. Instinctively, they raised their heads, in order to search the ceiling of darkness that replaced the sky for the origin of the familiar noise.

It was that made by the engines of an aircraft in flight.

Surely, there was an error. How could one imagine, in fact, and aircraft flying within the Earth? Vast as the pocket in the bosom of which they found themselves might be, even if it presented the dimensions of a world, one could not suppose the existence of a civilization advanced enough for its inhabitants to be provided with flying machines.

Jean Chapuis as, therefore, very close to believing himself to be the victim of a hallucination or attributing the sound to a different origin when, casting a glance at Tai, he saw him trembling.

The little subterran seemed to be very frightened, ready to hide. Thus he did not know the origin of the sound and was not accustomed to it.

Very emotional, Cyprienne clung to her fiancé. "Can you hear it?" she murmured.

"Yes—one might think it the throb of engines. We must have a buzzing in the ears."

"Why? If my father's genius has been able to reach this abode, Jean, it's necessary for us to expect the realization of the unrealizable."

"Alas, my dear Cyprienne, I can only repeat my previous objections: beware of exaggerated hopes. If my master has survived, he no longer has the free usage of his marvelous genius. Would not its initial manifestation have been to bring him back among us?"

The young woman bowed her head and sighed. She understood the accuracy of the reasoning.

Fortunately for human happiness, no logic, and no sheaf of arguments can triumph completely over the intuitions of our heart. Deep inside, Cyprienne sensed that, in spite of all reason, the current of confidence that impelled her could not be deceiving her.

Through the terrestrial mass, iron sends the mysterious influence of the magnet; the young woman was drawn—captured, we ought to say—by an energy of that order, as invincible and as inexplicable, but also as irresistible.

Suddenly, she felt Tai's head between her knees; crouching down, he was burying hits head in the creases of her tunic. At the same time, an exclamation by Jean made her raise her head.

From the vault of darkness, the luminous beam of a projector now fell; its radiance swept the ground, as if actively searching the corners of shadows.

There was no longer any doubt about it: an aircraft was flying under that sky of rock. An airplane! A searchlight functioning beneath the terrestrial crust!

Jean Chapuis thought he was under the empire of a nightmare, and Cyprienne felt her heart beating hopefully. To the latter, incontestably, that prodigious realization must announce the presence, perhaps nearby, of the great and omnipotent Oronius.

From the dark expanse, the bird whose fiery eye was searching the night suddenly emerged and appeared to the gazes of the little group. The projector came to cast its dazzling circle precisely over the engineer and his companions. Placed in full illumination, they could not escape the gaze of the aviators.

The scientific bird descended.

At the moment when it settled on the ground, a cry of amazement sprang from the lips of Jean Chapuis and Cyprienne.

"The Halcyon-Car!"

"Yes, the Halcyon-Car," riposted a joyful voice. "The ocean had made our luggage follow us. Boss, for his own count and yours, I have just taken delivery of it, a matter of claiming your spoils."

And Victor Laridon, beaming, leapt out of the cabin of the marvelous apparatus. In his turn, following him, Master Julep emerged, showing all his teeth in a broad smile.

The explanation of the miracle did not take long; the mechanic had finished giving it before the voyagers had recovered from their stupor.

The Parisian was a devil of a fellow, and no mistake. According to his own confession, he was not easily wonderstruck, so he was always ready to believe in the favors of chance and to welcome them as his due. When, after sliding down the flank of the gigantic wave swirling in the fashion of the maelstrom, he had found himself deposited on the submarine floor with no other damage than a moment of intense emotion, he had said to himself that it was necessary to believe in his luck, Being thus manifest, it could not restrict itself to that debut and abandon those it had come to protect in such a perilous situation. The revelation of the subterranean grotto and the events that had followed had only confirmed the mechanic in that good opinion.

An optimist, he was convinced that if humans had been able to endure such a frightful fall without injury, there was no reason not to predict a similar fate for the cargo of *La Stella*, infinitely better wrapped. That precious cargo, which constituted the equipment of an expedition, had also arrived at the bottom of the abyss. Laridon knew that; he had recognized the crates in passing, carried away by the torrent precipitating into the funnel of the grotto.

Then he had murmured: “I’ll wager that it will arrive at the destination before us.”

In order not to give his companions a hope that risked being dashed—with great difficulty, because he was loquacious—he had kept the heavy secret to himself. He had not made anyone party to his observations and the deductions he had drawn therefrom. Having arrived at the bottom of the descent, however, in the great obscure hall, before proceeding in caravan all the way to the luminous mountain, he had wanted to make sure personally of the good foundation of than hope;

he had slipped away secretly, taking Julep with him, whose aid would be necessary if he found the cargo.

"Well," he concluded, "The packaging being solid, everything has resisted. We only had to reassemble the Halcyon-Car and stow the provisions in the cupboards in the cabins. Now we're equipped for a trip in the belly of the globe. Name of a rat's moustache! Nothing's lacking in the hold. One could believe that Mamzelle Cyprienne had foreseen the tumble when she drew up the list of what we had to bring and prescribed a mattress capable of resisting any pile-up."

The young woman exchanged a glance with Jean Chapuis.

"I followed the inspiration that you know," she said. "My friend Jean, do you still doubt that the spirit of Oronius is with us and protecting us?"

In order to understand the joy of the young people and to appreciate the miraculous aid that the mechanic's discovery had brought them, it is necessary for us to give a few details of the Halcyon-Car and the treasures that it bore in its flanks.

It was not only the most advanced of aircraft, endowed by the science of Oronius with a secret mechanism making it the king of birds, it could also, according to need, be instantly transformed into a rapid auto, a tank braving all obstacles, an electric launch or a submarine. It was at home in the bosom of all the elements, under the surface as in the depths of the sea, in the air as on land, at the will of those directing it; the incomparable apparatus could run, jump, climb, fly, float or dive.

The equipment that its compartments enclosed was no less exceptional, and gave it an incontestable superiority over everything that had been conceived and executed in the same genre.

Henceforth, having reconquered that fortress auto-transportable in all elements—for it could traverse fire, clad in asbestos—the passengers of the Halcyon-Car could envisage the future with an entire confidence. They were certain of being able to confront any adventure.

Having shaken the hands of the ingenious and devoted mechanic effusively, Jean Chapuis had everyone installed aboard the aircraft. Having become a captain again, he cried enthusiastically: "Cast off, Victor, and en route! Now the exploration of this subterranean word will become child's play."

They were constrained to carry Tai into Oronius' cabin, where Cyprienne was installed. The bird that he had seen descend from the obscure vault struck him with a religious terror. He prostrated himself face down on the ground and refused obstinately to get up again Laridon had to take him in his arms in order to pass him to the young woman. The latter had all the trouble in the world calming the little being's fear. he groaned and addressed incomprehensible supplications to everyone. He calmed down, however, as soon as Victor had stepped on the gas. He saw the aircraft lift off without experiencing any harm, and when he could see himself being carried through the air his physiognomy took on an expression of ecstasy. He put his hands together and started to chant a sort of invocation, punctuated with cries of joy.

"You haven't seen anything yet," the pilot-mechanic said to him, without taking his eyes off the steering apparatus and without worrying about whether Tai could understand him. "It's up there, in the sunlight, that it's necessary to see this. An airplane in a cave doesn't show you anything."

The dimensions of what he called disdainfully "a cave" were, however, it was necessary to recognize, very impressive. The beam of the searchlight could find no limits to it, and The Halcyon was able to rise to nearly two thousand meters before he perceived above its flight the rocky vault that closed the strange sky.

In front of him, he did not encounter any obstacle. The pocket of shadow had to extend for hundreds of kilometers.

In the inky blackness of that night the apparatus continued its silent flight without encountering any hindrance. The searchlight beam studying the ground revealed a singularly chaotic landscape, uniquely composed of mountains, rocks, dormant lakes with sinister waters, and crevices that resembles the craters of extinct volcanoes.

On the horizon toward which the course of the great bird was directed, the luminous strip had had struck the explorers' gaze when they were still on the ground broadened and was amplified from one moment to the next. Jean Chapuis had naturally selected it as a point of direction. Was it not the center of this word, or at least the unique hearth of any life that might be encountered here? It was toward that point, in any case, that Cyprienne Oronius' thought was attracted, as if by a magnet.

As they drew closer the band soon changed into a large patch of light, and the Halcyon penetrated into the illuminated region, flying over a vast plain of luminous ground.

A hundred years earlier, a spectacle that had brought crowds flocking had been that of a ballerina named Loie Fuller,[4] who appeared to be dancing in the midst of flames because she moved on a transparent table illuminated from below. Well, that plain, immeasurably greater, had all the qualities of that theatrical trick, since the light came from the translucent soil.

Life animated it! Beneath the Halcyon, there was a multitude of creatures similar to Tai; there were also animals, buildings and vegetation.

But what was most disconcerting to the human eyes called upon to contemplate that unaccustomed spectacle was not finding any of the colors of the solar spectrum there. There were others, to which our explorers could not even give a name. They were unknown colors, different from those that make up our terrestrial landscapes; and that gave the singular world an unreal, not to say spectral, aspect.

---

[4] Loie Fuller (born Marie Louise Fuller; January 15, 1862 – January 1, 1928), also known as Louie Fuller and Loïe Fuller, was an American actress and dancer who was a pioneer of both modern dance and theatrical lighting techniques.

The entities agitating on that radioactive soil were really alive, however, and doubtless worthy of being observed at closer range.

They were about to be, for Cyprienne, still obsessed by the mysterious summons, could hardly wait to set foot there. In fact, she said: "Let's go down, my friend Jean. I'd like to make contact with these creatures. Via them, I sense, I'll find the trace of my father."

To that desire the engineer had no serious objection to oppose. The subterranean population appeared to be composed of inoffensive beings. Furthermore, the means of defense—and if necessary, of attack—at the disposal of the passengers of the airplane were of a nature to set aside any dread.

The Halcyon-Car therefore headed toward the ground, and settled lightly.

Chapter Seven
NATURE INVERTED

Of the first impression they received on setting foot in that bizarre world, the heroes of the adventure were to conserve an unforgettable memory.

While remaining awake they seemed to perceive sensations of dream, almost of nightmare. It was baroque and incoherent; it seemed to violate or invert all the laws of nature to which humans are accustomed.

First of all, the light, shining—as we have said—from the ground instead of descending from the sky produced, logically, the strange phenomenon of suppressing the shadows of objects; they were illuminated so bizarrely that they took on an appearance of unreality.

In the second place, the luminosity of the ground differed so much from solar light that it disquieted the eye maladapted to perceive it. Imagine that, on earth, the ultra-violet or infrared rays suddenly became perceptible to us other than by their beneficent or harmful effects on our organism. Suppose too that we could perceive their color. That was almost what Jean Chapuis and his companions experienced.

There was also the unfamiliar vegetation by which they were surrounded: plants with fantastic forms, grimacing flowers whose inverted calices were turned toward the ground, the source of light and heat, the illuminated parts of which were all below, while it was the upper side of the leaves and flowers that were in shadow.

There were the trees, finally: trees of Dantesque nightmare, the opulent foliage of which, avid for light, spread out over the ground, while every inverted trunk, projecting its base into the air, was crowned with roots that could be compared to the heads of gorgons.

In that landscape of wan ashen light, multitudes came running from all directions, stopping and prostrating themselves a few meters from the Halcyon,

Soon, an immense circle of subterran creatures surrounded the bird and its passengers, and thousands of wailing voices intoned a chant.

"A nice reception," said Victor Laridon, amazed.

"They mistake us for gods," explained the engineer, "or at least for *djinn*. We've fallen from the sky… from what they must call their sky."

"Then let's try to measure up," proposed the mechanic, swelling with pride. In order to take on the role, he struck a majestic pose, addressing gestures of benison to the crowd.

Tai, whom Cyprienne was holding by the hand, had to become a more appropriate interpreter; he started to address the nearest of its siblings with incomprehensible worlds. They were greeted by a great silence, succeeded by a formidable explosion of joy.

"He's introducing us and they're wishing us welcome," said the mechanic.

Doubtless obedient to Tai's suggestions, the members of the crowd got to their feet and formed a respectful double hedge, which seemed to want to trace a route to the Halcyon-Car. At the same time, all the little arms extended toward an agglomeration of buildings that had to be a village, and gazes were ardently fixed on the explorers, appearing to implore them.

Timidly, Tai tugged Cyprienne by her peplos; his gesture indicated the direction of the village.

"They're inviting us to come to their residence," the young woman translated. "In order to accompany these inferior humans, of whom I expect a great dead, Jean, fold up the Halcyon's wings and let's roll along the ground."

The transformation was immediately realized. In the middle of an admiring and respectful cortege, the automobile aircraft carried its passengers toward the village. From the height of its seat, Tai, now enthusiastic and exuberant, did not stop haranguing the crowd.

Cyprienne listened pensively. "It will be necessary for me to learn that language," she murmured. "I have so many questions to ask."

A few minutes later, the Halcyon-Car stopped in the center of one of the subterran agglomerations, which our subglobetrotters, from the height of their airplane, might have been able to mistake for molehills.

The aspect differed notably from that of our surface villages. Although the creatures discovered by the explorers of the unknown world belonged incontestably to the human race, of which they doubtless formed a lost branch, they had not followed their daylit brethren in the path of progress; their civilization remained rudimentary.

What struck the newcomers most of all about those troglodytes of the depths was the veil of melancholy that seemed cast over beings and things alike. The subterranean world appeared to be prey to an incurable sadness. That was doubtless related to the genre of light that illuminated it, and also to the depressing impression produced by the obscure and vaulted sky weighing heavily over the luminous plain.

The world was, in sum, only an immense cavern, and everything—humans animals and plants—must feel imprisoned here The temperature appeared to be almost constant, but as experience was later to inform Jean Chapuis and his companions, the electricity enclosed in the vast pocket could give birth to storms, and turbulence and whirlwinds sometimes agitated the air.

The entire village was constructed of the luminous substance that formed the ground, with the result that the exterior as well as the interior of dwellings was radiant, like everything else, and no restful shade could be found there. They did not contain any furniture, but only vegetable fiber mats and a few utensils and pots of primitive manufacture and vulgar form.

Ignorant of all refinements, the people did not know how to transform into a pleasure the satisfaction of a need. They vegetated sadly and miserably. One might have thought that they felt themselves to be the victims of some inimical condemnation and that they had lost all courage. They subsisted passively and could not even find the mental force to seek to soften it.

In contemplating those poor, chagrined and paltry beings, imprisoned in that inferno by the incomprehensible cruelty of destiny, Cyprienne felt moved to pity.

It was evident, however, that the appearance of the passengers of the Halcyon, brought by Tai, provoked a sort of awakening in the crowd. It must be considered by them as a fortunate and joyful event, for they were manifesting that in their fashion. The double intention of honoring Tai's protégés and conserving them in their midst stood out clearly in their manner of acting.

In the middle of the habitations, all small and low, a single construction of imposing dimensions rose up. It was not necessary to be an archeologist to divine that it was a temple of sorts. Its walls were not made of luminous stone but of a translucent substance analogous to glass; it permitted the interior to be perceived. A large portal gave access to it.

Completely empty, devoid of an altar, the temple seemed to be awaiting gods.

With enthusiastic clamors the crowd, harnessing itself to the Halcyon-Car, pulled it inside the building.

"They have flair, the marmosets! As garages go, there's none better," appreciated Laridon. He was not overly moved by so many honors. He only thought that the subterrans ought to leave them tranquil, now that they were in their "hotel."

"Sovereigns are acclaimed when they're outside, aren't they? But when they're washing themselves they're left in peace. Are these jokers going to peer at us from every angle without blinking? That's indiscreet, my word, now we're installed. One can't spend one's time smiling at them and blowing them kisses; we have our own affairs to discuss. What are we going to inscribe on the agenda, Boss? Was this the goal of our famous expedition? I'd like to have some grub, myself, so have us served. What do they make in his place?"

Jean Chapuis interrogated Cyprienne with his eyes. She alone could respond to the mechanic's question.

Thoughtfully, the young woman had placed a hand on Tai's head, and she was considering the little creature.

"I don't sense the summons any longer," she murmured. "But if we've been attracted into this lost world, it's not without design. How can I not believe that Oronius alone could have provoked the submarine eruption that opened the doors to this tomb to us? And then what was little Tai doing so far from his siblings in the dark, where we encountered him at a given point in order to serve as our guide? All that was planned and prepared by my father. So why have the signs ceased now? Why is nothing revealing to me the route to follow in order to go to him? If Tai could make himself understood, he'd doubtless explain to me a part of the mystery. Notably, he'd tell me what suggestion he was obeying in venturing into the tunnel where we found him. And he'd also tell me whether we're the first surface humans to penetrate into this abode."

"You expected to find your father here then?" asked the engineer.

"Yes," she replied. "I had that firm hope. It was one of those intuitions that one can't resist. Jean, do you remember the voice that we heard one day? Oronius is alive! He's cried that to us himself in a comprehensive fashion."

"How could he have come all the way here?"

"My father sank into the earth. You recounted the catastrophe of Belleville to me yourself: the explosion provoked by Jarrousse, Hantzen's envoy... Oronius' Villa sinking into a crater."

"Perhaps to be pulverized there."

"Nothing is less certain. The skeleton ejected was not that of my father, since we've heard his voice subsequently. By means of his science, Oronius commanded all the forces of Nature. He was even master of the elements. Have you been able to forget it? Where anyone else would have perished, he could have, must have, saved himself. My father was able to reach the center of the terrestrial globe safe and sound. That's why I can reasonably expect that these beings settled in the interior of the Earth are capable of informing me about the destiny of Oronius and taking me to him."

"I hope so, my dear Cyprienne; but while waiting for you to find a means of making yourself understood to them and enabling them to understand—or which would be better, waiting for Oronius to manifest himself again and furnish us personally with the means to rejoin him—don't you think that the wisest thing would be to explore this strange terrestrial cave in order to search for traces of your father… if any exist."

"Yes, Jean, that's necessary. Take Victor and Julep with you. I'll stay here with Turlurette and Mandarinette; I'll try to enter into communication with the little inhabitants of this sad world."

Chapter Eight
THE FLAMBOYANT TEMPLE

A crepuscular circle surrounded the luminous plain, and then the empire of darkness commenced in all directions. In that region there was nothing but somber gulfs and fantastic defiles plunging ever further forward into the bowels of the earth. They were too numerous for the engineer to think of exploring them all. To make a choice was embarrassing, and to follow a trail at random in the tangled maze of that eternal night was to risk not being able to return to Cyprienne.

Did Jean have the right to abandon the young woman whose safety he had sworn to ensure? No! He therefore limited himself to exploring the plain within the limits traced by the artificial daylight and visiting all the villages one by one.

Everywhere, the prostrate populations welcomed him, but nowhere did he succeeded in identifying the slightest sign permitting him to believe that Oronius had passed that way.

Oh his return, he found Cyprienne very excited.

"Great news, Jean" she cried, running to meet him. "First of all, an indisputable sign; by special favor, as if my ears had opened to the unknown language, I've just heard and understood everything that Tai and those of his race were saying around me. I've adapted myself, in an instant, to all the subtleties of that unknown language. That can happen, you know, in cases of hypnotism or clairvoyance. Entranced mediums have responded to certain questions posed in a language they don't speak. Now, who could have taken possession of my mind in order to realize that new prodigy, if not my father? It's certainly by means of him that it has been permitted to me to understand and speak the subterran language.

"This in what I've learned by interrogating Tai and his siblings: they take us for supernatural beings descended from the sky... from a sky that they imagine to have above them. What is extraordinary in that belief, the fundamental basis of their religion, is that the Paradise they have described to me corresponds exactly to the sunlit surface of our globe. They speak, as of supernatural regions inaccessible to the living, of all the splendors that are familiar to us. They have a prescience of our atmosphere, the sea, forests and blue-tinted summits. Isn't the divination unusual, Jean? For in reality, they're ignorant of the splendors of the surface that we take for granted. Their responses to my questions have proved that they don't suspect that it's a reality and that there's a different world above theirs… a paradise by comparison with their Gehenna. How can you explain that prescience and that ignorance?"

"In a very simple fashion," the young engineer replied. "Indubitably, we have before our eyes a branch of the human race, having a common origin with it. Without any possible doubt, the ancestors of these degenerate creatures, diminished by the lack of air and light, must have been born on the surface of the Earth, living there and aware of all its advantages. How did they come to subterranean life? A difficult question to resolve, but I imagine this: at a certain epoch of the tertiary age, in the course of one of the formidable convulsions that shook the globe then might have buried an entire country. Mountains torn from their bases, rejoining and adhering together, sealed the gulf. They form the ceiling of this gigantic pocket at the center of which life has continued. Buried alive and without the possibility of returning to the light of day because of the waves that have covered the surface, the unfortunates and their descendants must have adapted to subterranean existence. Gradually, the memory of the former existence led by their more fortunate ancestors has become confused and faded away. After a certain number of generations, it was no longer anything but a legend, and that legend became the basis of a religion. And that, my dear Cyprienne, is how Tai's siblings have been able to describe to you, in accordance with a conserved tradition, the marvels of our sky and the mildness of life in our verdant plains or on the edge of the blue and green waves. They speak of them as of a non-existent world, an Eden that only their spirits can contemplate after death."

"Poor folk!" said the young woman, sadly. "Now I can explain their belief in a divinity who will inform them of the road to paradise and lead them there."

"It's necessary to see in that myth the deformed memory of efforts their ancestors made to regain the surface."

"I understand now what prestige we borrow in their eyes. We descend from the sky. We might be the envoys charged with guiding them toward that existence of delights."

"Hmm!" said the young engineer. "It would be a scabrous mission and we'd be rendering a very poor service to the humans up above. Imagine, Cyprienne, what the invasion would be of these creatures so long confined in a kind of inferno? Emerged from Gehenna, they would no longer dream of anything but conquering all the ecstasies of the terrestrial paradise that was revealed to them. And as our landowners wouldn't see with a glad eye that invasion of intruders, careless of our customs and laws, it would certainly produce a bloody collision. I see an atrocious and merciless struggle between the former possessors of the surface, determined to defend their domain against any trespass, and these unfortunates, fighting desperately and savagely in order not to be cast back into their tomb. In fact, do we know how many they are? If they have multiplied in the same proportions as the surface-dwellers, we can fear that there isn't sufficient room for them up there."

"That's a terrible thought, Jean,"

"Alas, it's the law of existence. It assigns to everyone the place they must occupy, and its orders can't be transgressed without danger. So, for the tranquility of these unfortunates, we must refrain from revealing the truth to them."

Cyprienne sighed.

"They expect so much from us," she murmured. "We've awakened a splendid hope in them. We're the ones who were supposed to come, for whom they've been waiting for centuries. In their imagination, their god has finally been granted to them… for that's what I was coming to. That's the cause of the agitation in which you've found me; in an epoch that they can't specify but must be fairly recent, a genius was manifest to them. They could perceive him, contemplate him, hear him…for the magician spoke to then; they've described his formidable voice to me. The description immediately made me think of the Oroniphone, the marvelous loudhailer invented by my father, which permits him to be heard from one end of the world to the other."

Pensively, the engineer shook his head.

"In what place was that idol manifest?" he asked. "I've made the tour of the luminous plain, or very nearly, and I haven't perceived anything that could corroborate what you've learned."

"So far as I can understand, the apparition is visible, not in what they call their sky, as it would be logical to suppose, but, on the contrary, in the inferior regions, at the bottom of a kind of gulf, where we would be more inclined to situate the abode of demons. But isn't everything inverted in this bizarre world, where the light comes from below?"

"Have you been told where this gulf is situated?"

"No. They only speak about it with a superstitious dread. I think I've understood that in order to benefit from the contemplation of that superior being, it's necessary to submit to certain rites, probably at certain times at a designated hour."

"Well, my beautiful Cyprienne, we'll also await that time and that hour. Then we'll join the troupe of the faithful in order to take our homage to their living icon."

The young woman seized her fiancé's hand. "Oh, Jean!" she cried, emotionally. "What if…?"

"Shh!" replied the young engineer. Let's not hazard any supposition. It's unnecessary to prepare a disappointment for ourselves. We'll see with our eyes what it's necessary to think and believe.

The wait was not prolonged. In fact, a few hours after the conversation, a great rumor attracted the attention of our companions to the village.

Each of them carrying a fragment of luminous stone, all the subterrans were emerging from their dwellings and assembling in the square forming the parvis of the temple, and a long procession was beginning to wind through the streets.

Moved by a presentiment, the young woman interrogated Tai, who was giving signs of agitation himself. She divined the imminent realization of her desires.

As soon as she had heard the response, she summoned her friends.

"They're going to the flamboyant temple," she announced. "That's what they call the refuge of the god."

"Let's follow them, then," consented Jean Chapuis, knowing full well that it was the decision that Cyprienne was demanding.

Leaving the Halcyon-Car under the guard of Julep and the two soubrettes, he joined the procession in the company of Cyprienne and Laridon. All three were equipped with the light flying apparatus known as dragonflies, composed by a pair of mechanical wigs. They were thus able to fly over the column of pilgrims and then go on ahead of them once they were sure of the direction they were following. Furthermore, that direction was confirmed by that of convergent columns that were surging from all points of the luminous plain.

The three surface-dwellers, having attained its limit, plunged into the shadow. They were preparing to illuminate their little portable torches when the engineer stopped them.

"Look—that bright mist over there, above the gulf. Won't that be it?"

A few wing-beats brought them above the indicated abyss. Avidly, they plunged their gazes into it.

In the utmost depths, at an incalculable depth, which would doubtless have needed to be expressed in hundreds or thousands of kilometers, a brilliant dot was visible.

It was only a dot, but its luminosity was so intense that the particles of air above the gulf received the reflection of it and appeared to catch fire; the result was the radiant mist we mentioned.

Toward that fabulous and distant focal point, our friends, having knelt down, leaned over hopefully, in order to distinguish it more clearly but without being able to do so.

Behind them, the crowd of subterran beings was drawing nearer. Hundreds of faces leaned over the rim of the hole; thousands of hands brandished the radiant stones and a tumult golf cries rose up.

Then, from the depths of the abyss, the dot appeared to rise progressively and increase in size, then rise again, still growing, until it appeared to touch the edge of the gulf.

And the radiator of life took the form of a flamboyant palace, a palace of fire through which a majestic silhouette was discernible, a human visage with admirable eyes.

Succumbing to an emotion that was too abrupt and too strong, Cyprienne fell to her knees on the edge of the gulf, sobbing and joining her hands.

"Father…! Father...!"

The genius of the abyss whose image appeared to rise as far as the multitude of his worshipers, the god of the subterrans, was Oronius.

Chapter Nine
THE DIABOLICAL VACUUM PUMP

Still prostrate, Cyprienne continued holding out her arms and crying: "Father! You're alive! I can see you! What joy! Tell us what we have to do to join you?"

To pose such a question to someone who was doubtless separated by hundred of leagues might appear to be the height of naivety. Yes, if it had been shouted by anyone but her; but the daughter of the great scientist was not unaware that the Ear of Stentor, invented by her father, was collecting her speech and transmitting it, amplified, all the way to the bottom of the gulf.

The Ear of Stentor was the equivalent of a vocal wireless. That was so profoundly true that the Oroniphone transmitted the response instantly

"Descend all the way to the center of the Earth."

"By what route?" asked Jean Chapuis, in his turn.

Rising from the depths, the voice of Oronius came back, saying: "According to a old dictum, all roads led to Rome. Today, they all lead to where I am. Hurry; I sense an imminent danger."

Cyprienne and her two companions leapt to their feet.

"Soon, Father!" cried the young woman, whose eyes, still tearful, where shining with hope.

Resuming their flight, they returned to Tai's village, and a few moments later, having installed themselves in the Halcyon-Car, still equipped in its form as a rolling automobile, they departed at top speed across the luminous plain.

From the distance, roared by the powerful voice, one last item of advice reached them: "Prudence!"

The Halcyon-Car was all ardor and impetuosity; it devoured distance. With lightning sped it cut across the luminous circle and launched forth into the darkness.

Having switched on the searchlight, Jean illuminated the route.

He saw again the profound fissure already glimpsed, which plunged like infernal defiles into the terrestrial mass in all direction. Remembering what Oronius had said, Jean engaged the Halcyon in the first passage that he found before him.

Scarcely had the aircraft-auto been rolling for a few seconds in that canyon than, with the sound of an avalanche, there was a formidable landslide, A rain of boulders tumbling from all directions cut off the route.

With an extraordinary presence of mind, at the first sound, Jean Chapuis had put the engine in reverse and sent the machine backwards—but not quickly enough.

Leaning toward one another, the walls of the defile had just joined up. Behind, as before, the passage was obstructed. The irritated Earth had imprisoned its audacious violators.

In actuality, was it a revolt of the Earth that had provoked that quake?

Yes; at the entrance to the defile that had just been fatal to the subterranean explorers, a collapse had occurred. Bizarrely, the mass of earth and rock that formed it was not immobilized; it continued to be agitated by shudders, as if some gigantic animal buried in its bosom were seeking to free itself.

And now, in fact, the collapsed mass opened up, giving passage to a kind of giant reptile. It emerged, unwinding its metallic coils, shook itself, and started crawling toward the luminous plain.

Over the imprisoned Halcyon, the rock had therefore closed like jaws.

As the teeth of those jaws were constituted by corners of hard stone with sharp edges, the apparatus might have suffered severely from its bite; it might even have run a great risk of being crushed, but for two circumstances that must have preserved it.

Being transformed into an auto, it had, in effect, drawn back into itself all its fragile organs susceptible of dreading the consequences of a shock. Folded up along its flanks, its wings had been automatically covered by a metallic carapace. Entirely enveloped, the Halcyon had mutated into a smooth fat cigar. Thanks to the protection of that ingenious mechanism, it thus presented less surface and more resistance. Nevertheless, that probably would not have been sufficient to support the abrupt pressure of the rocky jaws, and Jean Chapuis would not have had the time to activate the magnetic current whose repulsive force could protect the apparatus, if hazard had not, at the moment of the collapse, caused a mass of clay to fall upon the aircraft-auto whose elastic envelope served as a shock-absorber. Sliding between the fangs of rock, which closed upon a void, the clay spindle that the auto-aircraft now was became lodged in a crack between the collapsed boulders.

Inside, they heard that rumble, and, on suddenly seeing that opaque envelope cut off the luminous beam of the search-light, the voyagers had experienced a minute of extreme apprehension.

The backward movement remaining ineffective, Jean Chapuis had hastened to apply his brakes. The Halcyon thus remained motionless, immured in its prison of clay.

The aforementioned protective carapace enclosed, after the furling of the wings, the entire body of the aircraft. It was made of an alloy discovered by Oronius, which combined the resistance of chrome steel with the translucency of glass. The engineer was therefore able to examine the situation and announce to his companions: "We're stuck in a pocket of clay. I don't know how we're going to get out of it."

More active than loquacious, he immediately switched on the fabricator of artificial air in order to ensure the passengers' respiration.

"Open the sudators, Victor," he commanded. "We have to try to soften that matrix of clay and pass through it.

The sudators were generators of emollient vapors of such force that even stone melted in contact with them; their emission took place on the external surface of the carapace by way of a system of minuscule holes that constituted veritable pores.

In a few seconds, the exterior of the Halcyon became as moist and shiny as an enfevered body.

The mechanic, placed amid the machines in the inferior part of the direction cabin, of which Jean Chapuis occupied the upper floor, got ready to obey, but a counter-order stopped him.

"No—don't touch anything... What's happening? We're rotating, as if..."

His breath was cut off by the involuntary somersault to which the movement of the Halcyon compelled him. preventing him from continuing.

Around him, as around Laridon, everything had suddenly began to turn, and that rotation accelerated by the second, becoming a kind of whirl.

In the passenger lounge, where the company was assembled of Julep, the little dogs, Cyprienne and her two soubrettes, the impressions were identical. They were all rolling pell-mell against the walls of the cabin, drawn by an infinitely disagreeable gyratory movement. They had the impression of being imprisoned inside a ball rolling down a steep slope, like the "love barrel" of ancient fairgrounds.

And that was really what was happening.

Outside, agitated by further shocks, the rocky walls of the defile, crushed against one another, had straightened up again; between them, the passage became free. But the seismic shock that had just shaken that part of the subterranean world must have aggravated the declivity of the ground singularly, for suddenly, a mass of earth and boulders—everything that was not adherent to a fixed point—started to slide and roll along the slope, plunging into an abyss of thicker darkness.

The enormous spindle of clay in which the Halcyon-Car was enclosed had been obliged to follow that movement, and if the passengers had been able to see the frightful course of their vehicle, turning and bounding in the dark, bumping into the walls of the oblique well in which they were engulfed, their hair would have stood on end.

It was truly fortunate that the Halcyon was protected by that thick armor of clay; otherwise, it would not have survived such a fall. But it was nevertheless the case that such a mode of locomotion constituted, for those submissive to it, an infinitely painful torture. At length, it would have produced serious disruptions in their organism.

Fortunately, Jean Chapuis and Laridon had not lost their presence of mind. As soon as the first bounds of the apparatus, they had cried in unison: "To the looping stabilizer! Engage the axial clutch!"

"That was a maneuver that was familiar to them, the possibility of which they owed to the inexhaustible Oronius. One day, having observed that glissades on the wing, descents like a dead leaf, loops and the various acrobatics of which certain aviators were fond could not have the same charm for uninitiated passengers, the scientist had sought, discovered and perfected a mechanism of cabin suspension that equilibrated them on a free axis, allowing the rest if the apparatus to rotate around them while they retained a horizontal position immutably. It was, in sum, the complete perfection of the invention made for the compass in 1302 by the Italian pilot Gioja,[5] obtaining rectilinear equilibrium for a median parcel no matter in what direction the envelope moved. It was of that device that the mechanic and the engineer had just thought, in order to nullify the disastrous effects of the rotational movement to which their apparatus was submissive.

Hanging on to the machines, they succeeded in seizing the necessary controls Immediately, the cabins ceased to spin and were no longer associated with the somersaults of the

---

[5] Flavio Gioia or Gioja (c. 1300 – ?) is reputed to have been an Italian mariner and inventor, supposedly a marine pilot, and has traditionally been credited with perfecting the sailor's compass by suspending its needle over a *fleur-de-lis* design, and enclosing it in a little box with a glass cover. He was also said to have introduced such design, which pointed North, in deference to Charles of Anjou, the French king of Naples.

tumbling mass, except for an imperceptible swaying movement that was quite tolerable.

They were able then to exchange their impressions with the passengers in the lounge-cabin, who disentangled their arms and legs.

"What happened, Jean?" asked Cyprienne.

Through the vitrified carapace, the young man was able to follow the vertiginous rotation of their envelope.

"We're descending," he said. "That's all that I can affirm."

"That's sufficient for me," replied the intrepid young woman. "Descending is following the right road, since our Rome is down below."

"No doubt," the young engineer could not help murmuring. "But descending at such a sped is called falling, and the heat disengaged by the velocity of our fall, accumulated by friction against the rock, must be sufficient for us to fear a rapid desiccation of our envelope of clay. If it cracks and crumbles, what will become of the Halcyon?"

"My father is watching," was Cyprienne's response.

"Do you really think that he's in a position to aid us?"

"His position doesn't matter. He's alive, conscious and active. Hasn't his brain, a generator of miracles, come to our aid in circumstances even more desperate?"

Jean Chapuis shook his head; he persisted in thinking that Oronius' situation limited his power; he saw the proof of that in the fact that the scientist, although he had survived the explosion of Belleville, had been unable to return to the surface of the earth by his own means.

But events were to prove his fears wrong, for after a time that appeared to him to last for years, the rotation of the ball of clay slowed down and then ceased.

The course of the conglomerated apparatus came to die on flat ground after having slid over several humpbacks on a gentle slope, which arrested its impetus and deadened the final impact.

Desiccated, as Jean had foreseen, the clay crumbled and the searchlight still switched on, illuminated the Halcyon-Car, immobilized at the entrance to a gallery, inevitably more obscure, which appeared to plunge in a steep slope into the eternal darkness.

The Halcyon had scarcely suffered. It recovered its aplomb on its six wheels, ready to roll.

The engineer was less hesitant to launch it forward again because the acoustic tube brought him Cyprienne's suggestion, like a plea: "Push on! Push on, my friend Jean!"

He therefore launched the Halcyon into the gallery—but, the light of the projector having shown him the frightful route, full of fissures and bristling with dangerous ridges, he shouted to Laridon: "To the tank-transformer, Victor!"

A few twists of a handle and the pressure of fingers on various buttons realized the prudent order. The wheels, in being rest, let pass a crown of teeth that were instantly engaged in the endless caterpillar-track of a tank. This transformed, the Halcyon continued to advance, crawling, ready to toy with all obstacles.

The power and perfection of the engines were such that the attainable speed remained considerable.

From his pilot's seat, Jean Chapuis surveyed the course and the perspective revealed to him as the luminous beam of the searchlight cut through the shadow.

Soon he perceived a distant noise that seemed to be coming from the depths of the gallery. As they advanced the noise was augmented, to the extent of becoming intolerable and deafening; one might have thought it the impact of thousands of hammers striking an infernal anvil in unison, and above that alarming cacophony rumbled the roar of a wind that could only come from a gigantic ventilator.

Suddenly, causing the glare of the searchlight to pale, the end of the gallery lit up flamboyantly, becoming a terrifying furnace whose sheets of flame, although distant, blinded the gaze.

Jean Chapuis uttered a cry, thinking that he understood.

"The central fire!"

Did so much matter in ignition announce the proximity of the terrible hearth? If so, it was toward a vat of molten metal, flaming gases and lava that the tank was sliding.

And yet, the temperature of the conduit was not augmented by the radiation of the monstrous oven.

But the excessively perturbed mind of the engineer did not permit him to sketch that remark.

He tried to stop the machine, but the Halcyon did not obey. Drawn by an irresistible airflow, as if by a diabolical vacuum pump, in spite of the hectic resistance of its engines, it flew through the gallery toward the fiery mouth.

"Cooked! Roasted! Flambé! Talk about a feast of chicken casserole!" moaned Victor Laridon, letting himself slide from his seat.

Jean Chapuis had let go of his indocile controls. Bewildered, he raced out of the cabin, traversed the fixation cell and attempted to immobilize the Halcyon. A childish remedy in the midst of that unleashing of tremendous forces! The electromagnetic currents no longer had any effect. The infernal vacuum pump, as if playfully, continued to draw in the tank.

Then, losing all hope and judging that their last hour was about to sound, the fiancé precipitated himself into the lounge, where Turlurette, Mandarinette and Julep were trembling, but where Cyprienne conserved an immutable serenity amid the tumult of the incomprehensibly joyful barking of Pipigg and Kukuss

"Cyprienne! Dear Cyprienne! We're about to perish!" sobbed Jean Chapuis, drawing his fiancée to his heart. "Adieu, Cyprienne!"

"Why perish?" she riposted, with a calm smile. "On the contrary, we're reaching the goal. Slow down!"

Swallowed, so to speak, by the prodigious vacuum pump, the tank emerged from the gallery at that moment and stopped in the middle of an immense grotto filled with a blinding light.

It was not the central fire. That legendary conflagration only existed in the engineer's imagination.

Looming up before his eyes, he only saw the flamboyant façade of Oronius' Vila, the famous Magical Villa, the pride of Paris, engulfed a few months before in the crater of Belleville.

And in the laboratory, a sort of fiery *djinn* surrounded by lightning, Oronius in person, seconded by a grimacing great ape, was directing the labor of thirteen mysterious metallic silhouettes, thirteen statues or iron or bronze, animated by an artificial life.

Chapter Ten
THE REDISCOVERY OF THE MAGICAL VILLA

At the beginning of the twenty-first century Paris had almost perished under a rain of fire, and had only owed its conservation to a rapid intervention by Oronius, the uncontested master of all the sciences. Scarcely had he proved to be the sovereign aegis of the capital of the United State of Europe, however, than an avalanche of sensational communiqués had informed the world of the scientist's demise.

All the libraries of the two hemispheres conserved preciously the summary story of the event. If the phonograms that constituted the newspapers of that epoch had been made to speak again, these are the terms in which they would have reported the disaster that had marked the disappearance of the scientist Oronius and permitted belief in his death:

Today, an inexplicable explosion, the consequences of which have been terrible, destroyed the Magical Villa belonging to the illustrious Oronius, situated, as everyone knows, on the heights of Belleville. At the twentieth hour, a formidable shock followed by a deafening noise shook Paris, and terrified spectators saw the master's dwelling sink into the ground. They were able then to observe that a crater had opened at the place where the villa had stood, from which flames and a rain of debris sprang forth.

Such a relation left no room for any doubt. It did not come to anyone's mind that Oronius might not have been killed in the catastrophe. However, things had not happened exactly as the Parisians supposed.

Let us first recall briefly the causes of the explosion and its circumstances. That evening, an emissary of Hantzen, the enemy and rival of Oronius, had succeeded in slipping into the scientist's laboratory. He wanted to extract from him the secret of his incomparable discoveries. He knew that the scientist was alone there, with no other defender than a great ape answering to the name of Bambo, of whose intelligence and devotion he had no suspicion.

The orangutan Bambo, seeing his master threatened by Jarrousse, Hantzen's envoy, had hurled himself upon the latter. In the course of the struggle engaged between the man and the animal, a flask containing a liquid explosive recently fabricated by Oronius had been overturned and broken.

An explosion had followed—an explosion of a very particular kind, for the product of Oronius' research, the nitrocolle, of which he was justly proud, did not act in accordance with the ordinary rules. Its terrible destructive power was not exercised immediately; it initially escaped in a gaseous form through the molecules of the substance that contained it, and its fracturing effect only followed a few seconds later. At that moment it was outside the villa and underneath it, for, instead of rising, it sank, perforating the ground, hollowing out a bottomless funnel, the void of which initially attracted everything that was above it before hurling it vertically into space.

On seeing the flask of nitrocolle break, Oronius had uttered an involuntary cry. As the scientist who had discovered it, he was not ignorant of any of the properties of the terrible explosive. He could have described minutely everything that was about to happen. In the first place, drawn into the well opened beneath it, the villa would not take long to be projected into the air, where the container and its contents would be volatilized.

But before that destiny, a few seconds would go by. Knowing the exact duration of that respite, the scientist took advantage of it. His glass villa, where so many dangerous forces were liberated, captured or manipulated in the silence of laboratories, had naturally been endowed by him with a protective system that would shield it from all accidents. It could be isolated instantaneously from the rest of the world by a combination of solaric and magnetic currents, which removed all its weight, rendering it insensible to the action of the unleashed forces. In that conjuncture, the villa was practically immobilized in space at zero velocity and it ceased to participate in the velocity of the surrounding bodies, submissive to their reactions or their attraction.

With lightning promptitude, at the moment of the explosion, Oronius bounded to the distribution panel and turned the commutator. The Magical Villa being henceforth isolated at the point in space at which it was positioned at that moment, the explosion of the nitrocolle could not have any effect on it; but a consequence was produced of which Oronius had not had the leisure to think.

The formidable pressure of the gases liberated by the explosive, in the impossibility of being exercised against the base of the villa or its walls, deviated laterally, enlarging the well that had just opened, then fusing around the glass construction and rising up again toward the open air.

Disaggregated by the violence of the explosion, the terrestrial crust had opened up to an incalculable depth, all the way to the igneous center. A volcano was born, the eruption of which was about to terrify the peaceful Bellevillois.

Meanwhile, stabilized in the middle of the volcano's chimney, the Magical Villa saw the Earth pursue its course in space. The orientation of that course was such that the walls of the volcanic chimney were displaced at a velocity of 30,000 kilometers per second alongside the villa, bringing it to the center of the globe.

What became of Oronius during that phenomenon, of which no other epoch had furnished an example, and which would have given the impression to less alert eyes of a fantastic and vertiginous fall into a bottomless well?

As one might think, he had been very busy.

His first gesture—a veritable reflex—had been to apply to his face a mask destined t defend him angst the nitrocolle vapors. For want of that elementary protection, Bambo and Jarrousse fell unconscious at the scientist's feet. He did not have time to help them; it was necessary for him to act.

In complete obscurity—for all the lamps had been pulverized—his extended had ran over a control panel with porcelain buttons, chose one of the latter and pressed it.

What Cyprienne's father wanted to do was to provoke the return of his villa to the surface by interrupting the action of the isolating currents above it, Submissive then to the attraction of everything that was between it and the open air, the crystal house ought to have risen up automatically until Oronius immobilized it again.

His fingers clutching the button, the scientist waited for the reappearance of daylight...

Suddenly, a violent shock broke off the button that he was touching, and he fell to the floor and remained there, stunned.

When he got up again, the Magical Villa was immobilized at the bottom of a well and all the needles of the position-indicator panel marked zero.

Oronius leapt to his feet and uttered a cry of amazement. That series of zeroes, telling him that he had just reached the dead spot where attraction ceases to be felt and where centripetal and centrifugal forces are similarly nullified, disconcerted him.

He had reached the center of the Earth.

Instead of rising up, he had descended. How had that happened?

He switched on a hand-lantern. Then a glance darted at the broken commutator that he was still holding informed him. He had made a mistake; it was the depth button that he had activated.

What rendered the error more serious—because it was irreparable—was that the impact had put his apparatus out of order. Neither the mechanism of ascent nor that of descent was functional any longer. Oronius and his villa were immobilized at the zero point of the planet.

He was alone, all alone, lost at a depth never attained, and with no other means of communicating with human beings except those inspired by his genius!

Alone? Well, no, he was not entirely alone. Jarrousse and the ape Bambo were still lying on the glass sheet that constituted the floor of the laboratory. The scientist bent down and ausculated them one by one. The ape was dead. As for Jarrousse, he was still breathing, and could be recalled to life.

What a problem of conscience was posed to the great scientist at that moment! It was a dangerous enemy that he had the duty of aiding, almost of resuscitating—an enemy with whom it would be necessary to remain in close company, and whom he knew to be capable of anything.

He meditated for a few seconds.

Oronius' mind always functioned with an extraordinary rapidity. He was able to envisage the facts and all their consequences at a stroke; he was able to weigh them, judge and choose. His decision was quickly made.

Before reestablishing the illumination, after a sigh, he got up and extended on an operating table, side by side, the inanimate body of Bambo and the still-palpitant body of Jarrousse.

Oronius was a surgeon of miraculous skill. He could dismantle and reassemble the human machine as a clockmaker could do with the mechanism of a watch or a clock.

In a lapse of time that would have frightened the greatest virtuoso of the scalpel and the disciples of Carrel, he removed from the living individual the unique organ containing the humans personality—which is to say, the brain—plus certain glands indispensable to organic life.

After that, he replaced by those borrowings the organs excised from the dead ape, reestablished the necessary contacts, reconnected the nerves, arteries and veins; then, having completed these various grafts, ligatured and scarred by ultra-rapid procedures employing radio-electricity, he carried out a blood transfusion from the living individual into the veins of the dead one.

Having done that, he went to place Jarrousse's body in a refrigerator and came back to extend his hands over the sutured skull of Bambo.

"Become an ape, Thomas Jarrousse!" he pronounced. "Be unaware when you awake than your bestial body contains a brain and human thought. Lose the memory of your humanity and that of hatred. Obey me henceforth as my poor servant did."

That was not a magic formula but simply a suggestion that Oronius, a master of hypnotism, imposed on his enemy.

That being done, when Jarrousse, thus metamorphosed, woke up, he would have become harmless; subject to the will of Oronius he would have thoughts in conformity with his new form.

Liberated from that care, the scientist could envisage the situation with a level head.

Ought he to abandon the treasures contained in his villa, the fruit of so many years of research and efforts, and try to return to the surface?

Apart from the fact that such an enterprise, since Oronius did not have any efficacious means to transport at his disposal, seemed to be beyond human strength, its execution would require a considerable delay. Before deciding on it, Cyprienne's father would have to make important preparations and create from scratch the resources and equipment that he lacked.

He was therefore forced to consent to a rather prolonged sojourn at the center of the Earth.

Resigned not too reappear very soon among humans, he had consoled himself easily for that. He was certain that his science could put that involuntary retreat to profit.

First of all, he had to occupy himself with resolving a problem that seemed rather delicate at first sight; from the center of the Earth, where he was henceforth a prisoner, he wanted to reenter into communication with humans and keep himself up to date with their actions and gestures. In particular, he was anxious to know what had become of his daughter, Jean Chapuis and all those in whom he was interested. Finally, he must not forget, either, that he had a powerful enemy in Otto Hantzen. The most elementary prudence commanded him to keep surveillance over his actions, while avoiding revealing the particular situation in which the catastrophe had placed him.

On reflection, Oronius decided that he could even obtain a certain superiority from that situation, by prolonging his adversary's illusion that he was now definitively harmless. For that reason, and although it would cost his paternal heart, the scientist decided not to reassure Jean Chapuis and Cyprienne immediately regarding his fate. It would be sufficient to follow by means of the Cyclopean Eye, his radiographic reflector, everything that happened to them.

That apparatus, of unlimited power and delicacy, was composed of a spherical mirror, on which the image could be reflected of any point attainable by a beam of Z-rays, the range of which could be regulated at will. Those rays, discovered by Oronius, could traverse any thickness of the terrestrial mass in order to reveal the landscapes of the surface and the beings moving there.

Handled by a skilful operator, that apparatus and its automatic magnifier, which restored the most minuscule images to their natural size, constituted a kind of precious telescope. It permitted following at any distance and through all obstacles the movements of a person or a determined group.

It was thus that, thanks to the radiographic mirror, Oronius had been able to follow step by step, so to speak, the adventures of Jean Chapuis and the other passengers of the Halcyon-Car. He was no less interested in his enemies, the baleful Hantzen and the mysterious Princess Yogha. We shall see later what he knew about them. Let us say for the moment that he had not ceased to intervene and guide those he protected by means of emanations of his thought launched through space as cerebral messages.

To speak, he had the Oroniphone, a marvelous loudhailer that transformed the slightest murmurs into a thunderous voice susceptible of resounding simultaneously at the extremities of the globe. To listen he had his Ear of Stentor, registering all the sounds of space.

In sum, he possessed an infinity of subjugated forces, commencing with the lightning that he had been able to capture and store.

His months of subterranean labor had been fecund. To the aerial forces he had joined other marvels, which we shall see appear in turn.

In brief, he was truly well-armed to play his god-like role, and the fashion in which he had just attracted his daughter and her fiancé to him, through the terrestrial crust, was sufficient proof of his power.

Chapter Eleven
THE CATOPTRIC BALL

The Halcyon-Car had, therefore, stopped outside the flamboyant villa.

Inside, Oronius held out his arms to his daughter, who was the first to leap out of the apparatus.

Still bewildered by the lightning descent that had brought them to the center of the globe, all of Cyprienne's companions, unbruised but slightly unsteady on their legs, hastened to descend n their turn.

Pipigg and Kukuss had precipitated forward first, barking joyfully.

The doors of the villa opened then and the scientist, accompanied by iron automata liberated from their tasks, advanced to meet his daughter, who fell into his arms, sobbing.

"Oh, Father! Good Father! I've finally found you again. I can embrace you!"

The illustrious castaway at the pivot of the world hid his real emotion beneath the mocking smile that was habitual to him.

"Bonjour, little daughter! Bonjour, my dear Jean. Bonjour, you others," he pronounced, with the slightly surly cordiality with which elite sensibilities willingly mask themselves. "Well, here they are, in a good enough condition, in spite of the steep plunge that I was obliged to inflict on them. Here's Laridon and Master Julep, and that scatterbrain Turlurette. And this one? Oh, yes, it's the little Chinese girl... Mandarinette, I believe. I only know her as yet via my revelatory mirror... we'll make a more ample acquaintance. My word, my brave friends, you wouldn't believe how satisfied I am to see you again. It isn't very merry at the center of the Earth, and I don't exactly have cheerful company here."

He darted a glance at the thirteen automat arranged around him and the ape, toward which the negro had just precipitated himself effusively.

But the individual that Julep mistook for Bambo did not appear to recognize him and only responded with the utmost coldness to his advances.

"Oh, that's true," sighed Oronius. "My poor Bambo was your friend, my brave Julep. Alas, you won't see him again; Bambo is dead."

"Dead, Bambo?" exclaimed the stupefied servant. "Oh, Master wants to joke. Here he is, against my heart.

"No. Evidently, they resemble one another closely—for it's even better than a resemblance, since you're contemplating the skin of poor Bambo, his camel-hair suit. Only, it's changed tenant. My friends, I present to you the former Jarrousse, to the intervention of whom I owe being here. He was an unsociable fellow, and particularly indiscreet, a little gift of my competitor Hantzen, to say all. Now, for the sake of my personal amusement, and taking advantage of the fact that the body of the devoted Bambo was vacant, I've made an ape of him."

At those startling words, Julep had stood aside fearfully. Jean and Cyprienne, almost sharing that sentiment, considered the ape-man with a visible revulsion.

"Him, Jarrousse?" articulated the engineer.

"Shh!" said Oronius. "I've persuaded him of the contrary. He believes that he's Bambo. Let's refrain from undeceiving him. It would be had for his docility."

"And these?" asked Cyprienne's fiancé, indicating with a timid finger the mysterious animate statues.

The face of the Master shone with pride. "My creatures! My masterpiece," he confessed, complaisantly. "Look at them; I've made artificial humans."

To tell the truth, the automata of which the illustrious scientist seemed so proud were not exactly beautiful to behold. Their strange and massive silhouette disquieted the eye; they were rigid, seemingly enclosed in prisons of steel. Their heads were only round balls, devoid of noses and mouths. Two holes in the formless mask allowed glass lenses to appear and two microphones occupied the placed of the ears.

"It's not extremely difficult to construct a man," he continued. "A network of electric wires can replace the nerves, muscles and tendons, animating the arms, the legs and even the heart. The artificial, in these different accessories, offers nothing very meticulous. The brain is another matter. Multiple trials had disappointed me greatly, for those I succeeded in realizing lacked the principal thing—which is to say, thought. In brief, I'd succeeded in constructing infinitely improved automata, but they were still automata, even so. It remained to animate them; until I found the solution to that problem I was keeping them in a cupboard. When I arrived here I thought of utilizing them in discovering a radium mine. I found my solution. The combination of radium and etherium renders the mechanical brains of these automata sensitive to cerebral waves. My thought directs them and activates their motor centers. They live my life; they realize the gestures desired by me. I no longer have only one body; I have fourteen of them!"

He stopped in order to enjoy the wonder of his audience, particularly that of Jean Chapuis.

"It's convenient," he concluded, summoning one of the automata and covering the metallic ball that served it as a head. "When their services are unnecessary to me, I only have to cut the communication and remove this."

He took out of the steel box a delicate mechanism, the central part of which was constituted by a series of tubes of radium and etherium. "The radioactive brain," he announced, "which is to say, a receiver and accumulator of cerebral fluid. Ours doesn't play another role; contrary to an opinion too generally admitted, the brain isn't the organic producer of thought. That is nothing but a special kind of electricity. It exists throughout space, more or less abundant or rarefied; it passes in the form of innumerable currents, and the brains that it bathes store it in passing."

The theory of that new paternal discovery only interested Cyprienne mildly. She was entirely given to the joy of seeing her father again, and could not weary of manifesting it to him. And she had so many questions to ask! The adventures of the stubborn struggler impassioned her more than the story of the automata.

"Wicked Father," she said, drawing him into the villa whose disappearance was lamented by the Parisians "Why did you leave me so long in that terrible doubt? Why didn't you let me know immediately what had happened to you and how we could reach you?"

Before responding, Oronius made sure that the iron automata, aided by the ape-man, were taking care of the Halcyon-Car and putting it in a safe place. Closing the door of his laboratory then, he opened a tap. Immediately, a cloud of vapors flowed between the double walls of glass and extended like a curtain between the external world and the scientist's guests.

"Thanks to that precaution, I'm assured that no indiscreet person can discover my secrets," he explained. "Those vapors absorb thought-waves and prevent them from reaching other brains that can equip themselves with amplifiers of the Aqueduct of Silvius, the name give by me, as you know, to my cerebral listeners. The conquests made by humanity on the path of scientific progress complicate existence greatly. Once, in order to keep a secret, it was sufficient to keep quiet and not to write... Now, those who have an interest can even eavesdrop on our thoughts. Fortunately I've found a means of avoiding that inconvenience."

"Do you fear someone, then?" asked Jean Chapuis, paling slightly, for he anticipated the response.

"Yes," said he scientist, respiring forcefully. "And that's why I don't want anyone to know about the state of immobility I'm in at the bottom of this well. That was the reason for which I had to use illusory subterfuges in order to bring you here without revealing my retreat. In truth, I scarcely fear an attack on their part of my adversaries, although they aren't disarmed, nor to be disdained. I have the wherewithal to riposte. The only thing that worried me was seeing you exposed to their thrusts.

"Seeing us?" queried the astonished engineer.

"Of course, yes, seeing you. I haven't lost sight of you for a single instant, and it's quite unnecessary to seek to relate your misadventures to me. I've lived them with you, I can assure you., minute by minute."

"How?"

"Thanks to this mirror."

They all grouped around the marvelous optical apparatus designated by the scientist. The first examination disappointed them. It was a simple ball of silvered glass isolated and suspended in the middle of a cage made of a tissue of threads so tenuous and transparent that they were invisible. It was necessary to touch them with a finger to observe their presence between the spectator and the ball.

Its diameter was about three meters; but, singularly, although the silvered and polished layer that coated it gave it the aspect of a mirror, no image seemed to be reflected there. And yet, by reason of its dimensions, it would have been natural for it to send back, considerably magnified, the anxious faces that were leaning toward it. There was nothing of that, and hat surprised the young engineer. Did the network of invisible threads surrounding the ball have the property of stopping luminous rays?

"On the contrary," responded Oronius, to whom Jean Chapuis expressed that suspicion. "It receives them and directs them, amplified, at the reflective surface of the mirror globe. But it's only distant images that form there. Nearby objects can only be seen there by means of a special focusing device. In fact, you have before your eyes a representation of the terrestrial globe. It's the perfection, attaining the supreme degree, of the ancient catoptric mirror of Patras. A beam of radiation departed from the center of that sphere, which I direct as I wish by means of these commutators, can go to illuminate any part of space; its image is then reflected on the surface of the mirror-globe. I can determine and choose the point of observation at will, thanks to this vertical needle, the tip of which can move over this graduated planisphere. It's the region depicted by the point at which the needle is aimed that is illuminated and reflected. This wheel permits me to circumscribe or extend, bring closer or move away the field observed. Look, here's the point of the ocean where you were engulfed."

"I can't see anything," protested Jean Chapuis, squinting in vain.

Oronius smiled. He had just placed a sort of crown on his head, equipped with a system of lenses ad prisms.

"Put my spectacles on," he said, simply, holding out a similar object to the young man.

Jean Chapuis had already recognized it. He understood. It was the Cyclopean Eye, a marvelous enhancer of vision, adapted to the relativity of time and space. When focused, it could provide a magnification of several thousand times and render perceptible the most distant objects or those most infinitesimal in relation to the human scale.

Scarcely had the young engineer placed it before his eyes than the surface of the globe and was illuminated and amplified. He saw the extent of the ocean before him and the infinity of the sky; he distinguished the waves, which had become peaceful again.

For her part, Cyprienne admired a similar spectacle

"You see, it was easy for me to follow you with my eyes," said Oronius. "Day and night, while my automata, inspired by my thought, accomplished my work, I never ceased to accompany you. I even saw things that escaped you. Do you remember your escape from the tower of Everest, the lair of Hantzen and Yogha, where our brave Jean came to deliver the imprisoned Cyprienne?"

"How could we forget those hours of anguish?" murmured the young woman, emotionally.

"Fallen himself into the power of the infernal Yogha, Jean ran as many dangers there as you, my little Cyprienne. If Victor and Julep, the devoted lads, had not succeeded in introducing themselves into the tower, the adventure would have turned out very badly for you. Fortunately, I was watching. I was able to transmit a few cerebral messages, which they received without knowing it, for, also unknown to them, I had previously endowed the with my amplifier. Inspired by me, they extricated you from the hands of your enemies, whom you believed that you had punished by destroying their lair."

"They suffered that fate," said Jean. "They could not have escaped. And the tower was destroyed behind us by an explosion that I had provoked."

"Child!" riposted Oronius. "They escaped."

"How? Deprived of sentiment, they were incapable of moving!"

"Little inconsequent! You were unaware of the hidden presence of one of their accomplices, that Wiwar, placed with me to spy on me, who rejoined his masters after my disappearance. While you were quitting the tower, Wiwar recalled Hantzen and Yogha to life. They had the means to flee. There again, you did not advise yourselves—and yet you had experienced personally the qualities of the *Spherus*, that extraordinary metallic Montgolfier that can be directed at a distance by Hertzian waves."

"Could, you mean?"

"Well, no, I saw the *Spherus* fly away. Hantzen, Yogha and Wiwar were inside it."

"But the apparatus could only be moved and directed by the action of Hertzian currents," objected the engineer. "Hantzen's tower, which emitted them, thus constituted the directing station indispensable for the utilization of the Spherus. The destruction of the tower should have left our enemies helpless, in consequence, without a means of guiding the curse of their aerostat."

Oronius shrugged his shoulders.

"Scatterbrain. Could a man of science, in such a case, not discover a means of getting out of difficulty? I didn't follow the course of the *Spherus*; you interested me more. I don't know what has became of it, but I can guarantee that it descended to earth again and that it brought the worthy Hantzen and his coterie down safe and sound. The trio must only be dreaming of revenge. I have all the more reason to be anxious about their projects because..."

The scientist's brow darkened and furrowed anxiously. Without finishing his sentence, he forgot himself in a silent meditation that they refrained from troubling.

Finally, he raised his head. "This is what worries me," he confessed. "I have, as you can imagined, tried several times to reestablish to my profit contact between me and the suspect individuals. In your interest and that of humankind I needed to discover what they might be plotting. Now, something bizarre happened. In spite of the means of investigation at my disposal for searching time and space, the trio has escaped my grasp. I sensed them, I divined them, I brushed them, but I could not attain hem, perceived hem or touch them. Sometimes, my detector of cerebral currents and recording apparatus, specially constructed, signaled some threads of thought to me, immediately blurred and indecipherable. They emerged from the brain of Hantzen and immediately escaped me, leaving me full of apprehension because of what I had surprised. Evidently, the scoundrels are meditating terrible reprisals… the total destruction of humankind, apart from themselves. Can you imagine the world reduced to that trio of bandits?

The Master waved his arms furiously.

"At any rate," he went on, my efforts to discover Hantzen's projects have remained unfruitful. The plagiarist must have discovered the secret of one of my thought insulators and is using it; I'm reduced to admitting it. It's also necessary that he has reconstituted my famous formula of translucent substances. The exposure of the human body for a given time to the action of certain radiations renders it permeable to light; all rays traverse it, none is reflected. Practically, the body becomes invisible, our eyes unable to perceive its contours or its surfaces. That's the only explanation I've found for the astonishing disappearance of Hantzen, Yogha and Wiwar. It's necessary for us to be strictly on our guard, for they might be able to follow in your tracks, and who can tell whether they might not already be in pursuit of you in his subterranean empire? The might have thought, if they suspect my survival, that you would guide them to me. I represent, in Hantzen's judgment, a threat too serious for him to risk carrying out his plans before having eliminated me."

Cyprienne and Jean Chapuis had listened to that explanation with an increasing anxiety. When Oronius stopped talking, they looked at one another.

"Master," pronounced the engineer in a trembling voice, "I ought to talk to you about a fact that might give reason to your fears. When, after quitting the luminous plain, we wanted, in conformity with your indication, to launch ourselves into one of the defiles susceptible of leading us to you, we were the victims of a singular accident. Was it you who provoked it, Master? Did you cause the landslide and the earthquake that nearly imprisoned us?"

Oronius shook his head. "No; it wasn't me."

"And you suspect...?"

"Nothing! I search. For your accident, my surprise was equal to yours. When my instruments informed me of your proximity to that bizarre seismic shock, I started to investigate. Your embarrassment having been revealed to me, I did what was necessary to unleash the further shocks that got you out of it, Apart from that I don't know what to think about the initial phenomenon."

Turning suddenly toward the mirror-bal, Oronius maneuvered the mechanism, after having replaced the Cyclopean Eye on his forehead. "Let's explore the theater of the accident," he proposed. "Perhaps we'll discover traces there susceptible of clarifying the enigma."

Jean had imitated him. On the surface of the reflective sphere he saw the image of the landslide form.

Directed by Oronius, the ray-projector must then have penetrated the collapsed mass in order to search it, for the engineer saw the image gradually transform and become confused...

A kind of rip having suddenly shown itself there, and having been patiently brought into focus by the scientist, he was able to see a breach in which the beam of rays was engulfed. Illuminated, the wall of a tunnel that went back up through the terrestrial mass appeared.

He imprinted the catoptric globe with a movement of rotation, which caused to file before Jean's eyes at a vertiginous speed the entire extent of the tunnel.

At such a speed—which must have been that of light—the surface was soon attained.

"I suspected as much," said Oronius, with satisfaction. "There's the thread. If something came down, it was by that route. I confess, however, that I can't divine what sort of beast or machine could dig through the terrestrial crust like that and open a route to such a depth. That devilry bears the mark of Hantzen."

"If it's him, what could he be attempting?" asked Cyprienne. "Whatever his audacity, he couldn't think of attacking us head on. And we're together again...what have we to fear?"

"What have we to fear?" Oronius repeated, slowly.

The question is understandable; he was posing it to himself.

The impetuous Laridon knew no such doubts. He had a blind confidence in the science and omnipotence of the Master.

"If he has entered the realm of the moles, so much the worse for him," cried the engineer, impetuously. "He can't succeed and you'll stick it to him. Let's admit that the fellow comes to knock on this door—aren't we here to receive him and give him the politeness he merits? We won't even need to get mixed up in it. Hasn't M'sieur Oronius got the trump card? He only has to say the word and all the inhabitants of these caves will fall on the hides of Hantzen and Yogha. Those monkeys are people who have religion. If necessary, they will come to inquire of their Buddha. They're too good! Remember their genuflections, Mamzelle Cyprienne! They won't lose their faith so soon."

Scarcely had he finished that profession of faith than an immense clamor filed the eternal silence of the central space.

That rumor was so tragic and so menacing that it made a frisson run over the skin of those who heard it. It emerged from the immense well by means of which Oronius communicated with the inhabitants of the somber world and offered himself to their adoration.

Chapter Twelve
THE IMPIOUS REVOLT

They all looked at one another, troubled and impressed. What did that tumultuous plaint signify? Who was provoking it and what events did it announce?

It was, in any case, impossible to mistake the sentiments that it expressed. It was a storm of anger confining frenzy.

Supposing that the vociferation was the voice of a crowd—and everything indicated that, since it was made up of thousands of voices—the crowd was out of control and had attained the paroxysm of irritation; there could be no doubt about that.

Without turning round, Oronius had sketched a mute gesture; immediately, the thirteen silhouettes of metallic men came to form up before the villa, into the interior of which the man changed into an ape reentered.

"To the niche," Oronius commanded him. "We have no need of you for the moment."

And the human animal, obedient to his dominator, went to lurk in a small lodge, where he was immediately imprisoned.

"Now let's go up to the observatory," said the scientist, having recovered his calm. "It's necessary to know what's happening up there. If necessary, I'll talk to the simpletons, whom some event must have panicked."

"Can it be them?" said Jean Chapuis, astonished. "Do you think them capable of those cries of fury and hatred?"

"It seems so," replied Oronius, shaking his head.

"For what cause? If they were in danger, I thought them more likely to cry their distress. It's supplications that you ought to be hearing."

"Or those cries aren't addressed to you," suggested Cyprienne.

"Who knows?" said Oronius, dubiously.

And as Laridon seemed indignant, ready to express in energetic terms an opinion unflattering for the "tenants upstairs," the Master added: "Are you forgetting human versatility? They can't be different from crowds on the surface, always ready to jeer and tear down the idols they were acclaiming a moment before. The gods of humans, in any epoch, are not sheltered from these disgraces. Let's go up."

They went up the glass staircase and reached the terrace of the villa.

Oronius had installed various items of apparatus here, including an array of projectors whose beams could be concentrated on an enormous crystal lens, under which he placed himself.

Having done that, he turned the commutator that produced the light, and his silhouette, greatly magnified by the lens, must have appeared fully illuminated to the crowd massed around the rim of the well.

The clamors redoubled; thanks to the amplificatory microphones, the scientist was able to distinguish, if not the words, at least the tone.

Oronius was an accomplished polyglot who, having studied the mechanics of all human languages and knowing all the sounds capable of emerging from a human throat, could assimilate any language in a matter of hours. It was thus relatively easy for him to divine the meaning of the subterrans' cries. They were expressing insults and threats.

As it was the apparition of Oronius that had just unleashed that new tempest and had increased its violence, the scientist could not be under the slightest illusion; the insulting tumult was definitely addressed to him.

As he had foreseen, the subterrans, instead of prostrating themselves, stood up and brandished menacing fists at their god.

Their inexplicable anger did not stop there. They had to have serious grievances against their innocent idol; or—which came to the same thing—they had allowed themselves to be persuaded that they had.

In fact, combining hostile gestures with the abuse, they suddenly began hurling a hail of luminous stones into the well, which rained down on Oronius. The faithful were stoning their god!

Certainly, the scientist was not a man to be moved by the sacrilege. His philosophy enabled him to be indulgent to poor humanity. The specimens to whose stupid fury he was presently subjected were among the most disinherited, and consequently among the least responsible. However, if the Master's self-esteem did not suffer overmuch from such a reversion and the loss of a popularity that he had not solicited, it was not the same for his person and the objects surrounding him. The hurricane of stones risked damaging his precious apparatus and himself.

Thus, he resigned himself to extinguishing his projectors, in order to disappear temporarily from the gazes of the furious.

Then, aided by Jean Chapuis and his mechanic, he hastily extended a protective net over the villa. Having thus interrupted the rain of stones, or having at least rendered it inoffensive, he then made use of the Oroniphone to launch a sincerely felt rebuke to the angry people in his turn, in an irritated voice.

As his discourse was naturally pronounced in the subterran language, neither Jean nor his companions understood its meaning, but they divined nevertheless, by the gestures and the intonation, that Oronius was expressing his discontentment and his indignation, and that he was striving to calm the rebels down and threatening them with legitimate reprisals.

In spite of his eloquence and the power of the onoriphone, he failed completely in his design, for a veritable tempest of cries and roars never ceased to respond to each of his admonitions. Far from convincing them, they appeared to exasperate the terrible little iconoclasts.

Chagrined, the scientist ended up abandoning the game.

"They're stubborn," he observed, moping his brow. There's nothing to be done. Their Manitou appears to them henceforth to be a simple creature, on which they are heaping anathemas and derision. That transformation cannot be spontaneous; it has a cause. For the moment, the cause escapes me. In any case, those people, who honored me and admired me are treating me at present not only as a false prophet or an impostor whose lies have been discovered, but also as an undesirable whom they want to call to account. Patience! Although the matter is presently incomprehensible, we'll clarify it eventually. Let's proceed in order. We ought to commence by returning the furious to reason. A little lesson, I think, will suffice to reinculcate the respect that is due, if not to my person, at least to my age!"

He smiled and murmured in an aside: "If I told them that I was already alive in the epoch when their ancestors were buried, they'd be very surprised. What would be the point?"

"Don't be too severe," begged Cyprienne "Remember that these poor beings constitute an inferior race, disadvantaged with regard to intelligence. It's necessary to treat them like children."

"That's certainly my intention, my darling child. However, the greatest service I can render children of that sort is to correct them when they aren't well-behaved. At least that will prevent them from pushing their stupidity as far as the irreparable."

"Might these rebellious and badly-behaved children not constitute a danger?" hazarded Jean Chapuis. "Their number is considerable. If they can't be brought back to reason and are obstinate in demonstrating their hostility to you, perhaps we'll be constrained, in order to defend ourselves, to make veritable hecatombs among them."

Cyprienne shuddered, pale with horror.

Smiling paternally, Oronius hastened to reassure her. "We won't be reduced to that extremity," he declared. "I can attain them without there being any direct contact between them and me. Our sole means of communication is this well, the opening of which I've just obstructed. I've therefore reduced their maleficent action, already very limited, to nullity. For the rest, they're too far away from me to be feared."

"Might they not have the idea of trying to come down here?"

In response to that question from Jean Chapuis, Oronius sketched a disdainful grimace and riposted: "Let's see, my friend; let's reason a little. With what are you fabricating your scarecrow? You've seen these people at close range and have been able to judge the rudimentary state of their industry and their civilization. All science is unknown to them. They're reduced to the miserable conditions of existence of the first ages: no machines, no other weapons than those of the Stone Age. How could they attack, and by what means could they cross the distance that separates then from us? It would take them years. In any case, even if that became possible for them, nothing in the world could convince them to leave the field of the protective radiations, to the action of which centuries of adaptation have habituated them, in order to plunge into the tenebrous routes that lead to the center of the Earth."

"You're exaggerating their fear of the dark," the engineer objected. "The enterprise before which, you claim, an entire people would recoil, one paltry and isolated creature has dared."

"You're alluding to Tai?" said the Master, smiling. "Know that that one was sent by me to serve as your guide. I insufflated him with the necessary courage, and my will never ceased to inspire him. He believed, in any case, that he was reaching paradise—or, in other terms, climbing the route that leads to the sky, the legendary sky that we, the humans of the surface, know is not a chimera."

"Why, Father, did you toy with the faith of that unfortunate?" said Cyprienne, in a tone of reproach.

"Tai has had his recompense," Oronius assured her. "He has glimpsed the sky of which he dreamed. His wonderstruck eyes, guided by me, have seen the ground and the ocean open. For two or three minutes, they were able to contemplate the dazzling infinity that is the celestial immensity. And they witnessed the miracle of the descent of envoys of the gods. In you, Tai could not see anything else. Having had the privilege of guiding you, nothing can corrode his faith henceforth. He will conserve it even if all his brethren lose it—which has doubtless occurred. I'll wager that he is not among our lapidators. Who knows? Perhaps he has undertaken my defense and has exposed himself to the reprisals of the furious."

"Oh, Father! If that's the case, can't you do something for him?"

"If he's still alive, I can extract him from their hands," Oronius promised. "If he has suffered because of us, I'll give him the finest recompense that a subterran can receive: I'll bring him back to the world of men."

For a few moments, the engineer reflected. "Master," he said, finally, "What you've just said enables me to draw the conclusion that there's a mean of acting on the minds of these creatures, that a means exists of triumphing over their fear and leading them to brave the terrifying unknown of the dark. If Tai, inspired by you, launched himself into it with the ardor that brought him all the way to us, how much more easily could an entire crowd be impelled?"

"For millennia that crowd has been living in the luminous crevasses of the globe, Monsieur Chapuis, for millennia its priests have been lulling it with the same legend and the same hope, without that legend and that hope inciting the subterrans to explore the entrails of the globe and to seek a route to the surface. They don't suppose that human feet can follow he route to the sky. They only believe it to be practicable for the dead. Tai was an exception inspired and willed by me. His brethren, whatever the eloquence of their leaders, will never quit the luminous plain."

Jean Chapuis shook his head. He was not convinced.

For a long time, however, the cries had ceased to resound above their heads. The impressive silence was reestablished. Without admitting it, the engineer was slightly more anxious about that than the noise.

Why had that calm suddenly returned? What had appeased that fit of delirium? Above all, what had provoked it?

Those two questions constituted a single enigma, and Cyprienne's fiancé had a presentiment of a further danger, much closer at hand.

But he was in the villa of the omnipotent Oronius, surrounded by the Master and his devoted servants, with his fiancée beside him. Could he be seriously worried?

Oronius raised his hand. "Listen," he said. "They've become quiet again. I knew that it wasn't necessary to take it seriously. Now they've stamped their feet and made a diabolical racket, they'll sulk. It's only necessary to leave them to it. When they've had enough, they'll come to beg my pardon and implore me to reappear. Let's go back downstairs. You doubtless won't be sorry to pass through the chamber of repose. It's a long time since you've led the normal life of civilized people. When you've been remuscled, we'll envisage the future. Your arrival and that of the Halcyon-Car have opened new perspectives for me. We can think about returning to the surface—you'll understand me better when I've brought you up to date with my adventures. But one question remains in suspense: that devil Hantzen and his clique. What are they doing? Where are they?"

A distant rumor of a crowd running and vociferating drowned out the Master's speech.

Everyone listened.

Thousands of creatures were descending through the somber galleries toward the central cavern and the villa.

"It's them!" exclaimed Oronius, unable to believe his eyes. "They've found a way! They're coming! They're here!"

Chapter Thirteen
THE MOBILE PYTHON

This is what had happened since the departure of the Halcyon-Car from the luminous plain.

The airplane-automobile had scarcely engaged in one of the defiles than the rocks had closed over it. A kind of giant serpent had then emerged from the collapsed earth and rocks: a singular monster that had began to move in the direction of the luminous plain, unfurling its metallic coils.

That had been seen and noted by the companions in the Halcyon-Car, and although their realistic science protested against such a fabulous existence of prehistoric fauna, they would retain the anguishing memory for a long time. But Jean Chapuis not had the time or the means to examine it sufficiently.

In fact, although, viewed from a distance, the serpent could have the appearance of an apocalyptic beast, one of those obscure monsters that terrified the embryonic humankind living in caves, seen at closer range it would have been identifiable by virtue of certain details as a mechanical simulation of those legendary creatures. One would immediately have taken account if the fact that its carapace was made of articulated metal plates fitted in such a way as to be reminiscent of the scales of a reptile. That structure evidently had the objective of permitting the machine, which only had the appearance of a beast, to make evolutions analogous to those of a snake. It advanced by imitating the movements of reptiles.

It might have been a dozen meters long and the diameter of its carapace was about two meters in the median part; it diminished in the anterior and posteriors parts which thinned and flattened in a fashion to simulate the head and tail of a veritable cold-blooded and bare-skinned crawler.

The head, in particular, presented bizarre details; it terminated in a burrowing muzzle armed with a drill. Such a device could only have one purpose: to permit the machine to hollow out a rapid passage through soil and rock. All of that supposed an interior mechanism powering the strange machine. In consequence, it must be inhabited, for a human intelligence must be contained within that carapace.

After the disappearance of the aircraft-automobile, and as if it had only been waiting for that disappearance in order to show itself, the steel python had launched forth across the luminous plain.

The head of the articulated monster had eyes. They could occasionally project light into the obscurity but sometimes must serve as simple windows in order to illuminate the progress of the conductors. The perfectly reasoned evolutions of the metallic serpent demonstrated that. Having hesitated momentarily to zigzag across the luminous plain it ended up heading for the villages inhabited by Tai's compatriots, who had doubtless perceived the people contained in the Pythonmobile.

The speed of the serpent's reptation was admirable; it contracted and then extended; its rings appeared to enter into one another in the direction of progress; then the anterior part extended again, stretching the long body. And all those movements were accomplished with such rapidity that the serpent seemed to fly over the surface of the ground.

That silent and contorted progression had something frightening about it; the apparition of such a monster could not fail to provoke fear, particularly in simple and superstitious populations.

That was, indeed, what happened.

When the mobile python arrived in sight of one of the villages and its approach was signaled, a veritable panic was produced and the people fled in disorder in all directions. In a few moments the nearest agglomeration was completely deserted.

The village was the same one that had welcomed the passengers of the Halcyon-Car, in whom, under the influence of Tai, the subterrans had seen envoys of the gods.

This time, they were obliged to believe that the metal monster was a delegate of the infernal abysms. Their terror was great.

Perhaps, moreover, they were not mistaken in their appreciation, for the reptilian machine, like the Trojan Horse was sheltering beings who really were demons.

At any rate, finding the terrain before it free and without appearing to be moved by the terror it had inspired, the monster continued to advance. It soon penetrated into the village and finally came to a halt on the luminous ground in front of the building elevated in the form of a temple, which had served as a garage for the Halcyon-Carr and had lodged its voyagers.

There, unfurling its coils in imitation of a fatigued beast, the serpent remained inert and flaccid, like a sated boa whose stomach is delivering itself to the difficult work of digestion.

Some distance from the village, the fugitives had looked back. Understanding that they were not being pursued, they relented their exodus and ended up stopping. Timidly, and encouraging one another, they had taken a few hesitant steps in the direction of their habitations. They remained on the alert, however, ready to flee again at the slightest alarm.

None was produced. Nothing emerged from the village.

The subterrans drew closer and eventually arrived at the entrance to the modest fortifications constructed by them with the luminous stones for the possible circumstance of resisting attacks by certain marauding tribes.

From there they could see the elongated serpent, as motionless as if it were dead.

That thought must have occurred to Tai's compatriots, and they doubtless wanted to verify the hypothesis. Picking up sharp stones, which seemed to be the only weapons used by those primitive people, they threw them at the serpent.

The projectiles rebounded from the carapace without even provoking a shudder.

In the minds of the naïve spectators, the matter then seemed obvious: the monster was dead or asleep. It became less terrifying. They dared to draw nearer.

After an hour of timid advances and abrupt fearful retreats that nothing justified, the boldest of the groups surrounded the metallic reptile. Almost reassured by its inoffensive immobility, some pushed audacity so far as to touch its flanks and then to climb on to the monster's back. The perplexity of the greater number remained real.

What was it? An animal? But then, why was it showing such forbearance? Had it really chosen that place in order to die there? Or was it rather a machine like the one brought by Tai, which had disappeared?

Yes, it might be a new machine, similarly inhabited by envoys of the god, who were waiting for homage to be rendered to them before showing themselves.

The only subterran perhaps capable of furnishing the fearful multitude with information in that regard, Tai, was not in the group of his anxious compatriots. Anxious and distressed by the disappearance of those he imagined to have descended from the sky—the gentle Cyprienne and her sympathetic entourage—Tai was wandering lamentably in the confines of the luminous plain, searching for traces of his marvelous friends.

But the least stupid of his friends remembered the fashion in which he had made them act during the first appearance of the celestial envoys. So, as intelligent organizers, they made the entire assembly kneel down and commenced to intone their prayers, as they had done when the Halcyon-Car arrived.

They did not have to wait long for the result.

Slowly, a scale with invisible grooves opened in the flank of the monster and three human silhouettes appeared.

The subterrans prostrated themselves face down on the ground, dazzled and fascinated by the marvelous adornments of the new envoys from above, doubtless dignitaries superior in rank.

First there was a woman of dazzling beauty, splendidly clad. She wore the veritable ornaments of an idol.

She was accompanied by an individual of repulsive ugliness but a powerful forehead; he had a body of elephantine amplitude, supported by short barrel-like legs, with the consequence that his appearance was that of a deformed and monstrous dwarf.

The third individual, a being about fifty years-old, offered nothing remarkable; his attitude, in any case, indicated the effacement of a servant.

It was Princess Yogha, flanked by Otto Hantzen, her associate, and Wiwar, their manservant.

Oronius' enemies had just set foot in the world of the damned—incontestably theirs.

Chapter Fourteen
POSSESSED BY INDRA

Our readers who have followed the previous adventures of the mysterious Princess Yogha and the malefactor Otto Hantzen will doubtless be astonished to find the people that Jean Chapuis thought he had destroyed alive and well. The explanation give by Oronius to his daughter and his pupil has already lifted a corner of the veil from that mystery. It is easy to understand how the world had not been purged of those demons.

We shall now go back to those events to which the scientist had made allusion while specifying the reason for his fears. We left Yogha and Hantzen in the invisible Tower elevated by them on the summit of Everest and enclosed in an artificial atmosphere.

The hour of punishment having sounded, Hantzen and Yogha were about to receive the price of their crimes by sharing the fate of their lair, which an immense explosion was about to project to the four winds of space.

Both of them were lying unconscious, Hantzen because he had been coiffed by Victor Laridon with a thought interrupter, and Yogha because her vanquishers had shut her in a glass cage submissive to the action of soporific gas. But, as Oronius has informed us, Wiwar, a creature of the two evil geniuses, whose presence neither Jean Chapuis nor Laridon had suspected, had emerged in time from his hiding-place. He had liberated his master from the interrupter, opened the cage of glass and roused Yogha from her torpor.

Awakened, the two accomplices envisaged the sad reality of their situation at a glance; they, the dominators, had been vanquished and condemned. In order to escape the destiny that menaced them, only flight remained.

Was that possible?

Yes, thanks to the imprudent neglect by Jean Chapuis of the *Spherus*, the enigmatic apparatus that Hertzian waves ordinarily directed across space, in accordance with the desires of Yogha. The *Spherus* was waiting at the top of the Tower, balanced on its pneumatic alveolus. Enough energy was stored therein to enable it to depart.

Without losing a second, Yogha dragged her two companions into the broad conduit that put the uppermost floor of the tower in communication with the inferior opening of the *Spherus* and enclosed herself in the apparatus with them. She did not have a choice; in order to escape the immediate death that she felt inexorably suspended over them, it was necessary to launch into space in the belly of that machine, previously obedient but which it would be impossible henceforth to steer once the tower was destroyed.

It was not, therefore, assured salvation, but a purely temporary solution.

For the moment, Yogha, mad with terror, Hantzen, still under the shock of his recent defeat, and the petrified Wiwar did not even want to think about the fate that awaited them. They were fleeing the death that was ready to seize them...

When the *Spherus*, rising into the sky, had carried them away from their tower, where they had been able to know fear and to dread the throes of a terrible agony, they breathed more feely.

The velocity of the singular aerostat was considerable. In a few minutes it had traveled an incalculable number of kilometers. None of the aeronauts heard the noise of the formidable explosion that pulverized the tower and caused the high summits of Gaurisankar to collapse.

Already, Yogha and Hantzen, recovered from that urgent alert, had recovered some of their sang-froid and were seeking a practical means of picking themselves up for a better future.

Their panic had thrown them into an inextricable situation. They were in the grip of chance, carried away by an airship devoid of a helm.

Hantzen knew that the *Spherus* could remain in the air for an unlimited time. Abandoned to itself it would circle the earth eternally. A new satellite, it would be discovered and catalogued by scientists.

Save for an encounter, a collision, or an unforeseen accident that might have favorable or deadly consequences, the journey that Yogha and her companions had begun would have no end.

"What will our fate be?" murmured Hantzen.

"We have one chance in a thousand of falling back to earth, and one in a hundred million of falling back alive," explained the Hindu woman coldly. She was a fatalist. She lay down on the floor of the glazed cabin situated in the upper part of the *Spherus*, which we have seen serving as a prison for Cyprienne and Turlurette. In that indolent posture she abandoned herself to destiny.

Wiwar was trembling and groaning. Hantzen was muttering in impotent rage, biting his fists.

That agitation on the part of Oronius' rival was, in spite of appearances, infinitely less active than Yogha's simulated inertia. In reality, the Hindu princess was summoning and concentrating within her all the mysterious forces of which her brain and vibrant body were both the magical emitters and the living receivers. That woman of frail appearance bore within her a veritable accumulator of energy. Her extended through accomplished prodigies.

At that moment, while her gaze seemed to be lost in the contemplation of infinite space and only belonging to a dream approximate to the nirvana for which she was waiting, she was, on the contrary, ardently pursuing a solution to the problem of arresting the course of the sphere, and obliging it to descend and land softly on the ground without any injury to its passengers.

That appeared to surpass the limit of human strength, but let us admit that Yogha was rightly reckoned to be a superhuman creature, who could not be stopped by the most unassailable obstacles.

The *Spherus*, of whom there would be little point in repeating the description here, was, as we have said elsewhere, a marvel of mechanics. Constructed with a special goal, it could only be utilized on condition of receiving from the exterior the force necessary to the functioning of its delicate organs. Deprived of Hertzian waves, it was no longer anything but a soulless body, and even the presence of Yogha could not render life to its inactive engines. It was only permitted to float in space, delivered to the whim of aerial currents.

The Hindu—just like Hantzen, the inventor and constructor of the flying apparatus—knew that she was incapable, for want of the indispensable current, of animating the machinery that directed the course of the *Spherus*, and she made no attempt to do so. She searched elsewhere.

She found something.

The sum of energy that she carried within her, great as it was by comparison with ordinary human abilities had limits. She therefore ought to use it not in a continuous or renewable effort but, on the contrary, for a time as brief as possible. On that condition only, she had a chance of producing its maximum effect.

What did Yogha want?

To descend... to land...

Perhaps that was realizable solely by means of the power of her desire. At least, all the worshiper of Sakyamuni [6] would have affirmed that without hesitation, because in India the initiates of the sacred pagodas accomplish miracles daily.

Emerging abruptly from her apparent apathy, the Hindu stood up, extending her thin arms toward space, raised like two antennae.

Above her, above the appeal of her ardent eyes, radiant sources of a formidable will, the molecules of the air suddenly appeared to vibrate with an extraordinary intensity. It was as if a double current of imponderables, magnetically attracted by

---

[6] The Gautama Buddha.

Yogha, were descending along her slender arms and accumulating within her.

Her entire body, arched in an abnormal pose, unsustainable and only permitted to someone possessed by Indra,[7] began to vibrate and palpitate, shaken by the intromission of an invisible entity, which appeared to traverse everything.

She seemed to become heavier—immeasurably heavy.

Transformed into weight, the forces scattered in the bosom of the atmosphere passed into her.

Suddenly—a magical result—the *Spherus* began to descend toward the ground, as if weighed down itself by the weight of which Yogha was the ensorcelled tabernacle.

There was a rapid fall, which frightened Hantzen and Wiwar by virtue of its inexplicable suddenness. They could not understand; they thought that a catastrophe was precipitating them from high altitude.

A moment before, they had been trembling and lamenting because they believed that they were condemned to wander in the air until the end of time, or at least until their death. Now, surprised by that abrupt denouement, they found their previous destiny enviable.

The strange attitude and the bulging eyes of their companion completed frightening them. They thought that, like them, she was yielding to terror, and that the gesture of her arms signified an imploration.

"What's wrong, Yogha?" cried Otto Hantzen. "We're falling, aren't we? Are we not going to crash on the ground?"

The daughter of fakirs did not deign to reply; she did not pay the slightest attention to their fear. In order to reassure them it would have been necessary for her to waste precious particles of her strength.

The sphere continued to descend with the velocity of an aerolith.

---

[7] Indra is an ancient Vedic deity, a deity in Hinduism, a guardian deity in Buddhism, and the king of the highest heaven called Saudharmakalpa in Jainism.

Hantzen and Wiwar, estimating that they were doomed, fell to their knees with a mechanical movement and hid their faces in their hands.

Such cowardice would doubtless have provoked the scorn and mockery of the Hindu, but she did not divine it, not seeing anything. Stretched to breaking point, all the fibers of her being were transformed into conductors.

In the vicinity of the ground, her members relaxed somewhat… it was just in time for her.

The fall of the *Spherus* relented, Gradually, the Hindu's arms lowered, and ended up falling along her sides. At the same moment, with the light rebound of a balloon, the *Spherus* touched down.

"To earth!" ordered Yogha, in a strident voice.

Shivering, Hantzen and Wiwar opened bewildered eyes. But, instinct drawing the, before comprehending, they obeyed. The Hindu, having opened the exit valve, leapt out of the cab-in. Followed by her two companions, she took two or three steps across the meadow that welcomed them, and fell on the grass, exhausted by the terrible effort that she had just made.

At the same instant, freed from the weight that the body of the Hindu had stored, the *Spherus* made a formidable leap and regained the heights of the atmosphere, in the bosom of which it disappeared, to take its rank among the secondary planets.

Chapter Fifteen
INVISIBLE!

Snatched from a slow death by the exceptional power of Yogha, the trio, finding themselves on the ground, were nevertheless reduced to the most pitiful impotence.

What remained of the baleful and slowly-prepared endeavor that had intoxicated the vainglorious Hantzen to the point of causing him to launch his imprudent challenge to Oronius? What remained of the forces accumulated by the couple at the summit of the inaccessible Everest, the roof of the world?

They had landed feebler and more deprived than the least of beggars.

Apart from Oronius, whom they believed to have been annihilated by the Belleville catastrophe, none of their enemies had been reduced to nullity. Cyprienne was free and reunited with her fiancé. Oh, how many new reasons the jealous Yogha had for detesting and hating her! Jean Chapuis had escaped more than ever from the Hindu's influence, and she had to be desperate to subjugate him to her caprices.

Jarrousse—their faithful instrument—was presumed dead, a victim of their attempt against Oronius. Even if he were not dead, he was scarcely worth any more to Hantzen and Yogha.

Thus all their hatred and effort had ended in the complete ruination of their hopes.

Even regarding Cyprienne's farther, a doubt subsisted in the mind of the perspicacious Yogha. She had appeared to share the conviction of her accomplice, but on reflection, she was beginning to doubt Oronius' demise.

Truly, that formidable obstacle to their dream of world hegemony had been set aside too easily. Besides, certain incidents devoid of natural causes gave her to think that the Master's genius might still be intervening and causing their designs to fail.

Such was the final account of the struggle they had undertaken: they had lost everything and could no longer boast of any advantage.

There was worse; henceforth, they had everything to fear from their more favored adversaries, if they committed the imprudence of giving any signs of life.

One can understand why, in those conditions, the first cry uttered by the trio, when Yogha recovered from her faint, had to be: "What will become of us?"

The Hindu even added, with a wrathful smile: "Everything has to be recommenced!"

With as bleak expression, Hantzen gave his approval to that disastrous remark. Only Wiwar dared to manifest some satisfaction.

"We're alive, after all." he observed, judiciously enough.

"We've come a long way, there's not a shadow of a doubt," muttered Hantzen, dejectedly, "but it's a fine advance if it's to die of hunger and poverty."

Although much depleted by the hard effort that she had been obliged to make, Yogha took pity on the fat man and tried to shake him out of his prostration.

"If you're still alive, you owe it entirely to me," she said, dryly. "I wanted it thus, not being one of those who abandon a game. For as long as a breath of life remains to me and the possibility of conserving it, I'll retain the hope of taking my revenge. To live is to fight. We'll fight."

"With what?" said Otto Hantzen, showing his empty hands. "Deprived of our centers of attack, without instruments and machines, above all without the *Spherus*, what can we do?"

Yogha looked at him scornfully.

"You have a short memory," she snapped. "What did you possess when you appeared to me one day, years ago? You were then a scientist without a *sou* or a suitcase, and without renown. You'd just been humiliated. No hope remained to you. I dragged you out of your rut, however and put in your hand famous trumps, with which it was permissible for you to resume the game. That's what it's necessary to recommence."

"In that epoch, my dear Yogha, you were powerful and in a situation to help me. Is it still thus today? Alas, no. Your position is no more brilliant than mine."

The stubborn Hindu riposted: "It's when one is at the very bottom of the ladder, without having anything—which is to say, with nothing to risk or to lose—that it's easy to climb up again, unburdened, to assault the means and wealth that others have, The Romans once sank their fleets in order to remove all means of retreat. We're in exactly their situation: me rich in my hatred and my reckless will to satisfy; you rich in your science. Only gold is lacking for us to do again what we have done. It's therefore necessary for us to begin by procuring gold."

"I'd be content with a laboratory. My brain, fortunately, contains treasures that no catastrophe, except death, can take away from me. I could quickly reconstitute my arsenal."

"I'll procure you that laboratory," Yogha promised, decisively. "Exactly like you, I defy fate to despoil me completely. The precious power remains to me that I have from my ancestors, the yoghis. I can therefore subjugate to my will anyone susceptible of being useful to us. You were entirely wrong to abandon yourself to discouragement. Hantzen and Yogha are still fearsome. Their hour might come."

"Prudence!" murmured Wiwar.

The Hindu approved with a nod of the head. "We'll have it," she affirmed. "The moment has not yet come to raise our heads, and we'll doubtless be obliged to hide for many days. But let's see where we are, and where those that we can reduce are."

She closed her eyes and retreated within herself.

Hantzen and Wiwar were familiar with that genre of meditation; they knew how important it was not to trouble her at times when she was concentrating her will. Yogha exteriorized her thought and sent it questing through time and space: a prodigious faculty of which the daughter of the fakirs had obtained the secret from her forebears.

At times when the Hindu princess was entered into internal practice, her thought was duplicated by virtue of a sacred right, and could attain the confines of the universe, and which no psychic or scientific force had yet been capable of opposing.

When the young woman opened her eyes again she seemed as fatigued as a person arriving from a difficult and distant voyage, but a joyful animation was shining in her gaze,

"Destiny," she said, "has not been as contrary to us as we imagined. We've fallen in American soil, in proximity to the Rocky Mountains. By heading eastwards, at a distance that will be easy for us to cross on foot, we'll encounter the isolated observatory of a scientific mission. There, friend Hantzen, there is all the equipment you could desire."

"I won't ask you, friend Yogha, whether we'll be welcomed and whether whatever I judge I might need will be put at my disposal without indiscreet questions," sniggered Oronius' enemy.

"We're expected," she replied, with assurance. "My mental order will be obeyed."

Otto Hantzen knew the strange power of his associate too well for doubt or astonishment. Many times she had proved the ease with which her will could be exercised at a distance upon human brains and subjugate them to her influence.

"Guide us, then," he acquiesced, confidently. "I believe I can replace advantageously these cheapjack scientists, worthy at best of serving me as laboratory assistants. Wouldn't you like, my dear friend, to suggest to them that they accept that secondary role?"

"It will be as you desire."

Two hours later, in confirmation of the Hindu's promise, the adventurers found themselves installed as masters in the observatory lost in the middle of the granitic slopes, provided with a scientific installation very propitious to Hantzen's projects. They had found the personnel of the mission submissive to Yogha's hypnotic influence. The action of her unsustainable gaze completed their subjugation. Henceforth, and for as long as it pleased the young woman, they would be no more than slaves, unconscious and docile instruments in her hands and Hantzen's.

Very satisfied with his booty, since he could consider himself henceforth as the entitled proprietor of the buildings and equipment of the perfectly-provided station, the elephantine scientist, after having examined everything carefully, returned to his accomplice, smiling.

"My felicitations," he said. "We couldn't be better placed here, In addition to modern comforts, it doesn't lack any of the apparatus that I might need. I'll get to work and appropriate them to the service that it will be necessary for them to furnish. My studies, as you know, can only tend to the destruction of the human race in order to assure us of the empire of the word, where we'll reign alone."

Pensive, Yogha stopped him.

"I haven't yet made you party to my fears," she said. "I anticipate a certain danger held in reserve by contrary destiny."

"Are you talking about that Chapuis?"

"No... of that one and his entourage I'll make short work, if..."

For a moment, she appeared to hesitate to reveal all her thinking. Then, thinking that it would not be bad to stimulate all of Hantzen's hatred, she went on: "Suppose that, against all plausibility, Oronius is still in the world."

The fat man's adipose tissue shook, and he went pale. Such a hypothesis was infinitely disagreeable to him.

"Do you think so?" he stammered. "Where could he be?"

"Somewhere—here or there, something is interposed between him and me—I can't see him... he must be taking precautions in that regard. However, an occult prescience keeps me on the alert. At any moment, he might think about us, You know that, with other faculties than mine, his science is equal to my power. Like me he can see through space, and he can also hear. If he discovers us, be certain that he won't leave us to reconstitute our work in peace. What can you do to ward off that danger?"

"I possess the means to render us invisible," replied Hantzen, after having reflected. "Yes, I can realize that by rendering our bodies translucent to that damned Oronius' rays. Knowing his method, I've searched for the defense, and I think I've found it."

"Act without delay, then, Otto."

Hantzen's method was, in fact, the one that Oronius was to divine. He had subjected himself and his two companions to certain radiations destined to render their molecules permeable to light, Henceforth, and for as long as they continued the treatment, rays of any origin would traverse their bodies; it really was the invisibility promised by Oronius' rival.

The precaution was completed by the psychic isolation of their retreat. The principle of the thought-interrupter realized by a substance that had the property of refracting cerebral waves, served Hantzen to render vain the action of the wave-captor and the recording apparatus of which Cyprienne's father disposed.

Henceforth the two associates and their servant could work under shelter. Their persons, as well as their actions, would escape Oronius.

Several times, however, Yogha, extending her will, had been able to slip outside the ideal circle of protection and invisibility in order to attempt, by means of mental concentration, to discover and reach Oronius' retreat.

For a long time her efforts had remained unfruitful, Cyprienne's father was playing the same game as them and he was also able to shield himself from the Hindu's investigations It only happened that in the course of those attempts and in spite of the strength of her concentration, Yogha had let a few thoughts escape that had gone to disquiet Oronius.

Unfortunately, those warnings were too obscure to be veritably useful. They put Oronius on his guard, but nothing more.

On the other hand, and in spite of the discretion with which they had been surrounded, the communications that reached Cyprienne and the preparations for the expedition that were their consequence had not occurred without being captured by Yogha.

Since then, the seer, maintaining herself in constant psychic communication with the young woman, had contrived by follow her in her subterranean voyage. From then on, she had been certain; for her, Oronius' retreat was no longer a mystery.

And as, in the meantime, Hantzen had not ceased to deliver himself with a feverish activity to certain preparations, on the indications of his accomplice, on the day when she demanded it, he was able to put at her disposal the instrument capable of pursuing and attaining their enemies.

That instrument was the mobile python, the burrowing metallic serpent that, where it had to go, could replace advantageously the lost Spherus. It had been equipped by Hantzen with all perfections, as well as some of the frightful means of destruction which the malevolent couple made their ordinary weapons.

Their expedition being ready, they had plunged into the bowels of the earth in their turn. Having fallen on the traces of the Halcyon-Car, they had reached the luminous plain, almost in the heart of the world of the damned.

Under the terrestrial crust, the frightful battle was about to recommence. The implacable enemies of the fiancés were in pursuit...

They had already dealt a first blow, which they were able to believe efficacious.

In fact, from inside the bronze serpent they had unleashed the seismic shock that has so nearly contrived to bury the passengers of the Halcyon-Tank under a mass of rocks.

Chapter Sixteen
THE SACRILEGIOUS ATTACK

Before emerging from the *Snaky*—as they had baptized their reptator—Hantzen and Yogha applied themselves for some time to studying through portholes dissimulated under the annular scales, the curious people whose attitudes revealed a primitive mentality. They both foresaw what they might be able to get out of such a rabble, as impressionable and as easy to dominate as a class of infants.

Their eyes scanned the horizon of the radiant plain. They conjectured that other luminous fissures must exist in the depths of the terrestrial core analogous to this one and similarly inhabited. There was, therefore, an unsuspected force contained in the entrails of the globe. The active imagination of the cruel Yogha was already taking possession of it in order to exploit it and turn its against humanity. A plan was born in her maleficent mind.

Less inclined to generalizing, Hantzen abandoned himself uniquely to the preoccupations dictated to him by his personal hatred.

"If Oronius is hiding at the center of this hardened pulp, these manikins must know him," he murmured, designating the subterrans.

Yogha approved.

"Let's show ourselves to them and domesticate them," the redoubtable scientist continued. "Stupid as they are, perhaps they'll be able to lead us to the lair where our enemy is hiding."

"It will undoubtedly be possible to obtain more," replied the Hindu, pensively. "Let me do it, Otto; you don't know their language and won't be able to get anything out of them."

"While you hope to understand them and make them hear you" sniggered Hantzen, vexed.

"Of course."

"Have you become polyglot, my dear?"

To that question, posed with heavy irony, Yogha riposted dryly: "Your pride is harmful to your mind. They both take on the heaviness that affects your body. Know that I speak the only language that can be universal, the language of thought. Let's show ourselves, and I'll enter into communication with these beings."

Hantzen had too much at stake for him to take umbrage at the rebuke or to persist in his ironic attitude. He therefore obeyed without further objection and gave Wiwar the order to open the hatch that enabled the *Snaky* to communicate with the exterior world.

All three descended into the middle of the prostrate assembly of the wretched inhabitants of the underworld.

The latter showed marks of respect but not of terror, for the subterrans recognized in Yogha and her companions creatures similar to those whose previous arrival had filled them with joy and hope. They did not know that souls differ under equivalent aspects, and that in the lot of the human race, no particular sign distinguishes malefactors from honest people. Having before their eyes faces almost similar to those they had already contemplated, anatomies clad in similar fabrics, but much richer and more rutilant, the candid primitives thought, delightedly: *they are more envoys from the open air*.

A great hope animated their hearts, and the attentive Hantzen took account of that impression.

"They've seen humans before," he murmured.

Yogha did not appear to have heard him. Already at work, she was scanning the groups with her magnetic gaze, searching for a subject.

Suddenly, like the beam of a detector, the intelligent gleam fixed on a little creature similar in all respects to Tai. Dominated, that one got up and advanced meekly toward the drawer open in the carapace of the *Snaky*.

The poor fellow was trembling in every limb but, under the magnetic action of the dominating gaze, that tremor died down and the elect was able to stand straight and still, his eyes fixed on the double gleam that was searching them.

"Go inside and wait for me," murmured the hypnotist.

Obedient to that order, although it was murmured in a language that he did not now, the subterran penetrated without any mark of fear or hesitation into the bronze monster.

Yogha then extended her hands toward the multitude who were still kneeling, their foreheads touching the luminous ground.

"You see in us tutelary gods, superior in power to all your gods," she pronounced, in a musical voice.

A frisson passed over the subterrans. Prey to a sudden collective excitement, they got up and cheered. Then surrounding the monster and handing on to the asperities of its carapace, they steered it toward the temple, vacant since the departure of the Halcyon-Car.

In the place of the aircraft, and with the same marks of respect and adoration, the installed the new apparatus there. They went out thereafter and went to crouch in a semicircle some distance away, like respectful worshipers.

"Play your role," Yogha recommended to her companions. "I'll instruct myself in the mores and beliefs of these people, and everything that it's important for us to know. We'll see thereafter what advantage we'll be able to obtain from this encounter."

In her turn she penetrated into the carapace where the creature captive of her power was waiting.

An hour later, Yogha reappeared. Her triumphant expression was the indication of a complete success.

"I know where Oronius is and I've already drawn up a whole plan of action," she announced. "It will be easy for us to turn these naïve little dolls—or puppets, for one truly can't tell whether they're male or female—against him. They see him as a creator of sorts. Their history is rather curious and will certainly interest you..."

"Do you think you can get anything out of that vermin?" Hantzen interrupted, skeptically. "What could they do against

Oronius? One might as well launch a legion of ants or mosquitoes on his heels. He'll crush them by the thousand."

"Your comparison is quite just," Yogha approved, "but whatever you might think, an army of insects isn't to be disdained; the strongest man in the world would end up perishing if ants assailed him in sufficient numbers. It's neither the smallness not the individual weakness of an adversary that it's necessary to consider; volume increases in proportion to number, so it's how many legions it can launch into battle. If the waves are renewed incessantly, it will finally be victorious. No human resistance could be opposed to it. A swarm of irritated bees can put the king of beasts to flight—think about that!

"On the other hand, I don't believe that your Oronius is in a situation as brilliant as before. We've had our misfortunes, he must have had his, and he probably hasn't got out of difficulty, since he persists in hiding in the deepest entrails of the globe. Who knows? Perhaps it's impossible for him to quit them. It's not certain that he arrived here of his own free will. In that case, we have the upper hand, for it's no longer the unassailable Master of the Magical Villa that we're taking on but a diminished Oronius deprived of a good part of his means."

"Let's hope so, my dear friend," said Hantzen, his expression brightening.

"I've learned many things," Yogha went on. "I believe I know now the flaw in our competitor's armor. You're about to see the manner in which I topple the false god of whom this people expect so much."

"How are you going to do that?"

"Firstly by abdicating ourselves the quasi-divinity that we were on the point of usurping. The advantages would have been mediocre. We'll increase them by becoming human again and demonstrating to these primitives that the heaven of which they dream is a myth and its sovereign a fraud.

Hantzen tugged the caprine beard that adorned his chin anxiously. "I only ask to follow your advice, my beautiful friend," he assured her, "but your tactic doesn't appear to me to be without danger. In effect, you want to remove the blindfold that the course of the centuries has prudently knotted over the eyes of these myrmidons. We'd be destroying the beliefs that have given them the strength to endure this frightful existence. Won't they be enraged?"

"I certainly hope so. And in the riot that will follow..."

"Well collect a few bites."

"No, not us: Oronius, become a mere mortal again; Oronius, the false god who has deceived these worthy people by not revealing to them the seat of the happiness that he was content to promise them."

"I don't understand."

"You will."

The Hindu the explained to her accomplice of what the religion of the subterranean people consisted, and the vague tradition conserved by them, which made the sunlit surface a legendary paradise impossible to attain. Yogha's plan was simple. It was necessary to make the subterrans understand that the paradise in question existed and that it was inhabited by humans little different from themselves. It was also important to convince them that only Oronius could take them to that paradise, and that they could constrain him to do it.

At the mere thought of being so meanly deceived and turned to derision by that supposed supreme being, all those obtuse brains, initially disturbed, would end up exploding in anger. They would be all the more furious because, their ancient beliefs having crumbled, no moral brake would retain them any longer.

A people is unstable; its resignation is only apparent. If a marketplace orator comes to trouble its calm, mock its submission and persuade it that it will be sufficient to run riot to have immediate access to a place it believed to be forbidden, the indolence of the people changes into fever and gives way to a kind of savage fury. It sees red!

That was what Yogha was counting on. Having listened to her explanations, Hantzen ended up judging her hope perfectly reasonable. He no longer doubted that that it would be easy to utilize, unknown to them, the anger of the subterrans.

"I'll leave it to you," he said. "You're truly infernal, my dear." In his mouth that was a compliment.

Then, returning to the *Snaky*, the hatch of which she had left open, the Hindu raised one of her hands.

The subterran appeared. Still under the empire of hypnosis, he had the glittering, staring eyes, as if inspired, characteristic of visionaries and illuminates.

"Go," she instructed him, "and obey."

The poor little being immediately drew away with a automatic stride and was lost in the midst of the group formed by his brethren.

"I've schooled him," Yogha affirmed. "He'll go to spread the good word. Within an hour, we'll see and hear fine things. Just in case, let's go back into our machine and shut ourselves in, to await events."

Otto Hantzen willingly conformed with that advice. It was not a lightning war, for fatty degeneracy softens the combative forces as well as the muscles. He knew that popular anger could not be unleashed with impunity and that it was necessary to fear its outbursts.

"Let's be ready to take off if things go wrong for us," he advised.

"They can't go wrong," riposted the Hindu, peremptorily, "but in our *Snaky* we'll be better able to follow the progress of events and take a hand when the necessity makes itself felt."

The instrument that she had chosen must have done good work, for, less than an hour after his return among his compatriots a certain emotion was manifest—an emotion that did not take long to acquire the proportions of a rumbling effervescence.

A tumult of cries finally burst firth; and soon, a horde of subterrans, with a fanatic at its head who was still under Yogha's influence, climbed the steps of the temple. The exasperated individuals, unconscious *agents provocateurs*, had soon gathered around them all the groups that had previously dispersed and harangued them in loud voices, with a communicative vehemence. They were manifestly seeking to draw them and to associate them with a project before which the pusillanimous were hesitating.

Increasingly overexcited, the preachers of revolt increased their eloquence and excitement. Several times they were seen to wave their fists in the direction of the gulf at the bottom of which was the flamboyant temple—which is to say, Oronius' villa.

They finally prevailed. With crowds, the violent always prevail. And the maleficent trio watching through the serpent's eyes saw the demonstrators launch forth at a run, vociferating, toward the gulf.

Yogha was triumphant.

"All right! There they go!"

"Let's follow them at a distance," proposed Hantzen.

But the demonstration that was taking place could not satisfy them entirely. When the Hindu had observed that the vulgar popular vengeance was reduced to a simple projection of stones into the gulf, from which the villa could scarcely suffer, she emerged from the *Snaky* and mingled with the besiegers.

Her quivering hands, her gestures and the flashes springing from her eyes acted upon her neighbors like electrical discharges. Her hatred and her violent desires passed into the hearts and brains of the subterrans, magnetically dominated and subjugated.

Soon, there was a new exchange of animated words. And the delirious people, conducted by a few fanatics, finally yielding to the will of the daughter of fakirs, abandoned the rim of the gulf in order to launch themselves toward one of the defiles, the one whose steep slope fell in rocky cascades toward Oronius' refuge.

The stimulatrix was in their midst, pouring out her fluid and driving them like a flock.

Some way behind slithered the metallic serpent, in the interior of which Hantzen and Wiwar exchanged their impressions while supervising the mechanism.

"She's a masterly woman, she knows what she's doing," said the fat man, rubbing his hands. "With such a tigress on his heels, the old man will have a lot on his hands. On seeing one of those monkeys one would think, disdainfully: *What's the point? Poor thing!* But there are so many! They're pullulating. They're emerging from all the holes. Look, they've already formed more than an army corps; and others are flocking...more than we can count. It will be like a swarm of locusts. The stick can't do anything; it will cover everything. Oronius will perish in the vermin!"

While perorating thus, he had stopped the serpent in the middle of the defile. He was waiting for the return of Yogha in order to her the news, which would be, to say the least, a bulletin of victory.

However, he suddenly shivered and his repulsive face expressed the most abject terror.

A howling mob, which included in its ranks a considerable number of limping individuals, was returning toward the reptator, dragging with them the grim and somber Yogha.

Dragging? Yes—for that crowd seemed to have changed completely and the Hindu no longer presented a dominating figure in their midst.

Hantzen was afraid, and wanted to start the engine. If he did not succeed into turning round before being reached by the running tide, he was resolved to plow into the mass at speed, at the risk of crushing his own ally.

To have heart in the guts is a saying that one would be wrong to take literally in many cases. At that critical moment, Hantzen sensed a bravery that was confined to the heroic sacrifice… of his accomplice.

"Too bad for Yogha," he decided. "She didn't have to leave us. Forward!"

But on the point of pressing the starter button, his fingers were retracted painfully.

Was it an attack of articular rheumatism? No. The anguished Hantzen, felt weighing upon him the terrible will of the ferocious Hindu, which forbade him to flee.

The subterrans surrounded the serpent.

At their head, visibly exciting them, marched a little being enraged by lust for vengeance. Otto Hantzen, something of a physiognomist, sought to recognize in him the creature hypnotized by Yogha, but could not succeed.

In fact, it was Tai

Chapter Seventeen
THE IRON AUTOMATA

Otto Hantzen had not exaggerated in evaluating at more than an army corps the number of subterrans running through the somber defiles toward the flamboyant villa. The rumor matched the roar of the ocean on days of great storms. Their wave unfurled in the vast illuminated cavern with such impetuosity that it seemed bound to submerge everything.

Grouped around Oronius, Cyprienne and Jean Chapuis, Laridon and Turlurette, Julep and Mandarinette, watched that rush. Through the transparent wall of the villa, they could not contemplate without going pale the irritated faces, the eyes blinking under the dazzling light, and the swarm of extended fists.

Like Hantzen, they thought: *Nothing can stop them. Nothing can oppose the inexorable slide of that avalanche. We're going to be carried away, crushed...*

However, the Master conserved all his calm, and contemplated the multitude of assailants without hatred, rather with a sort of pity.

"Poor fellows" he was heard to murmur between his teeth. "I'd like to know the cause that has driven them to commit this act of dementia. Evidently it's not with kind words that it will be possible for me to bring them back to reason. I'll have to resign myself to giving them a severe lesson."

He sighed, and went to sit down in a glass armchair, from which numerous wires departed, plunging into the floor. The arms of the chair were fitted with a number of buttons forming a double keyboard. Oronius' fingers brushed them lightly, in the fashion of a virtuoso caressing the instrument that he is causing to vibrate.

Uttering frightful imprecations, the horde of subterrans approached the villa.

Cyprienne uttered a faint cry and hid her face.

"Only those whose lives are in danger ought to tremble," said Oronius. "We're not in that situation. Look, child."

In fact, the furious wave, which appeared to be about to carry everything away, broke at that moment upon an unexpected obstacle.

The left hand of one placed upon the right of another and forming a chain in front of the façade of the villa, the thirteen iron automata had suddenly advanced in a line.

It was into that insensible rampart that the wave of assailants crashed.

To judge solely by appearances, such an obstacle appeared very fragile to contain the surge of that human sea; it ought to have been broken by the first impact sand submerged by the wave

Nothing of the sort. At the moment of collision, fulgurant sparks sprang from the armor of the thirteen automata. At the first contact, the subterrans in the first rank uttered in unison a howl of dolor and rolled under the feet of the followers, licking their burned fingers.

The automata had endured the impact without flinching. They seemed unbreakable.

The misadventure of the first rank, however, could not stop the others. As always happens, the generous pressure of the rear, ignorant of the damage and still shielded from it, obliged the second rank to advance whether they liked it or not.

Successively, three or four lines, trampling the bodies already fallen, came into contact with the automata and suffered a similar fate. Lightning flashes sprang forth every time and the victims collapsed, immediately trampled underfoot.

In a few minutes there was a veritable rampart of the tangled burned and wounded in front of the men of iron, against which the flood was now breaking.

The cries of pain and heart-rending plants now dominated the vociferations of the assailants, driven back and furious at being prevented from entering the struggle.

Containing the mass of bodies, which the momentum of the besiegers was trying to push toward them, the thirteen automata formed an insurmountable barrier. The heap of the crippled fallen before them only served to reinforce them.

And above that rampart of swarming and moaning flesh, Oronius' creatures now projected long blue flames, which emerged from their hands, extended toward the crowd. Those silent flames, contact with which burned the rare rags in which a few were dressed, blistered the skin and caused intense pin, sowing panic among the subterrans. Directly threatened, the advanced ranks wearied, and tried to recoil. This time, it was against their brethren that they were fighting. Fists rendered furious by panic crashed into fearful faces; breasts were battered; there was a brutal exchange of blows.

Oronius smiled.

Was he about to make his automata charge and order a general massacre?

Moved by pity, Cyprienne raised her joined hands toward him. "Don't exterminate them, Father!" she begged. "They must have yielded to some excitation. They're not responsible."

"I'll be content to frighten them," the Master assured her. "However, it's necessary for me to complete the route and clear the area, while taking away any desire to return."

The index finger of his right hand descended on one of the buttons on his chair.

At that moment the desperate recoil of the nearest had gradually pushed back the mass all the way to the entrance of the dark tunnel; the struggle therefore continued in obscurity. But when Oronius had reassured his daughter and accomplished his gesture a sheet of green light sprang from the automata, as if from arc lamps, and illuminated the gallery.

The spectators of the scene would never forget the vision that appeared then before their eyes. Deforming the silhouettes, the strange light gave them a fantastic appearance. Instantly, the invading army, struck by fear, no longer offered to the gaze anything but the disordered aspect of a host of grimacing faces convulsed by terror. The cries resumed again, but they had changed character and tone. They were lugubrious lamentations. Under the caress of the green light, one would have sworn that the amalgam was composed of spectral apparitions howling at death.

Under the meager tunics of vegetable filaments, a few rich subterrans were agitating in the center of the great mass of unfortunates in their most natural costume. While colliding with one another in disordered bounds, as if struck by epilepsy, they were foaming at the mouth, their eyes glittering, their lips twisted into demonic rictuses rendered even more hideous by the fantastic reflections mimicking cadaverous decomposition.

Satisfied, Oronius turned another button. The green light disappeared to give way to a rubescent sheet, the flood of which blooded the floor, the vault and the walls of the gallery. The suddenly-flamboyant cavern took on the aspect of an infernal furnace, in the bosom of which demons were agitating, stripped of their skin and sweating blood.

The sinister howls changed instantaneously into howls of pain. The flayed individuals stamped their feet and capered madly, as if they could feel burning flames.

"Father, Father!" moaned Cyprienne. "You promised me to show them mercy, and you're torturing them frightfully."

"Error, little girl… illusion!" riposted Oronius, smiling. "I'm only inflicting a lesson that they'll remember, without having to bear the scars. It's a case of saying that they'll get away with a scare. Understand that the radiations by means of which I'm chastising them only act on the central nervous system; they produce disagreeable sensations but spare the individual, only giving, in sum, the illusion of sensation. They're not suffering; they only think they're suffering…and the impressions I'm inflicting on them vary with the color of the radiations. Do you want to see more examples?"

Without giving his daughter time to answer, he turned various buttons one after another. And, successively, the red inferno became a blue aquarium in which grimacing drowned bodies were floating; then, under a sunny hue, a host of yellow furies were seen; then a pink flood fell into empty space.

Incapable of supporting the luminous showers any longer, the army of assailants had fled in a stampede.

Before they disappeared, however, Cyprienne had had time to see, quite clearly, an unexpected intervention.

In fact, one little subterran creature, who certainly did not belong to the mob of the revolt, had run from the depths of the gallery and had set about abusing his compatriots, already discouraged, striving to simulate their retreat. His virulent objurgations, supplemented by the terror of each possessor of an epidermis exposed to the radiations, had no difficulty in completing the rout.

Cyprienne clapped her hands.

"Tai is making them go back!" she cried. "Brave Tai! He's remained faithful to us!"

Chapter Eighteen
THE GREAT SILENCE

Quitting his terrible armchair, Oronius had interrupted the projections and immobilized his iron servants, still arranged in battle formation before the villa.

Followed by Cyprienne, Jean Chapuis and their companions, he went outside and advanced as far as the entrance to the gallery in order to listen for any sounds that might be descending therefrom.

Silence was already reestablished there. The retreat of the vanquished had been definitive, Repelled and chastised, they must have renounced their project of constraining the Master to serve as their guide in order to reach the surface.

The scientist was still ignorant of that design, so he could not understand the aggression of which he had just been the object, much less the abrupt change of attitude of the sad creatures in his regard.

Nevertheless, he felt certain doubts obsessing him.

"Although we're rid of them," he said, "that's not sufficient for me. I want to understand, I need to discover where the blow departed from. In fact, mustn't it be a trick of Hantzen's? In that case, he must have others in reserve for me. Let's go and consult the spheromirocatoptric. If there's something suspect up about, I'll obtain knowledge of it."

Having become thoughtful again, he returned to the villa.

He pushed the door and was about to cross the threshold when a formidable din seemed to fall upon the villa: a sound of breaking glass mingled with a terrifying rumble. Knocked over by an irresistible gust of air, Oronius fell to the ground.

Jean and Laridon hastened to aid him, but the scientist was already on his feet and racing toward his laboratory. As he went in, a cry of dolor and despair escaped his lips.

Fallen from the height of the gulf at the bottom of which the villa had stopped, a veritable cataract had just broken the glazed terrace and the glass floors of its stories. The foaming torrent had even fallen on the mirror-sphere that contained the radioactive projector that Oronius used to search space. Henceforth, it was materially impossible for the scientist to survey the universe. The scientific Argus was deprived of his eyes.

At the sight of that irreparable disaster, Cyprienne's father would doubtless have fallen down, struck by apoplexy, if he had not had a quasi-divine power to put a brake on the revolt of his blood.

"Can I doubt it?" he only lamented. "There's only one man who could have unleashed such a calamity upon my treasures, and that's Otto Hantzen!"

Alas, the destruction of the marvelous mirror was not the only consequence of the catastrophe, and the damage as not limited to that. Not only was the Magical Villa and all that it contained threatened with annihilation, but the lives of Oronius and his guests were also in peril.

Jean Chapuis had the first intuition of that on seeing the waterfall continue its diabolical sweep, carrying everything away in its seething tumult.

"We're about to be dragged way!" he shouted. "Quickly, to the Halcyon-Car!"

Laridon and Julep leapt to bring out the apparatus.

"My discoveries! My instruments!" groaned Oronius. "Can I abandon all that?"

"Your brain contains creations a hundred times more precious!" shouted Jean Chapuis, in the midst of the deafening noise of the waterfall. "If you survive, it will be easy for you to repair this disaster. In any case, we can doubtless save a part of what your house contains. Order your automata to transport aboard the Halcyon everything that it can accommodate."

The advice was good; Cyprienne's father hastened to follow it. Under the liquid turbulence, which never ceased to harass them, the rescue was organized.

Without the men of iron, that removal would not have been possible, but they had a solidity proof against anything and inaccessible to emotion.

In the meantime, Cyprienne and her two soubrettes, and then Oronius, Laridon, Julep and Jean Chapuis, took their places aboard the aircraft-automobile. Jarrousse, the ape-man, was also accommodated. Last of all, after the loading of everything dear to the scientist had been completed by their cares, the automata were taken aboard. Then Laridon closed the hatch.

He was just in time. The bottom of the pit, having absorbed the initial surge of the fall, began to overflow. The water was arriving from all directions and rising rapidly; it was a frightful inundation.

To explain it, it was necessary to admit that criminal hands must have liberated simultaneously, by means of an explosive, the pockets of water contained in the upper strata of the subterranean world.

His communications with the external world destroyed, reduced to the sole refuge of the Halcyon-Car and the resources contained within its flanks, Oronius and his companions were forced to flee before the invasion of the waters.

To be sure, they were in no danger of being drowned, since the Halcyon could be transformed at will into a submarine and roll along the slopes even so.

Put yourself in the place of our savant adventurers for a moment; remember that their laudable devotion to saving Paris had been the initial cause of the fantastic and perilous excursion, and perhaps you can imagine what their state of mind must have been in the course of the terrifying flight in the depths of the obscure galleries departing from the center of the globe.

How long did the pursuit of the waters last? How could they get out of that infernal empire? What dangers would loom up in their path, and what traps?

Jean Chapuis, enclosed in the steel carapace of the Halcyon, had set a course and asked his tank mechanism for its full speed. He only had one thought, only one goal: to return as soon as possible to the luminous plain.

Via the subterrans, who it would doubtless be easy to intimidate and bring back to better sentiments, they would discover what had happened. And then, with the aircraft, reequipped with its wings, they would doubtless be able to set forth on the track of Hantzen. Like Oronius, at present, the engineer no longer had any doubt that their implacable enemies had ventured into the subterranean world.

They had the Halcyon; they had the iron automata. The conditions of the struggle ought to remain equal, at least. Oronius and his troops could confront them with every chance of success.

Along the almost-vertical slopes, bristling with redoubtable asperities, the Halcyon-Tank crossed hollow cliffs and rocky promontories with frightening somersaults without its passengers feeling the effects, climbing at running velocity.

Permanently lodged in the fixation cell, Oronius was ready, at the first sign of danger, to use the repulsive force of radiomagnetic currents for the protection of the Halcyon,

He did not need that recourse. No trap was revealed, The route was free, and without any hitch having stopped it, the tank emerged into the immense dayless grotto in the middle of which the luminous plain extended as far as the eye could see.

Jean Chapuis breathed more freely.

Bringing the transformer into play, he liberated the Halcyon from its carapace, withdrew the caterpillar tracks, brought out the wheels and deployed the wings. All those operations only took half a minute; the apparatus, reequipped as a bird, took off proudly.

"Let's see what our little topplers of divinity are doing," the engineer proposed.

In fact, although he was isolated on the upper floor of the direction cabin, he could chat with his companions, distributed in the various compartments. The wireless telephone and loudspeaker linked all the parts of the aircraft together. Thus, Oronius heard and replied.

"They must have returned to their huts and are remaining tranquil there, for nothing is moving on the plain."

"It's even too deserted, Master. This exaggerated calm and deathly silence give me a bad feeling. What can have happened?"

With that question, Jean Chapuis directed the course of the aircraft in such a manner as to fly over all the agglomerations successively, ending with the village from which they had departed.

To his great surprise—and, let us also say, to his increasing anxiety, everything seemed deserted. The streets were empty, the sound of the engines did not attract any of the representatives of the subterranean would outside their dwellings.

"What's happened?" Jean repeated, frowning. "This isn't natural. Where are the people hiding? In sum, they can't have been spirited away. Multitudes can't disappear like this, without leaving any traces."

"Let's land," said Oronius. "I'll send the automata to search one of these habitations. If the disappearance that intrigues you conceals a trap, I can certify that my artificial men won't fall into it."

Laridon would have liked to be authorized to join the scientist's silent patrollers. He was in the mood for a "stroll." He was not permitted to do it. Prudence demanded that they stick to the plan, and the disappointed mechanic had to stay with Turlurette while the thirteen iron pedestrians drew away. He did not refrain from grumbling, or from confiding a few subversive opinions to the pretty soubrette.

"Whatever M'sieur Oronius says," he murmured in the chambermaid's ear, "his ballheads, who can walk like you or me, are only tools. They're not worth as much as a natural brain, especially not that of a native Parisian. The gray matter, you see, is an article that can't be fabricated."

In spite of that denigration, the patrol of automata pursued its mission with a methodical regularity, as conscientiously as any citizen of Paris could have done. Oronius followed their evolutions by means of the Cyclopean Eye and applauded himself for his idea; but what those instruments of genius could not do was discover the inhabitants where they were not.

The village was empty—truly empty. By certain traces that the visit of the automata put n evidence, it was even necessary to conclude that it had been abandoned and that it inhabitants had left in a hurry, without any intention to return, for they had taken with them everything they possessed.

What purpose had that general departure, which strongly resembled a mass migration? Who had convinced or forced the poor people to act thus? Where had they gone?

The luminous pocket could not be unique within the terrestrial crust. Perhaps similar regions were inhabited. If there were any, and they were known, the little humans of the luminous plan had doubtless emigrated to one of them.

Those questions and that response necessarily presented themselves to Oronius' mind; he exposed them to his companions.

Jean Chapuis shook his head. Did he fear something else? What? He did not say.

"Here or there, all the subterrestrial crevasses must be similar," he explained. "It wouldn't be worth the trouble of moving."

In their turn, all the villages perceived were searched like the first, with the same result. Everywhere there was the same emptiness and the same silence. The frightful slumber of deserts reigned henceforth over the immense surface that had seen so many beings swarming.

Absolute, total silence?

No.

The men of iron, as we believe we have explained, were naturally provided with an auditory system, the impressions of which were transmitted to Oronius' brain. The scientist sent them ideas and formed gestures to be accomplished in reaction to the sounds heard. They were, in sum, only a prolongation of his physical means. Via them he could perceive and act at a distance. That is why he sent them forth with so much security. Less vulnerable than his self of flesh and blood, those mechanical and metallic aspects of himself could carry out without risk everything that he could have accomplished in person.

Traversing the last of the villages—which was the one in which the Halcyon-Car and the Bronze Serpent has presented themselves successively—the automata suddenly stopped. Their ears had just perceived a faint sound resembling a groan,

It departed, so it seemed, from beneath a heap of luminous stones.

Without having any need to exchange signals the thirteen automata approached and immediately began clearing the debris.

Under the last stones that they withdrew, they discovered a recumbent body. It was that of Tai, cut and bruised, covered in blood, as if he had been stoned. The poor thing was still breathing, very feebly.

Chapter Nineteen
KILLED AND RESUSCITATED

Cyprienne had seen correctly. It was, in fact, Tai who, running after his crazed brethren, had attempted to turn them away from their sacrilegious assault.

Abandoned by his new friends, the little guide of Jean Chapuis and the "men descended from the sky" had been wandering sadly in the darkness in search of the Halcyon when he had heard the tumult of the assault. Having immediately headed in that direction, he had only reached the location of the event in time to witness the rout of the assailants.

Apprised of the situation, and able to determine the appropriate course of action, it had not been difficult to bring his brethren back. On the way, the lame brought him up to date with the arrival of the serpent and the new strangers, as well as the provocative role played by Yogha and Hantzen.

The intelligent Tai, thus informed, had not had any difficulty, in his simple logic in judging severely the conduct of Oronius' enemy. As much as Cyprienne and Jean Chapuis had been and remained sympathetic to him, these newcomers, whose catastrophic work he had seen, awakened his antipathy. They could only be demons come to cause the doom of the subterran people. Was the result of the revolt provoked by them against "the god of the gulf" not a sufficient demonstration of that belief?

Tai set about adjuring his brethren not to listen to the perfidious tongues of the devils any longer. They then explained to him that, on the advice of Yogha, they had wanted to oblige the god of the gulf to deliver a secret that he held.

"Brother," one of them said to him, "the sky exists. The open air is a real paradise. The marvelous abode of which our religion speaks and which is promised to us after death we can reach while alive, and now. It would be sufficient for the god of the gulf, who is not a god but a man like us, although belonging to the race up above, to consent to inform us of the route. Up there, above the ceiling of rock obstructing the open air, another limitless world commences, in which an incomparable light reigns and where there are extents of which we can have no idea. All delights await us there; everything there is joy and pleasure, a feast for the eyes and the senses. Over our heads we would no longer sense those somber vaults weighing that oppress us. For up there, no matter how high one rises, one does not encounter any limit. Above the head there is nothing!"

Tai did not put in doubt the reality of the existence of that superior world so well endowed. The suggestions of Oronius, as well as what he had glimpsed, prepared him to believe. Nevertheless, he remained suspicious and was not far from believing that the "people of the serpent" were seeking to push his brethren into a trap. Did he not remember, in fact, how the scrap of sky had closed up again? He still had the formidable rumble of the ocean in his ears, making its liquid walls collapse in order to imprison in a subterranean tomb those it had just allowed through.

He therefore listened with mistrust and skepticism to the conclusion of Hantzen's extollers.

"Everything depends on the good will of the god-man, Tai. Thus far, he has lied to us and abused us, since he hid his science from us and let us implore him for an ineffective protection when he could have given us happiness right away. That's why, resolved not to allow ourselves to be deceived any longer, we wanted to oblige him to serve as our guide."

"You tried to do that, in any case," Tai replied, "in the most maladroit fashion. At present, whether he is a god or a simple mortal, the inhabitant of the gulf could not be more ill-disposed in your regard. In reprobation of your actions, he has just proved his power; it's necessary to lose all hope of seeing him lend himself to your plans. In any case, why do you add faith so easily in the perfidious advice of the strangers, of which the clearest result has been to make you commit that error? For myself, I doubt that the god of the gulf has any knowledge of the upward route."

"He knows it! Does he not come from up there?" someone riposted victoriously. "If he hadn't followed it in order to descend, he wouldn't be among us. And if he was able to find the path of the descent, he must be able to find it to ascend again."

"But in that case," said Tai, "the people of the serpent must be no less well-informed; have they not come from the same superior place?"

That adroit argument appeared to make an impression on his listeners. Tai concluded, without further ado: "In those conditions, those whose advice has put you within an inch of extermination could serve you as guides just as well of the god of the gulf. Why did they not offer to do so? Might they not be even more villainous that the person they are trying to blacken?"

At that direct blow, so well placed, they all began to grumble against Hantzen and Yogha.

The latter, enraged by the defeat that she had just witnessed, had lost all measure, and, for want of being able to insult them, she was threatening the subterrans with gestures, leaping about like a Megaera. She was pointed out to Tai.

"She led you to death," he observed. "Now she has a duty to lead you to life. You have a right to demand that of her."

That reasoning could only seduce and convince those infertile brains. In an instant, all the crowd so well informed by Tai rushed on Yogha and dragged her toward the serpent.

It was that mob that Hantzen and Wiwar had seen coming, with a legitimate anguish, and which they had proposed to flee.

The Hindu, we now, aware of her accomplice's lack of courage, had opposed that cowardice. By concentrating her will she had stopped the gesture sketched by Hantzen and immobilized the *Snaky*.

Did she not know that the game was not lost, and that it would be easy to recover her ascendancy over that imbecilic crowd. It would be sufficient to employ her ordinary trickery—which is to say, to interrogate the hypnotized subject. Through him, Yogha would learn what was happening and would be able to act in consequence.

The subterrans, overexcited and pressed to follow Tai's suggestions, had just had the same idea. They wanted to have recourse to the one of their number who could communicate with the stranger and who was endowed with the faculty of translating her words. Reciprocally, he could make known to her the will of his brothers. Yogha's interpreter was, therefore, apprehended and charged with going to expose his congenerates' complaints. The Hindu had just reached the serpent. He entered it after her and all the people, very excited, surrounding the diabolical machine, awaited the result of the embassy.

Inside the *Snaky*, Yogha first had to reassure Hantzen and Wiwar; having done that, she interrogated her subject.

In that way she learned how and why her popularity had been compromised and what, on Tai's advice, those she had made to obey were now demanding of her.

Knowing that she was secure now that she was within the carapace of her strange and redoubtable vehicle, such a threat could only make the Hindu smile. She did not care about the anger of her dupes, knowing full well that they had no means of constraining her yield to their demand. Like Oronius, Hantzen was equipped to teach the presumptuous primitives a lesson. Thus, the eventual anger of the little people could not have any weight in Yogha's decisions. She need not allow it to impose a line of conduct.

But there were other considerations.

Where were they in regard to Oronius? What could they still do against him? The first attack had just failed and had proved that the subterrans were insufficient to wage her war, although their multitude, the magnitude of which Yogha knew, thanks to her questions and her subject's responses, certainly represented an army susceptible of being exploited.

Jean Chapuis had had a presentiment of that. Released among the people of the surface, those millions of beings, drunk on light and space, would certainly deliver themselves to frightful depredations. In all innocence, and struggling for their expansion, they would practice pillage and murder; they would ravage the lands they traversed. Their invasion would be the equivalent of the worst of plagues.

The infernal smile reappeared once again on the Hindu's lips.

She asked the being she had subjugated a few questions. The responses manifestly filled her with joy. Turning then to Hantzen, she said in an enigmatic tone: "They want to be guided by us to the surface. I think it would be maladroit not to satisfy that very legitimate desire."

"You're abandoning the struggle against Oronius?" said the astonished Hantzen.

Yogha smiled.

"You don't know me very well, my dear. It's a matter of a simple change of tactics. I have reason to believe that by acting as we're going to do, we'll be infinitely more disagreeable to the immortal Oronius than by launching the cohorts of the imps of this inferno against his legs. When he learns about the fantastic emigration that we're about to provoke, he'll regret keenly, believe me, not being on the surface to receive all these undesirables appropriately. At that moment, perhaps he'll decide to abandon his dear Magical Villa, fully collapsed, in order to launch himself n our pursuit. I'd like nothing better. So, in order to encourage him to make that decision as quickly as possible, we're going to make arrangements to render his dwelling uninhabitable."

After those preliminary remarks, she exposed her plan. It was nothing less than the unleashing of a flood that would expel Oronius from his subterranean palace.

The information obtained from the hypnotized subterran had shown the Hindu that that result could easily be obtained. An immense lake existed in the vicinity of the gulf. It would be easy to make it pour into the great pit.

With the collaboration of the indigenes, that task could be carried out in a few hours.

"I'll take charge of convincing them and obtaining their benevolent aid," said the young woman. "I also want them to punish this little Tai so ill-disposed toward us. We can do him the bad turn that he tried to do us. Anyway, these cretins will do whatever I want if they know that we're ready to realize their dream, and that the promptitude of that realization depends uniquely on their docility."

In fact, when Yogha's messenger had returned to announce the result of his embassy, the enthusiasm was unleashed. It was obvious that the stranger's new promises enchained the naïve people even more tightly to her will. They all declared themselves ready to accomplish the simple tasks that she demanded of them, provided that they could be accomplished rapidly in order not to defer the great departure for the surface.

It mattered little to them to hollow out a drain. They did not worry about the ravages that the waters of the lake might cause in falling into the gulf. Of their own accord they had not even tried to penetrate Yogha's designs.

But Tai divined them immediately and his heart was squeezed by anguish at the thought that the god of the gulf and those to whom he was attached might be about to perish. He tried to turn his brethren away from that deadly work. He only succeeded in attracting their anger to him, slyly stimulated by the servile creature of Yogha.

Tai was stoned and abandoned, dying, under the heap of luminous stones gathered to ensure his execution.

At the same time, through the contrived outlet, the waters of the lake were precipitated into the gulf and made to cave in all the horizontal planes of the glass villa.

Yogha's two vengeances were accomplished simultaneously. Nothing more remained than to draw away, in the wake of the *Snaky*, the credulous people of whom she wanted to make a scourge.

On her order, the great migration commenced.

Gently, with the same precautions that Oronius would have employed personally, two of the automata lifted up the dying individual found under the stones and carried him to the Halcyon.

The Master examined him immediately. With tears in her eyes, Cyprienne awaited the result of that examination.

"He's in the process of rendering the last sigh," announced Oronius. "Practically, he's dead. But..."

"Good Father!"

"Dry your eyes, little girl. I was about to add: but I'll resuscitate him."

Shutting himself in one of the compartments of the Halcyon-Car with the body of the unfortunate Tai, the Master immediately put his prodigious surgical talent to work to repair and resuture the broken cadaver. When he had returned the essential organs to a good condition and only a motor was lacking to make the mechanism function, he incised one of the veins and put it in communication, by means of a rubber tube, with a receptacle filled with a red liquid. That liquid was reconstituted artificial blood, for Oronius had been able, after much research, to realize the synthesis, basing himself on the previous findings of Berzelius and isolating the aqueous fibrin from seventeen other principles. A pneumatic pump added him to pass a sufficient quantity of that compound into Tai's circulatory system. After that, scarring the opening of the vein, he restarted the heart by means of electricity. Then, the blood having resumed its circulation and the heart beating, Oronius only had to activate the respiratory machine by means of rhythmic tractions of the tongue. The resuscitate lived!

A few moments later, Oronius presented the reanimated little creature to Cyprienne, and Tai, full of joy, began the story of his adventure and the events that he had witnessed.

That story confirmed all too fully the fears that the passengers of the Halcyon-Car had experienced, as well as the dark suppositions of the Master. Hantzen and Yogha, seconded by Wiwar, were indeed the authors of their woes. The two demons, having succeeded in recovering part of their power, had resumed the struggle.

But that was not the most terrible thing. The cause of the departure of the subterrans, now clear, worried the Master and Jean Chapuis much more. Guided by Hantzen and Yogha, the inhabitants of the interior were en route for the surface. No more redoubtable invasion had ever threatened humankind. What horrors would such troops accomplish under the command of the abominable scientist and his Hindu tigress?

"At all costs, it's necessary to prevent that!" exclaimed the engineer, rising to his feet, very pale. "Without losing a moment, we must lunch ourselves in pursuit of the evil scientists and their army.

"Let's go, Hunters—on campaign! I'm in, since I'm Laridon… don… don!" sang the mechanic, who was only dreaming of wounds and bumps. "No more laughing! With M'sieur Oronius and his pretty torches, you're talking about a hunt that won't end without the quarry at bay. What do you say, Bout-de-Zan?"[8]

Bout-de-Zan, or Master Julep, rolled his eyes without replying.

Oronius, whom Jean Chapuis' words seemed to have plunged into a profound meditation, finally raised his head.

"Yes," he said, with the admirable energy that radiated from his person as from a luminous source, "We must pursue them. Let's not dissimulate, though, the perils to which we are about to go with cheerful hearts. Between the Halcyon and the instrument that you designate by the name of a mobile Python, and which they call the *Snaky*, the contest will be terrible!"

---

[8] A fictional enfant terrible created by filmmaker Louis Feuillade in 1912. He was played by René Poyen who was four at the time.

Chapter Twenty
TOWARD THE ETERNAL FIRE

The determination to launch themselves in pursuit of the subterrans, and consequently Hantzen, was not sufficient, It was necessary to have the ability, and first of all, to determine the route that they had taken,

Now, an elementary prudence had certainly prescribed to Yogha's associate that he ought to hide his traces.

Although he was drawing an army in his wake, that precaution was easily realized; it was sufficient to charge the rearguard of the marching people to provoke a few landslides, in such a way as to block the passages employed.

Nevertheless, given the Master's resources, that method could only delay the pursuit without stopping it. In fact, an explanation of the openings of the galleries existing around the circular plain, particularly those whose entrances seemed deliberately obstructed, ought to furnish the pursuers with the necessary indications.

That preliminary exploration, the passengers of the Halcyon decided to undertake immediately. In order to carry it out more rapidly, they divided to two squads which, departing from the same point and taking opposite directions, were to meet up after each having explored half of the perimeter.

The first was composed of Oronius and Julep, taking with them the ape-man and six automata. Jean Chapuis and Laridon formed the second, with the other seven iron men. For the direction of the latter, the Master had given the engineer his powers, with as small adduction in the receiver of each apparatus.

As for the Halcyon, piloted by Cyprienne, it was to float around the illuminated terrain in a circle, keeping in constant communication with the two groups by wireless. At the first signal, alerted by whichever of the groups discovered the right path, the aircraft had to take aboard the unlucky explorers and join the others.

Tai, Turlurette and Mandarinette remained with Cyprienne, who, in order to warn her in case of any surprise, also had Pipigg and Kukuss, her devoted papillons, with her.

The exploration commenced. There was no lack of defiles that appeared to rise up toward the surface. Several were obstructed, but it was easy to determine that the clasped that forbade access to them dated back to an era already distant.

Jean Chapuis had an idea then, very susceptible of putting an end to their embarrassment.

What Tai's story had permitted them to deduce regarding the qualities of the burrowing serpent led him to think that Hantzen, in order to return to the surface, might have taken the route by which he had descended. That was, in sum, the only one of which he was certain, the only one capable of taking him back to a determined point of the continents.

Thanks to his crawling perforator, it had been easy for him to fray a passage for the army of emigrants through the blocks of stone that dissimulated the issue. He must then have got away with replacing those blocks.

The engineer knew the approximate location of that tunnel. It was near the defile in which he had just engaged the Halcyon at the moment when Hantzen had attempted to bury it.

Having made those reflections, Cyprienne's fiancé immediately steered his troupe toward that place, and did not take long to find it.

Or at least, he thought he had found it.

Immediately putting his automata to work, he did not take long to find himself in the presence of two orifices. In one of them, a vein of clay allowed him to recognize the place where he had nearly perished. The second, recently enlarged and abundantly trodden, finished removing his final doubts. It was by that route that the army led by the escapees of Everest had passed.

He immediately telephoned Cyprienne, and shortly afterwards, the Halcyon-Car arrived, bringing its passengers, rejoined by Oronius' group.

The Master, having checked Jean Chapuis' observations, approved them. "You've discovered the right track," he affirmed. "We'll follow it. I think that with all the impediments he's dragging in his person and his troops, Otto Hantzen can't advance very rapidly. The speed of our Halcyon will permit us to catch up with him in no time."

All the chances seemed, in fact, to favor the aircraft, which was obliged to become a tank again for the circumstance. Since that transformation did not detract at all from its speed, the match seemed to be settled in advance; Hantzen and his people were about to be overtaken at the beginning of their journey, necessarily slow and long.

Alas, the unexpected takes charge too often of deceiving human hopes.

The Halcyon-Tank had just engaged in a narrow and low tunnel hollowed out in the heart of a bizarre rock, which Oronius would have examined more closely in any other circumstance, when the engines abruptly stopped working.

"The rattletrap is crocked," observed the mechanic.

In his eccentric language, "crocked" meant that it had broken down—an improbable incident, given the perfection of the apparatus and all its organs. However, the fact was there. Immediately, Jean Chapuis and Laridon proceeded with a rapid check, in order to discover the cause and remedy it.

Almost immediately, a double exclamation of amazement escaped them.

"What do we have here?" Victor asked.

"Unusual! Astounding!" cried the engineer. "Master, we're victims of a failure of radioactivity. Our reservoirs of solarium, radium and etherium are no longer emitting any radioactive force. They only contain dead matter, emptied of its substance."

Oronius bounded into the reservoir cabin. He could only observe the exactitude of what Jean had announced. The source of radioactive energy represented by the enumerated substances had abruptly and mysteriously run dry.

"Can it be a trick on the part of Hantzen?" growled the Master, frowning. That was evidently the first thought that had occurred to him. But how had his rival contrived to capture the precious energy in the Halcyon's reservoirs?

Oronius took his head in his hands in order to concentrate better; he left the aircraft and walked back and forth in the tunnel. At one moment, his gaze having arrested on the wall, he shuddered and started running his slender fingers over the spongy matter of which the rock was composed.

"A radiophilic stone… or, more precisely, radiophagic!" he exclaimed, despairingly. "Jean, Cyprienne! Come and see the explanation of our misfortune, an evil without remedy. We've fallen into a trap… this rocky mass, into which that damned Hantzen has led us, extracts and absorbs radioactive emanations to the point of exhausting their source."

At the Master's appeal, the engineer and the young woman had emerged from the Halcyon. Laridon and the others listened curiously. Everyone's consternation was great.

Immobilized in that somber corridor, the Halcyon could no longer be any help to them.

"Master," Jean Chapuis suggested, "Can't this radiophagic rock restitute what it has taken? Can't we use it to charge our apparatus? It seems to me that, being saturated with radioactive energy, it ought to be able to drive our engines."

"No," Oronius replied, shaking his head. "The precious emanations penetrate into its mysterious mass never to reemerge. They're lost there and unite with it in combinations, which it would be necessary for me to study in order to discover whether it would be possible to isolate radium or thorium therefrom. There's only one thing to do if we want to continue our route and get out of this inferno, and that's to descend from the Halcyon and have it towed by my automata. We'll continue on foot. Victor, and you, my dear Jean, will illuminate our march. I'll form the rearguard with Julep and my ape-man. For more security, an automaton will precede us and another will follow us. The other eleven ought to suffice to drag the tank. Fortunately, I equipped them with a double source of energy; the one originating from solarium and other radioactive sources is certainly drained, but my fulgurite is still sufficient to animate them. More than ever, I congratulate myself for having succeeded one day in stealing the fire of the heavens!"

"It's the lightning, then?" said Jean Chapuis, astonished.

"It's the lightning, or at least a portion of the lightning. In sending it over Paris, Hantzen scarcely suspected that he was offering me an indefectible force."

On the order indicated by Oronius, the caravan resumed its march. A certain dejection reigned. The engineer, in particular, was desolate at the thought that they would now arrive too late to oppose the terrible invasion.

For her part, Cyprienne was not thinking without apprehension about the ordeals that they might yet have to undergo. Certainly, having obtained that first success, the malice of Yogha and her acolyte would not stop there. She would have other surprises in store for them.

It was necessary to advance, however—which is to say, to march toward the danger, and perhaps the suffering.

The tunnel that had been deadly to them, they observed with an increased chagrin, was only prolonged for a few meters. On emerging from it they found themselves in a wider conduit, which expanded into a cavern.

Unfortunately, with the exhaustion of the solarium, the possibility had gone of making the aircraft's searchlights function. Deprived of that source of light, they were reduced in order to illuminate their march to using long silent flashes that Oronius drew from the bodies of his automata. Those fulgurations, which succeeded one another at regular intervals, permitted them to glimpse the vast cavern, but rather confusedly, and without being able to distinguish the details.

In any case, as soon as they had entered it, a terrible incident deflected their attention from any serious examination.

From the ceiling of the cavern enormous black masses were detached, and precipitated upon them with strident cries. Cyprienne and the two soubrettes uttered exclamations of horror.

Frankly, they were not wrong, for the monsters that were attacking the caravan were gigantic bats with wingspans of several meters, the bodies of which attained the size of a veal-calf. Those nocturnal mammals were armed with formidable claws capable of inflicting mortal wounds.

At the first glance, Oronius understood the magnitude of the danger.

"Retreat!" he shouted. "Everyone into the Halcyon! Let the metal men act. Only they can confront such adversaries, for they're vampires of prehistoric dimensions."

In the blink of an eye, all the passengers had taken refuge aboard the tank, the hatch of which was closed precipitately.

In the darkness furrowed by flashes, a frightful battle commenced between the men of iron and the winged monsters.

Rendered furious by the invasion of their domain by animate beings, and even more so by the flashes with which Oronius; automata never ceased blinding them, the giant bats attached themselves to their impassive adversaries and tried to suck their blood, which they were very surprised not to be able to attain. Their clawed fingers scratched the armor plating, and dull impacts resounded.

For their part, the artificial men commenced a terrible massacre. With their heavy gauntlets they stunned the vampires and threw them to the ground, quivering, where they trampled them.

But further bats descended continually from the vault and flew to the rescue. The combat seemed endless. Were they condemned to remain there until the slaughter was concluded by the extermination of all the monsters?

Ordering his automata to cease a futile combat, Oronius had them harness themselves to the Halcyon again, which they dragged through the cavern in the midst of the bloodthirsty swarm, which attacked them relentlessly.

Fortunately, the invulnerability of the men of iron permitted them to endure the furious assaults without sustaining any damage, and to reach the extremity of the cavern.

A narrow tunnel resumed there, into which they toward the Halcyon.

After having attempted vainly to pursue them, the bats, hindered by their wingspan, were obliged to return to the ceiling to await less well-protected prey. A large number of them were lying on the floor of the cavern, and were devoured by the others. Wolves do likewise.

Informed by that experience, Oronius engaged his companions, before risking themselves outside the aircraft, to don protective armor and to equip themselves with the electric weapons that were included in the equipment of the expedition.

It was in view of subterranean exploration that the suits of armor had been fabricated. As that had been under the inspiration of Oronius, they were coated top and bottom with an asbestos fabric. The Master had, in fact, foreseen that the explorers might encounter, in the course of their descent, if not the central fire, at least one of its flow-paths. It was therefore necessary to be able to withstand the infernal furnace and traverse waves of lava.

For the moment, it was not against such encounters that they were thinking of protecting themselves; but as the asbestos suits were the only ones at their disposal, they put them on.

Another preoccupation, in any case, did not take long to take possession of Cyprienne's father; the narrow corridor in which the automata had engaged the Halcyon on leaving the cavern of the vampires was no longer rising; instead, it was descending.

The discouraging truth imposed itself: the voyagers had quit the route followed by the invasion that Hantzen was directing. At a given moment, whether at the exit from the cavern or before the entry into the deadly tunnel, they had deviated from the good route. It was certainly the abominable association that had prepared that guidance toward the only two paths left open by the profusely-strewn obstacles and the final bottling of their pursuers.

Now, they were no longer going toward the surface, and the temperature was augmenting at every step. Without the asbestos armor it would already have become unbearable. Did not prudence command that they retrace their steps and resume the search for the right route?

Oronius wanted to do that.

Unfortunately, it was only possible to realize that desire on condition of abandoning the Halcyon, because the exiguity of the tunnel into which Hantzen had had the skill to lure them opposed any turning around. The Master perceived that with anguish. Immediately after the passage of the transformative apparatus, the walls of the tunnel began to sweat, and that leakage, hardening progressively, diminished the diameter of the conduit in a matter of minutes, to the point of rendering it impracticable.

In order to take account of the gravity of the menace, Oronius, accompanied by an automaton, went back some fifty meters. He was then able to observe the frightful phenomenon visually; the crystallization of the abundant tears—which, preceded by successive falls, were superimposed—ended up obstructing the corridor completely. The passage was therefore closing automatically behind the Halcyon.

Hantzen again! The implacable Hantzen, determined to vanquish and destroy!

More worried, Oronius rejoined his companions. They were condemned to march forward. But if the Master could not discover a source of energy capable of substituting for the solarium and other radioactives, he had to fear remaining a prisoner eternally in this forbidding part of the earth's core.

The route that they were following, forcibly now, must be a path of terrors, since it had been chosen by the jealousy of a hateful rival.

It was certainly by design that, taking care to close the passage behind them, he had nevertheless left the way forward open. Why was the sweating only produced after the passage of the caravan? If it had been generalized along the length of the tunnel, it would probably have required all the effort of the thirteen automata to prevent Oronius and his company from being buried alive. In that hypothesis, the Halcyon could not have been saved and they would have been obliged to abandon it. If Hantzen had not used that means of termination and was permitting the crew of pursuers to continue their march, was it not because he reserved a worse fate for them?

Mute, all his faculties extended to find the necessary riposte, the scientist had resumed his position at the rear. Jean Chapuis and Laridon, preceded by an automaton, continued to guide the little troupe.

Once again, after a rather steep descent, the passage broadened out and a new caver appeared to the eyes of all, bizarrely illuminated by the flashes of the automata. And there also, a double exclamation on the part of Jean and the mechanic stopped the convoy dead.

"Halt! Battle stations! We're about to be attacked!"

Obedient to the mental impulsion imprinted upon them by the directive mind of the Master, the thirteen men of iron abandoned the Halcyon and deployed their protective line ahead of the voyagers.

In the shelter of that powerful rampart, the engineer, Laridon, Julep and Oronius prepared their electric weapons. Next to the Master, Jarrousse, the ape-man, stood meekly. Finally, ready to go back into the Halcyon-Tank if events required it, the three young women formed a final group with Tai and the little dogs.

To tell the truth, the spectacle presented by the cavern justified those preparations, both prudent and bellicose. Colossal dark masses were moving slowly there, barring the passage.

They were strange animals covered with black pelts, attaining the dimensions of an elephant. However, instead of standing solidly on powerful legs, like the animal revered by the Hindus, their mass scraped the ground, crawling, dragging their tails behind them. The advanced sweeping the dust with their formidable and bizarre heads, which terminated in a burrowing muzzle.

Singularly, those animals, which were traversing the cavern in all directions to plunge into the opposite walls, which they perforated irresistibly with the tips of their muzzles, did not seem to pay any heed to the intrusion into their home of the new arrivals.

Could they even see them? No—they were blind. One might have thought that they were moles.

And, to tell the truth, they were nothing else. But these mastodon moles belonged to a special race. Having developed in the depths of the ground, they attained a gigantic size. On considering them curiously, Oronius was better able to understand the multiplicity of the galleries hollowed out in all directions and forming an inextricable labyrinth. They were simply the traces of the passage of the giant moles. No mountain or rock could resist those powerful burrowers.

Laridon, to whom Jean Chapuis explained that, suddenly proposed: "What if we were to capture a couple? They'd be a famous haulage team! For a start, the automata would no longer be reduced to the role of dray-horses. And then, with our Hantzen moles—for that fellow is also a son of elephants, since he has the paunch of one—we'll be able to go anywhere, even where there isn't a route. That will enable us to give the finger to the homonym of our nags!"

"Better to ask them politely to withdraw and leave the way clear for us," muttered the scientist. "This time, the task appears to surpass the strength of my automata. Their combat against the bats and the successive efforts I've demanded of them have necessitated an exaggerated expenditure of fulgurite. What will become of us if that last energy source susceptible of animating my artificial men loses its efficacy? Don't forget that I no longer dispose of any radioactive substance and, in consequence, the vitality of my automata is already greatly diminished. In these conditions, would they be able to fray a passage if these mastodon-moles come together and limit themselves to opposing us with the force of inertia?"

"Friend Victor is no longer laughing," observed Julep.

That was true; Laridon was no longer laughing.

"In that case, we'll remain in perpetuity in this bottomless pit? Thanks very much. Necessary to find a trick to let these iron men have a rest and recuperate. Me too, if that's agreed."

The fears expressed by Oronius had not been exaggerated. Overtaken by a sudden caprice or because their instinct had alerted them to a danger, the elephantine moles had, in fact, assembled, cutting the grotto in two by means of a living barrier that it would not be easy to breach if it did not open of its own accord.

Intrepidly, before anyone had time to oppose his design, Victor Laridon emerged from the ranks of the little troupe and advanced alone to meet the monsters.

"We'll soon see if I have a vocation!" he murmured. "When I was a kid it was a kind of obsession; I wanted to be a boxer, in order to get my nose flattened, which was too prominent; a matador, in order to upper-cut goats; or a mahout, I don't know why… well, here's a good opportunity presenting itself; let's see if we can ride."

And the reckless fellow, having stealthily approached one of the moles, which as presenting its tail to him, suddenly took hold of the animal's rough pelt with both hands and launched himself on to its rump. The giant burrower did not even flinch. The mechanic's audacious ascent produced no more effect than if an insect had landed on its back.

But Laridon, whose asbestos suit, marvelously articulated, took away none of his agility, continued to crawl along the ridge of that mountain of flesh and fur. He reached the neck, and then the head, on which he installed himself in the fashion of a mahout. One of his childhood ambitions was thus realized. Although it was a trifle belated, he experienced a legitimate pride.

"Now there's no more to do than find the sensible spot," he estimated. "I'll tickle the beast, Necessary for it to move, or say why not."

And the imprudent youth, sliding his stick along the muzzle of his mount, started teasing its extremity.

That stratagem achieved a complete success—too much success, we ought to say. For the monster, after having shivered all along its spine and snorted noisily in order to rid itself of that disagreeable sensation, suddenly broke away and started fleeing on its short legs with a promptitude of which one would not have believed such a mass to be capable.

Carrying away its bewildered rider, who had instinctively clung with both hands to the fur in order not to be thrown to the ground, it plunged into one of the lateral corridors.

As if that had been a signal, the entire troop of elephantine moles broke away simultaneously, similarly fleeing in all directions.

At first, Cyprienne and Jean Chapuis had instinctively uttered a cry of amazement, while Oronius shouted in an anxious voice: "Victor!"

But already, muffled trepidations of the ground announced the flight of the herd. The monsters were drawing away, carrying the imprudent mechanic into the depths of the labyrinth.

And the unfortunate fellow was alone.

Alone? Well, no.

On seeing his friend, a joker but good to him, similarly a victim of his foolish temerity, Tai, modulating a bizarre shriek with his lips, had suddenly leapt on to the back of the last mole, And as if it were obeying an order, the latter had immediately plunged into the same gallery that Laridon's monstrous mount had taken.

All that having been accomplished in less time than it takes to write it, silence was reestablished. Around the automata, the Halcyon-Car and its consternated passengers, there was no longer anything but solitude and darkness.

"Forward!" decided the engineer. "We can't abandon those good companions."

"Yes, yes, let's go!" Oronius consented, visibly anxious.

The diminished troupe set forth again, followed by the automata harnessed to the auto-tank.

The temperature became suffocating. Without the envelopes constructed on Oronius' inspired plans, no living creature could have supported its oppression.

The Master could no longer have any doubt; they were descending, and doubtless traversing a hot zone of which the first, excessively rapid, descent had not permitted them to remark the effects.

But the asbestos garments—with which Pipigg and Kukuss had just been provided—not only prevented them from feeling the effects of the excessive temperature but also enclosed an inhaler furnishing an abundant current of fresh air.

His brows furrowed and his lips taut, Oronius marched without saying a word. What could he have communicated to his companions that was not of a nature to discourage them? No word of hope was possible. Every hour aggravated the Master's concern and rendered the situation more critical.

They were descending! That meant that they were plunging at hazard through the terrestrial mass and that no goal could replace the original objective, from which the maleficent Hantzen had been able to deflect them.

That was nothing; but every forward step they took further eroded the provision of fulgurite, the supreme resource of energy and light—a resource that could not be renewed. Thus, each new step, forward or backward, gradually diminished the Master's power. Between his unusable Halcyon and his automata, whose accumulators were about to be drained, Oronius could not be without dread. Since the destruction of the villa-laboratory, buried henceforth underwater, his enemies had not ceased to strike hard and accurately, without him being able to return a single blow. Would he be able to ward off the supreme attack? That would doubtless not be long in coming, and Hantzen would then have every facility to triumph over an adversary reduced to the last extremity.

That could not be! Thus the Master growled, internally. But he was marching with his head bowed, very close to discouragement.

The darkness became heavier and more enveloping. In order to conserve his fulgurite, the ultimate resource, Oronius had to reduce the emissions of the blinding jets with which he was illuminating the march.

Firstly, the number of iron men charged with those emissions was limited to six, then to five, and then four. In the end there was only one. Soon, the last one spaced out the flashes more and more, with the result that the troupe, exhausted and bleak, was marching for long minutes in profound obscurity.

Suddenly, that obscurity was brightened, faintly at first, and the more. But the luminous source, this time, did not originate from fulgurite. It was distant, but seemed to be coming closer. The light was coming from the end of the gallery that they were following, lamentably, calling from time to time, always in vain, to Victor Laridon and Tai.

Jean Chapuis felt hope reanimating within him. He touched Oronius' arm.

"Master, what if that were the luminous plain? What if, in zigzagging through those disagreeable conduits, we were descending toward it again?

The luminous plain—that immense field of radioactivity! What inexhaustible resources it offered to the passengers of the Halcyon-Car! The science of Oronius would certainly be able to utilize the strange substance to recharge the aircraft's apparatus; the provision of energy would be reconstituted. The iron automata would recover their unlimited strength. They would resume the route to the surface, but this time they would avoid the terrible radiophagic rock.

Splendid hope! Intoxicating projects!

How disappointed they were about to be!

Attracted toward the light that had caused a rebirth, they all ran forward. Even the men of iron towed the Halcyon-Car with an increased ardor that was only the reflection of that of their creator. Oh, that hearth of hope! Quickly, quickly!

They reached the exit from the corridor… the luminous source...

They saw...

They all experienced a frisson and they all went pale under their asbestos masks. Pipigg and Kukuss recoiled, emitting suffocated yaps.

It was not a mountain of solarium. Oh no! It was an immense, unimaginable, extraordinary conflagration

Yes, it was the terrestrial inferno with its roaring flames, its torrents of lava, its metals in fusion: a blaze extending over a surface area a hundred times that of Paris, and projecting its tongues of flame toward a vault perforated by invisible chimneys, the probable bowels of volcanoes.

They had reached the central fire.

Chapter Twenty-One
THE SEA OF GOLD

As before the maw of an active blast furnace—and this one offered no point of possible comparison—they wanted to recoil and flee.

Why would they have persisted? The moles could not have carried Laridon and Tai through that ocean of flames; their route had certainly not passed over that ground hollowed out by ditches of lava.

"Back!" Oronius commanded his automata, mentally.

Giving the example at the same time as the signal, he took a few steps back into the interior of the subterrain.

An appeal from Jean Chapuis made him turn round.

"The Halcyon! The automata!" stammered the young engineer, horrified by fear.

No less terrified, her eyes bulging, trembling in ever limb Cyprienne clenched her fingers on her fiancé's shoulder, rooted to the spot. Julep also seemed transformed into a statue of terror. All three of them were looking backwards, in the direction of the infernal furnace.

Was the terrible lesson of Sodom about to have its second edition here? Would the Master be condemned to see his daughter, his future son-in-law and the faithful servant petrified by the mortal hypnotism of the accursed fire?

Seeking to understand, he turned back, imitated them… and he too was turned to stone.

For the first time, the artificial men were disobeying his order. Instead of retracing their steps, as he had signaled, they were pursuing their route… with the Halcyon-Car.

Had another will than that of Oronius taken possession of them, then? Was it that antagonistic will that was inspiring that revolt and launching them through the flames, over ground liquefied by the atrocious heat?

Stupefied, the scientist distinguished the strange silhouettes through the curtain of smoke and flame. They were drawing away. *But they were not walking*! It appeared, on the contrary, that they were being carried away by a force against which they were struggling, as if that were the instinctive desire of the Master. And they were not hauling the aircraft. It too was bounding forward of its own accord, in jerky leaps that were not provoked by any visible means of traction.

In addition, those strange bounds, abnormal and as if, so to speak, obtained by a tractor running out of fuel, were only repeated two or three times. Then the phenomenon ended, immediately replaced by another, no less astounding.

A few meters from the place where Oronius, Jean, Cyprienne, Julep and the two soubrettes were standing, the iron automata and the aircraft were suddenly immobilized.

By means of his will, previously the unique animator of the artificial men, Oronius remained in communication with them. He felt, in the same way that he had felt the material force that was drawing them away, the formidable resistance that was now attaching them to the ground, neutralizing his own efforts.

He understood, and shivered.

The automata and the Halcyon, similarly metallic, had just been attracted by a magnetic mass emerging from the ground. Now that mass was holding them imprisoned.

Oh, if Oronius had been able to give birth to and utilize the radiomagnetic countercurrents uniquely capable of combating and annihilating the influence of the magnet, how rapidly he would have snatched away its prey. Superfluous regrets! The vanity of his science! He was disarmed, impotent.

So he stayed there, downcast by that final disgrace, the consequences of which would be fatal for all of them. Abandoned henceforth by their only normal means, without a refuge and without protection, he and his friends, before the forces conjured from nature, whose secrets he had dared to violate, were about to suffer its implacable riposte.

A frightful dilemma, the unique alternative offered to them was to confront the torment of the fire and risk being doomed there or to throw themselves into the darkness of the subterrestrial labyrinth and wander therein until death came to claim them.

And did they even have that choice?

No! A series of shocks initially muffled an distant, and then more violent, incessantly approaching, shook the gallery at the entrance of which they were standing. The shocks were dislocating their refuge; the vault and walls were cracking. Through a rain of debris, Oronius and his entourage perceived, with a mixture of wrath and terror, a sinuous form that was hastening toward them.

The *Snaky*!

That was, indeed, what it was. The mechanical reptator was bringing Hantzen, Yogha and Wiwar to the place chosen by them for their imminent and definitive revenge.

While the subterrans were climbing up toward the surface, following the way opened to their invasion by the passengers of the *Snaky*, the latter had turned around and returned in haste to witness the defeat of Oronius and, if necessary, to complete it.

At that moment, they had not yet discovered him; they were searching for him.

The Master perceived that and was able to envisage, in an instant, the possible consequences.

If he remained where he was he could not fail to fall into the power of Yogha and Hantzen, and Cyprienne and Jean Chapuis with him… as well as Turlurette, Mandarinette, Julep and the two little dogs… and even Jarrousse the ape-man!

All the survivors of the terrible adventure would become Yogha's captives.

The man whose science had saved the capital of the United States of Europe from destruction could not support that thought. As long as a breath of life remained in his body, he wanted to employ it in the struggle. Rather the eternal fire, with all its perils! It would be more clement than the associate of the Hindu princess.

"*En route!*" cried Oronius. "Not backwards, forwards! Let's plunge into the middle of the flames, my children. Our garments will protect us and perhaps the fire will save us from a more implacable peril!"

The humans and animals only hesitated for a second, and the entire troupe raced into the furnace.

Despairing as they were, that frightful refuge made them go pale. It cost them far more to abandon, without hope of ever finding them again, Victor Laridon and Tai, the Halcyon-Car and the men of iron. It was, however, necessary.

On the heels of Oronius, they all ran through the flames.

Could they recoil? Could they even hesitate, whatever the horror of the spectacle that was offered to their eyes—perhaps the torture to which they were abandoning themselves?

They fled the *Snaky*, which had entered the diabolical crucible behind them in order to search for them. They were probably only separated by a curtain of red embers.

To stop and turn back would be to risk running into the fabulous reptile; so they went forward, and they truly required the heart of triple bronze of which Horace speaks in order to dare to confront Satan. Blinded by the swirls of smoke and flame that whipped their masks, they could not see any obstacles that loomed up in front of them or beneath their feet. The brazier hissed and roared; showers of matters in ignition and lava flows, fell upon them; their feet were wading in a thick mud of molten metal, from which they could only extract them at the price of great efforts.

To advance in such conditions was exhausting. To succeed in it and not be doomed, they took one another by the hand and marched in Indian file.

At one moment, lifted up on a crust of burning ground suddenly inflated by an enormous blister or abscess, they had felt that crust open up and give passage to a geyser of green-tinted flames and nauseating vapors. Knocked over by the violence of the it, they had fallen to the ground.

An anguishing minute! Each of them wondered what had become of their companions. All were able to believe themselves the sole survivor, or even to dread that, if the others had survived, they would not be able to rejoin them. From all parts, therefore, cries went up. As they got to their feet, they all called out.

First of all, by groping, Jean Chapuis found Cyprienne and was able to gasp her hand. A moment later the young woman collided with her father, who was wandering, moaning, under the burning shower of that infernal pus.

An initial chain was thus reformed. Voices informed them that a second group, similarly, had reconnected, which ought to consist of the other members of the caravan. Julep was leading it. holding on to Mandarinette, who was holding on to Turlurette.

The two groups joined up again, and the forward march resumed. The chain lacked one link, however; Jarrousse, the ape-man, was no longer there. Oronius realized that and called out.

A moment ago, alongside his creator, the ape-man had slipped like the others, but now he no longer responded to the appeals and no one could tell what had become of him. If he had gone astray in the midst of the furnace, they could consider him as lost.

"Adieu, then!" pronounced Oronius, already consoled. "No bond of affection existed between him and us. It's no great loss, and it would be stupid on our part to shed a single tear in his regard."

The double chain continued on its way, staggering and splashing, paddling though the boiling flood that covered the ground. Both parts could only advance by yielding almost completely to chance. If Providence is the fortunate hazard of believers, simple hazard can be providential to the scientific, generally devoid of any belief. We ought to think so, since it certainly showed itself favorable to our people. Before them, the wall of flames, without any apparent cause, suddenly became less dense.

The smoke was diluted. It was soon no more than a mist, in the semi-transparent waves of which they were able to see one another and recognize one another.

One last effort brought them out of it, and they found themselves safe and sound on rocky ground bordered by shadow, a few meters from the terrifying conflagration.

So much effort and so much anguish had left them exhausted; they let themselves fall to the ground.

They had traversed the central fire and they were still alive!

They had seen the *Snaky* and they had escaped it!

Was that madness, miracle or magic? For the scientist, very realistic, it was simply a matter of chance: a double sign of the protection of destiny.

"We'll get out of this," he affirmed. "The important thing is not to allow ourselves to be beaten."

"But Victor probably won't get out of it!" moaned Turlurette, wiping tears from her eyes.

That was also the secret terror of Oronius and Jean Chapuis. Dominating it, and in order to comfort the poor young woman, who was about to need all her courage in order to continue the march, they pretended to conserve hope.

"Who knows?" said Jean. "Laridon can get out of troubled if anyone can. Doubtless, thanks to his mount, he's already regained the surface. Let's do likewise... we'll find him again up above."

Turlurette did not allow herself to be persuaded.

"He risked himself to save us," she insisted. "If he'd been able to render himself master of the elephant or jump off, he would have rejoined us. We won't see him again."

"Tai is with him," Cyprienne observed, gently, "And Tai has proved his worth to us."

"Furthermore, Tai is a native of the land," Oronius added, confidently. "I'd give a good deal to have such a guide at present. Before lamenting the fate of the brave Victor, give some thought to ours, young Turlurette. Presently, you see, we're not lodged under a better sign. And yet, I won't concede victory yet to the fabricator of cardboard thunder. So, on your feet, everyone. Let's move on!"

His voice was persuasive. Everyone obeyed. Had he not taken them into the inferno from which they had emerged? Turlurette uttered a deep sigh, and followed the movement.

This time, moreover, it was no longer a matter of resuming the terrible route. On the contrary, they could turn their backs on the visible danger and draw away from it. It was sufficient for that to lunge into one of the passages that traversed the granitic wall before which our friends had stopped.

Again, obscurity was the sole obstacle to confront there. On the other hand, the narrowness of the corridors guaranteed the fugitives against a silent pursuit by the reptilian machine. If Hantzen and his bronze Python wanted to engage in it they could only do so by perforating the granite wall, in which case the noise of the burrowing would alert Oronius.

What would they find beyond the rock?

For the moment, he question did not come up. It was only a matter of putting a barrier between the Master and his enemies.

Having reconstituted their chain, they resumed walking in order; Oronius took the lead, and Jean Chapuis covered the rear in case of a possible surprise.

They traveled several hundred meters thus. Then, once again, light cut through the darkness. Was it the eternal fire again, toward which they had returned? In darkness it is impossible to take account of the direction one is following. They had seemed to be walking in a straight line, but they could easily have described a curve and returned toward their point of departure.

However, the light bore no resemblance to the shifting fulgurations given off by the infernal brazier. It was uniform in color, constant and calm. No redness traversed it; nothing could be seen of the surges of flame and swirls of smoke that had been raging a little while before, indicating a fire in full combustion. This resplendence, which resembled the dazzling reflection of the sun in a mirror, was evidently coming from a motionless light source.

"Could it be an aurora borealis?" the engineer thought aloud.

"Come on, my dear friend," retorted the scientist. "Underground—do you think so? Where could the sunlight that could produce it be coming from? Between us, it must be the reflection of a large lake, but its color surprises me somewhat. What odorless liquid—for we can't smell anything—has that hue?"

"Picric acid?"

"Yes, a few particles of that compound would be sufficient to turn a pond yellow. But why conjecture? Let's go forward and see what it is."

They followed him with confidence, and as the corridor widened, our comrades emerged from it abreast.

Then all their breasts dilated and a similar cry of admiration escaped their mouths, while their dazzled eyes closed.

They were on a sort of strand running alongside an immense lake—a sea! But it was not water that extended as far as the eye could see; the smooth, calm surface, perfectly motionless, was resplendent, and the yellow gleam that it emitted caused the brilliant rocks that reflected it sparkle with magical glimmers.

"A sea of metal! A sea of gold!" cried Jean Chapuis.

"Yes, a sea of molten gold," Oronius specified, having knelt down in order to examine the singular liquid "And a sea of gold reflected by mountains of diamond. This unique spectacle represents fabulous treasures. The gold of this lake and the diamonds of that open mine, I dare say, would be sufficient to multiply the wealth of humankind a hundredfold—or ruin it, by rendering gold and diamond so common that they would lose all value."

"Then let's refrain from making our discovery known," joked Jean, "and scorn treasures that could only impoverish us."

That was not the opinion of Julep, excited by the sight of those inestimable treasures.

What! He only had to bend down to enrich himself, and he, Julep, the poor servant, would miss such an opportunity? Oronius had to be joking!

"Julep wants some! Julep wants to become rich! Julep brings back lots… lots!" he cried, dancing a frenzied *bamboula* on the edge of the marvelous lake.

He was delirious, struck with vertigo by the dangerous scintillation that has made many a human being lose his head. Could the brain of a poor servant be any more solid? Could he resist the temptation?

Momentarily, Julep's companions feared that he might precipitate himself into the golden flood; already they were advancing in order to retain him. But he polychromatic servant contented himself with kneeling down and leaning over in order to plunge his hands—fortunately gloved with asbestos—into that liquid fortune. He had united them in the form of a cup and attempted to bring them back full of the precious metal. Was it not thus that one slaked one's thirst when a favorable hazard put one in the presence of an opportune spring?

Unfortunately he had reckoned without the diamond that closed his asbestos gloves; that diamond caught fire on contact with the molten gold; through the gap in one of the gloves a drop of gold ran and made a hole in the unfortunate's hand. Uttering a howl of pain, Julep hastened to withdraw his empty hands.

"A cruel lesson, but a salutary one," said Oronius, to console him. "So it goes all too often with the misdeeds of that vile metal toward its worshipers! Learn to your expense, my lad, that gold can burn the avid fingers that reach our for it imprudently. Let's leave this igniter of war and purveyor of felonies where it is, and follow us. We can't try to cross this sea of gold... and yet it's important to put it between us and Hantzen. I reckon that if he follows us in this direction, it will be sufficient to delay him for a while, for he's certainly as unreasonable as you, my good Julep. So let's go around the lake. Beyond it there's security."

Confused and a little disappointed, the negro had the wisdom not to recriminate. From time to time, while following his master he darted glances charged with rancor at the sea of gold.

"That's not good," he muttered. "A trap for a poor black man. Bad gris-gris underneath. Makes fire to burn fingers!"

And he shook his damaged hand.

The shore extended interminably. Certainly there was enough there to cover half the world with golden palaces. The piercing eyes of Oronius searched in vain for the other side.

After an hour of walking a rumble struck their ears. The mass of gold, immobile a moment ago, began to ripple; a current was designed on its surface."

Further on, it became more rapid, and soon, irresistibly drawn toward a breach opening in the middle of the ring of mountains, it was precipitated thereinto with a dull crashing sound—the sound of molten lead falling from above.

Oronius and all the members of his caravan ran toward the fall. They remained in ecstasy before the grandiose spectacle presented by that sheet of molten gold falling more than a hundred feet into a second seething basin, from which purple vapors rose.

Like the others, Cyprienne, simultaneously seduced and terrified by the grandiose horror of the spectacle, leaned over in order to try to perceive the bottom of the extraordinary cauldron.

Suddenly, it seemed to her that she was shoved forwards, and she fell into the seething mass, uttering a heart-rending scream of agony.

Chapter Twenty-Two
THE METAL CATARACT

Jarrousse, the malevolent individual doubly metamorphosed into an ape by Oronius, had lost both human appearance and human thought. Since the operation by means of which the great scientist had imposed his new form on him, memory had been forbidden to him; he was only living in an unconscious state. In all circumstances, the conviction, hypnotically suggested, that he was an ape made him act like a quadrumane.

It was thanks to that stratagem that Cyprienne's father had been able to make of that enemy a docile servant, replacing adequately the veritable orangutan who had died in the laboratory of the Magical Villa during the explosion provoked by the breaking of the nitrocolle receptacle.

Thus, his human thought, having been rendered torpid by the will of Oronius, no idea of revolt could be born in the cranium of Jarrousse-Bambo, so he had followed his master meekly into the furnace, after having been clad in an asbestos garment, like the others.

At the moment when the spontaneous geyser of fire had caused him to roll on the burning ground, however, a singular phenomenon occurred within him. Either because the violence of the shock had shaken the ape-man's nervous system and returned to activity certain cerebral cells put to sleep by the will of the Master, or because the latter, ordinarily extended, had relaxed under the empire of the emotion. Jarrousse suddenly found himself partially liberated from the hypnotic suggestion that maintained him under the domination of the man he had tried to murder.

That was a very confused impression. It could not be assimilated to the reawakening of the personality and free will. Nevertheless, for the first time since the descent to the center of the earth, a parcel of the veritable soul of Jarrousse agitated within him. He experienced, confusedly, a great reluctance to rejoin those from who he had just been fortuitously separated. A sort of desire for liberty and flight was reborn in his partly-recovered brain, to the extent that when he got up, instead of responding to the appeals and rejoining Oronius' companions, he hung back and ended up frankly retracing his steps. The ape-man was, therefore, not dead, as Oronius had supposed. On the contrary, more alive than ever, he had reconquered his liberty.

Not for long!

His personal luck determined that he emerged from the eternal fire a few paces from the *Snaky*, and was immediately spotted by Yogha.

He was, as we have said, masked and armored with asbestos. His silhouette was thus that of a veritable human being, and nothing could reveal that inside the envelope in question, nothing would be discovered by an ape.

Om perceiving him, the Hindu thought that she had put her hand on one of those for whom she was searching. She signaled his presence to Hantzen, and the latter, having judged the prize good, charged his accomplice with operating the capture. Yogha therefore gave Jarrousse a mental command to stop and then to rally to the serpent.

Without being equipped to resist a summons of that genre, the ape-man was in no hurry to obey; he was in a period of relativity, neither human nor beast; only within him, the former species was seeking to take a step beyond the latter.

The intervention of Yogha completed the disintegration of the mental prison in which Oronius had maintained the mind of his captive artificially, and Jarrousse suddenly recovered consciousness of his humanity. Memories returned to him in a host, but those memories were all anterior to the Belleville catastrophe. Between that moment and his original recuperation of the self, he remembered nothing. The influence of Oronius and the hypnotic dependence in which he had been maintained prevented him from retaining any image of events.

All of that was limited to a vague impression of having lived a horrible nightmare.

Things happened, therefore as if nothing had existed between that awakening and his loss of consciousness. He could not take account of the time elapsed and was unaware of the enormous lacuna that existed in his memory.

He had felt a terrible pain and had lost sentiment in the middle of a clap of thunder, in Oronius' laboratory; he remembered being surrounded by horrible flames, two paces from a strange animal, an apocalyptic monster.

At first he experienced a sentiment of fear, and wondered whether he was still alive.

As he had no consciousness of his transformation, he tried to cry, in accordance with the formula adopted by people emerging from a faint: "Where am I?"

He was astonished by the exaggerated effort that he had to make in order to articulate those simple words. They seemed to rip his throat and he was frightened by the hoarse and inhuman sounds that emerged therefrom.

What was wrong with him? What had squeezed his throat to the point of only permitting inarticulate sounds to emerge?

But the will of Yogha drew him at that moment inside the *Snaky*. He yielded to it unconsciously and slipped into the opening revealed to his eyes. There, suddenly finding himself in the presence of Yogha, Hantzen and Wiwar, his emotion equaled his amazement.

By what miracle did he find them reunited, a few minutes—it seemed to him—after the terrifying explosion of Oronius' laboratory?

Pass for Wiwar; he admitted that the spy attached by Otto Hantzen to the person of the great scientist of Belleville had remained in the vicinity. But the Hindu and her associate? How did they come to be so far from Everest, where he knew that he had left them in their cloudy tower?

For Jarrousse naturally imagined that he had not quit Paris. For him, the abominable vision that he had just had of the eternal fire was simply the consequence of the already-distant explosion, and he had not been unduly moved by it.

His gaze, however, lowered mechanically toward the asbestos suit in which he was clad, and he was more seriously astonished by that useful masquerade. By whom had he been thus protected? Combining his attire with the fact that he did not seem to have suffered very much from the explosion, and that someone must, in any case, have pulled him out of trouble, he concluded that it had been an amicable intervention. The presence of Yogha and Hantzen naturally suggested to him that he owed that help to them, and perhaps his rapid recovery too.

An entire world of ideas was colliding in his head. He began to deduce that his unconsciousness must have lasted much longer than he had supposed, for important events had doubtless occurred in the course of that lapse of time.

Understanding then that he ought to express his gratitude by means of amicable signs, for want of emotional words, since his tongue was functioning poorly, he held out his hands abruptly to the two accomplices.

It was the turn of Yogha and Hantzen to be invaded by amazement.

Who was this mysterious prisoner, then? Why was he behaving so bizarrely? They thought they had captured in him one of Oronius' companions, if not Oronius in person, and now, instead of trembling before them or manifesting chagrin at allowing himself to be caught, he appeared to be experiencing on seeing them a kind of satisfaction. He seemed to want to thank them!

It was inexplicable.

"Who are you?" demanded the imperative Yogha.

There had been no need to employ suggestion to force him to explain himself; Jarrousse asked for nothing better than to respond and be recognized. For a second time he tried to articulate the human syllables so painful to his anthropomorphic throat.

"Jarrousse! I'm Jarrousse!" he tried to say. "Don't you recognize me? It isn't you, then, who has saved me and cared for me?"

Pronouncing such syllables was a task beyond his possibilities. His second attempt was no more fortunate than the first. In spite of all his efforts, he only succeeded in making a horrible gurgle emerge from his throat:

"Ooousse! Ummm ouououusse."

And as the three inhabitants of the serpent considered him with bewildered expressions, impatient and vexed by not being able to make himself understood, he took off his mask and his asbestos suit, thinking that his appearance would explain everything and produce a marvelous effect on his friends. The effect was produced, you can take our word for it, but absolutely not in the sense that Thomas Jarrousse had counted on.

Instead of the cry of welcome that he expected, and the cordial welcome to which he thought he had a right, he heard exclamations that were incomprehensible to him:

"An ape, my dear!"

"That's true... it's only an ape!"

A mountain falling on Jarrousse could not have crushed him more. For a good minute, he stood there open-mouthed, his eyes ready to spring from their orbits. He felt as incapable of thinking as he was of speaking.

He only heard the words disdainfully repeated by Yogha:

"It's only an ape! It isn't a human!"

A commotion finally shook the simian body of Jarrousse; the meaning of that remark reached his brain. Mechanically, he looked down at himself.

What a roar escaped his throat then!

He expressed the most intense amazement that any human creature had ever felt—and the fear and the anger, and the pain and the shame!

Jarrousse had just seen his deformed and hairy body, his immeasurable orang's arms, and his enormous belly.

There was a mirror on one of the walls of the cabin. He bounded toward it and darted a glance at his visage.

Then, uttering a frightful plaint, he veiled the hideous face with the flattered nose that he had just seen with his hairy hands with terrible fingernails. Then, folding himself up, he began to sob violently, humanly.

Yogha's exclamation was explained; it was true, he was only an ape.

Alas, alas, how had that transformation been produced? Whence came his misfortune?

Meanwhile, the attitude of their unusual prisoner, in whom she had initially only seen a man of the woods, intrigued the Hindu to the highest degree. The spectacle of that dolor was particularly eloquent: the individual expressing it could not be a beast.

Pressed to fathom the mystery she sensed, the Hindu approached and touched Jarrousse on the shoulder.

"Why are you crying? Do you understand me, then?" she interrogated.

The ape-man uncovered his eyes, the expression of which had become human again. This time, he did not try to speak. The revelation of his transformation had explained his impotence to express himself in speech. He contented himself with staring and Yogha, pointing at his throat and shaking his head.

For her part, the Hindu looked at him intently, and direct communication was established between them. The young woman easily read in the thoughts of the ape-man the responses that he was making mentally to her questions. The following dialogue was established:

"Who are you, who have the form of a beast but weep and suffer in the fashion of a man?"

"I *am* a man. Can't you recognize me Yogha? And yet I was one of your faithful followers! I'm Thomas Jarrousse!"

"You, Jarrousse."

The Hindu's eyes finally opened. A few questions finished enlightening her. She glimpsed what had happened.

Then, using her habitual method, she plunged the ape-man into a hypnotic sleep, and made him relive all the scenes that had succeeded one another since the explosion in the laboratory.

When she had clarified everything, she woke Jarrousse and told him about the vengeance of which he had been the victim and the strange servitude in which the Master had kept him.

When she has reawakened his memory and resuscitated in his consciousness, the sensations that had remained until then in Jarrousse's unconscious—which is to say, when she had rendered him the possibility of remembering the hours lived with Oronius in the form of an ape—Jarrousse got up with a bound and rushed to the door with a terrible growl.

"Where is he going?" asked Hantzen, anxiously, on seeing him launch himself outside and plunge into the obscure corridor.

"Let him be," Yogha intimated, with a cruel smile. "He's going to avenge himself. And we're going to follow him."

Jarrousse was not running at hazard. The inspiration of a seer was guiding him.

It was, therefore, easy for him to avoid the eternal fire and to reach, through a corridor, the shore of the sea of gold. He set out along it, and did not take long to perceive the group formed by the Master and his entourage, stopped on the edge of the infernal groove hollowed out by the incessant fall on the precious molten metal.

Above the seething of its vapors Cyprienne was inclining her charming head.

A demonic inspiration traversed the mind of the ape-man. Two flames sprang from his pupils; he had his vengeance. It would be the most terrible that he could inflict upon the author of his degrading transformation.

The rumble of the golden cataract, falling from the lake into the gigantic crucible, covered all other sounds. Jarrousse was able to approach the group without being heard.

When he was at a favorable distance, suddenly bounding forward upon the engineer's fiancée, he precipitated her into the abyss.

A quintuple cry of horror accompanied that fall. Terrified and desperate, Oronius and the two soubrettes extended their arms toward the gulf, into which Jean Chapuis, mad with dolor, had just leapt in his turn.

Jarrousse's vengeance was more complete than he had hoped: the gulf in which there was nothing but molten metal and rock, and from which nothing emerged but smoke, had just devoured its double prey.

Would he be able to savor that vengeance in peace?

Furious yapping suddenly resounded.

While Cyprienne's father and devoted servants, crushed by their grief, remained kneeling, absorbed in the contemplation of the tormented gulf that had just swallowed the young woman and her fiancé, instinct had warned the two little dogs of the presence of an enemy.

Only Pipigg and Kukuss had understood the drama. With a common accord, as brave as they were minuscule, they launched themselves at the aggressor of their young mistress.

It did not enter into Jarrousse's intentions to stand up to them. He immediately ran away—but Julep, Turlurette and Mandarinette had already turned their heads. They perceived the ape-man, saw him fleeing, and understood the role that he had just played.

Horror and anger were painted on their faces. In the wake of the two little dogs, they launched themselves on the track of the murderer.

On the edge of the crucible, which he had not ceased to fathom with his moist eyes, Oronius remained alone.

Vainly, his gaze tried to plunge into the pit and to pierce the thick veil of vapor. He could not distinguish anything of the epilogue of the drama; and the rumble of the golden cataract, colliding with gold, prevented the cries of the victims reaching his ears.

What was happening below him? Were the fiancés still struggling amid the boiling of heavy liquefied matter that natural alchemy was brewing in the depths of the vat? Had they perished, or was it still possible to render them assistance?

Oronius stood up. Curbed by his initial, his unique, despair, he moved along the edge of the outlet; but the toxic vapors incessantly emitted from it prevented him from seeing, and even from breathing.

Time passed… probably hours. Sunk in his grief, he did not take account of it. He kept moving forward, suffering from feeling disarmed before the terrible misfortune. It was his daughter and the man he loved like a son who were agonizing in that giant cauldron cooking the metal for which humans killed one another… agonizing or, doubtless, dead…but he, who could resuscitate the dead and hold the forces of nature in check, could do nothing for his children! All the miraculous arms forged by his marvelous brain had escaped him.

Where were the treasures saved from the disaster of his laboratory and contained in the flanks of the Halcyon? Where were the thirteen iron automata, by means of which he could have sounded that abyss? All of that was lost… lost forever!

Cries extracted him from his reverie.

Having become indifferent to everything that was not the gulf, at first he paid no attention to them; but the cries redoubled and drew nearer. Familiar barking as mingled with them—that of the little papillons so dear to his Cyprienne. Then he distinguished the voice of Julep and, hectically, those of his daughter's two devoted soubrettes.

"Help, Master!"

"Monsieur! Monsieur! Protect us! Save us!"

Oronius turned his head, and he saw Julep and the two young women, preceded by the bounding Pipigg and Kukuss, returning toward him a top speed.

A metallic monster was pursuing them: the *Snaky*.

What had happened can easily be understood. Fleeing before the dogs, and above all before Julep, Turlurette and Mandarinette, Thomas Jarrousse had returned toward Hantzen's crawling machine.

For her part, as we know, Yogha had convince her ally to set his machine in motion in order to go after the ape-man.

She had a plan.

As soon as she perceived the pursued and the pursuers, she had the *Snaky* stop and she opened the panel in order to allow Jarrousse to take refuge under her protection.

After that, he mechanical reptation resumed.

As one would imagine, at the sight of the *Snaky*, Julep and the young women had turned on their heels, and ran away as fast as they could.

"What you've done is stupid!" moaned Hantzen, shrugging his shoulders. "Why, instead of running at those chasing Jarrousse, did you stop our charger? It was a good opportunity to collect them all."

"Not all of them," Yogha riposted. "My count wasn't full. Let's let them run and content ourselves with following them. They'll go to find the rest… the whole lot!"

And she put herself in mental communication with the ape-man again, in order to learn from him the result of his expedition.

When she discovered that the crime committed by Jarrousse had had the result of pushing Jean Chapuis to throw himself into the liquid furnace she flew into a violent anger.

Yogha, it ought not to be forgotten, had particular views regarding the young engineer, since she had not ceased to pursue him with her advances. The hatred she had for Cyprienne and her father originated, primarily, from the disdain testified to her by Jean Chapuis, in whom she wanted to inspire a very different sentiment. If her jealousy had not had such motives for desiring the doom of Cyprienne and the humiliation of Jean Chapuis, Hantzen would never have obtained her constant association with his projects. So, on learning of what she called "the young engineer's fit of madness" she heaped Jarrousse with the worst insults.

Hantzen interrupted the flood brutally. "Oronius still remains," he said rudely. "Let's occupy ourselves with him. Afterwards, you'll have all the leisure you need to abuse this poor fellow. He hasn't worked so badly. Furthermore he has enough personal grounds to complain of the treatment he has endured."

Yogha looked at him severely. Oronius' rival did not seem unduly moved by that, and launched his serpent on the tracks of Julep.

A few moments later the crawling machine arrived within sight of the golden falls...and within sight of Oronius.

The two soubrettes and the negro, along with Pipigg and Kukuss, had just rejoined the Master. They all formed a group toward which the *Snaky* immediately raced, and as it was finally showing its true speed at that moment, the unfortunates understood very quickly the impossibility of escaping it by means of a new flight. It described rapid semicircles, which enclosed them in an ever-narrower space and obliged them to retreat to the edge of the crucible.

Hantzen's maneuvers appears to be driving them implacably toward the gulf in order to precipitate them into it in their turn. Their foreheads glued to the glass plates that simulated the eyes of the bronze reptile, Yogha, Hantzen, Wiwar and Jarrousse feasted on the spectacle of their victims' terror.

Only Oronius conserved an impassive attitude and awaited death with a steady footing. In order to confront his enemy better, he had removed the asbestos mask and uncovered a firm visage unadulterated by any terror.

That sang-froid and scornful attitude exasperated Hantzen, who went pale with chagrin.

By contrast, the mysterious smile had reappeared on Yogha's beautiful calm face.

"Let me act," she said to her associate. "You can see that you'll never succeed in troubling that heart of bronze. Do you think you can impress him with this infantile procedure? You lack imagination, my dear. That death will be too quick and too mild."

"Have you something better to offer?" growled Hantzen, eagerly seizing the opportunity to vent his spleen.

"Can you doubt it?" replied the hyena with the cruel smile. "Remark that by throwing those people into the fall you'll lose the spectacle of their agony. That's a waste. Let's take possession of them; I'll be able to devise unprecedented tortures for them."

"A fine project, in truth," sniggered Hantzen. "Do you believe it easy of realization? I have too profound a knowledge of Oronius' intractable pride to hope so. I'm sure that he's rather cast himself into the beyond than permit us to lay a hand on his divinity."

"Believe me, I won't give him the time. You've lost your memory, my dear, or you doubt the petty talents of your serpent. Quickly! Activate the fascinators! Have Wiwar prepare to open the mouth in order to catch its prey. I'll draw them in by means of the pneumatic aspirator."

Those words were a flash of enlightenment for the malevolent individuals. They leapt to the apparatus indicated by the young woman and released the various mechanisms.

Immediately, the vitrified eyes of the metallic monster were animated by a strange gleam, the immediate effect of which was to immobilize Oronius and his companions. Nailed to the ground by the fascinating force, they felt their gazes invincibly attracted and riveted to the captivating source maneuvered by Hantzen. Without being able to struggle against the disturbing attraction, which had the authority of a psychic magnet, they saw the menacing maw opening.

Before them they felt the cold of the void and, slowly sucked in, they took a step toward that maw...and then another.

"They're coming...! They're coming...! They're ours!" sniggered the Hindu princess, whose nostrils were palpitating with a ferocious lust. "Your inventions are admirable, savant Hantzen... but on condition that it's me who utilizes them.

Gently does it! Small steps! Very small steps! It's necessary to give them time to sense our power… and for us to savor our pleasure... it's so amusing to see them approaching gradually, of their own accord, the maw that awaits them... one more step… and another. There they go… it's almost a pity."

But at the moment when she thought that one last inhalation of her apparatus would attract her prey inside the gaping mouth, a flash of lightning sprang from the heights of the cavern. A terrible electrical discharge was engulfed in the interior of the serpent, sending Yogha and the enemies of Oronius sprawling pell-mell, howling with pain.

Instinctively, Hantzen's hand closed on the lever that set the serpent in motion, and the monster, closing the mouth that had not been able to snatch the prey, writhed, bounded and fled as if it had been attained itself and cruelly stung by the electrical discharge,

Joyful bursts of laughter saluted that precipitate retreat.

They seemed to depart from the sky, if one can use that term in speaking of the ceiling of rock that closed the subterranean world.

Stupefied and saved, Oronius, Julep, Turlurette, Mandarinette and the little dogs raised their heads.

Then they perceived, floating proudly above the gulf, the Halcyon-Car, manned by Laridon, Cyprienne and Jean Chapuis.

And, tracking the bronze serpent, the retreat of which they were trying to cut off, the thirteen reanimated automata came running.

Chapter Twenty-Three
IRRADIUM

Projected by the cowardly aggression of Jarrousse into the basin into which the fall of boiling gold poured, with a thunderous din, Cyprienne had instinctively uttered a scream of terror and anguish.

In reality, the young woman did not lose her sang-froid for an instant. Although blinded by the green vapors disengaged by the continual turbulence of the brew and deafened by the whistle of the liberated gases, she had the presence of mind immediately to open the air-taps of her asbestos envelope.

Spreading through the interior of her suit, that air, previously condensed and suddenly dilated, inflated the garment in an instant and transformed it into a kind of balloon, so that it sustained the young woman's descent and permitted her to land lightly on the surface of the burning crust.

The asbestos protected the young woman against any burn; her diminished weight prevented her from sinking. She was able to get up and to move in an upright position over the tormented but almost solid surface.

At the same instant, Jean Chapuis fell in his turn. Coming as a rescuer he had not neglected to employ the same procedure used by Cyprienne. Like her, he landed without a jolt a few meters away from her. Through the fog of vapors the two fiancés perceived one another.

He could not distinguish her clearly because of the veil of vapors that enveloped both of them, but he divined her and, invaded by a hectic joy, he repeated to himself, marking the flight of the seconds by the precipitate beats of his heart: "Cyprienne is here… nearby... safe and sound... alive... the infernal crucible has not been able to kill her!"

At that thought, by virtue of a reaction familiar to all those who have suffered or trembled, the exultation suddenly enveloped them of a radiation like the joyous flame springing unexpectedly from a dark star. The sentiment of mad joy that suddenly took possession of him could not be analyzed; he had a desire to weep and laugh, to shout and sing, to dance and fall to his knees. It was an extravagant delirium, and simultaneously the sweetest of emotions.

Cyprienne was alive. All his terrors and all his anguish of the previous moment immediately vanished. The memory of what he had just suffered was abolished in him.

He opened his arms and pressed to his heart the golden-haired fiancée, who abandoned herself, palpitating with emotion, no less happy.

Amour, a grand amour, made those two hearts beat in unison, forcefully, while they held one another enlaced.

They forgot the situation. For lovers, no threat and no danger can exist while they link their hands and are able to exchange kisses.

"Jean! My Jean!" murmured Cyprienne. "You threw yourself into death in order to follow me!"

"Cyprienne!" he sighed. Looking passionately into her eyes, the color of forget-me-nots "Could I accept to survive you? Could I even accept for a second time the ordeal of a further separation? Have we not suffered enough? I shiver at the mere thought of the torture that I would be enduring at this moment if I were still up there, ignorant of your fate."

They contemplated one another. He caressed her with his hands, seemingly unable to sate himself with the sight of her.

"My darling! My adored beauty!" he stammered again, under the effect of his emotion. "I was so frightened... so frightened!"

Hugging his fiancée convulsively in his arms, feeling her breast palpitating against his heart, he lived an unforgettable minute of ecstasy. having completely lost sight of the fact that they were both in an open tomb—the most frightful of tombs!

"No one can tear you away from me now," he said, with an energetic candor.

“Why? Why? The danger isn’t so great,” riposted the young woman, smiling tenderly, very glad to find herself loved like that. “Have we not traversed horrors that were equal, if not worse?”

“We traversed them together, my beloved, and it’s not the same thing. One can’t see things with the same eyes when there are two lovers supporting one another. Now that I can feel your heart beating against mine, it seems to me that I’m sure of getting us out of this.”

“How? Have you forgotten where we are and how we got here?” said Cyprienne, with a sad smile that chilled Jean Chapuis’ enthusiasm.

She was right. It was necessary to be mad—mad with happiness—to talk tranquilly about getting out of that terrible place, as if it were the most peaceful in the world.

But the lover wanted to put on a brave face. With a tenderly protective gesture he put his arm around his fiancée’s shoulders.

“We’ll get out of it,” he repeated. “And even if we had to die in the bottom f this pit, we wouldn’t be separated. Cyprienne, my beautiful Cyprienne, tell me, wouldn’t it seem to you less harsh to die if death were to carry us away together?”

At those words, pronounced in a firm and tender voice, the young woman’s heart melted. She leaned her pretty head on her fiancé’s shoulder.

“Ingrate that I was!” she exclaimed. “If death came to take us thus, I would bless it, my Jean!”

Again their lips met.

But at their age, could they resign themselves to disappearing before having attempted everything?

Jean Chapuis still felt energetic; Cyprienne had proved many a time that she did not lack strength or courage. In those conditions, ought they to despair?

Closing one’s eyes is pleasant when one can feel a dear head with blonde curls on one’s shoulder, when the warmth of a palpitating bosom lingers against one’s breast and two soft arms make a necklace of tenderness for one's neck. But that huddled treasure, that delectable burden gives too much value to existence for it not to attach you to it ingenuously.

While talking about dying, Cyprienne and Jean searched for a means of salvation.

Enlaced, they examined the terrible ravine with their gaze, which was like the antechamber of annihilation.

But because of the supple waist that he was surrounding with one of his arms, Jean Chapuis could not succeed in envisaging the supreme sacrifice with serenity. Incessantly, regrets, more or less dissimulated, escaped his heart; and his eyes fixed their mute adoration on the delicate face haloed with gold.

In the depths of the terrifying crucible, over that shifting perfidious foundry, side by side, they slid, almost dancing, without saying anything further, Side by side, also, they pursued a dream—the same dream: that of escaping, together, that new ordeal, in order to be able to drink for a long time from the cup of happiness, in accordance with the promises of their youth.

Sustaining one another mutually, they looked around. Their march, joined and rapid, had drawn them away from the fall. Under their feet the seething was attenuated; the liquid metal was in the process of cooling and was already forming a near-solid crust, which easily bore the weight of their bodies, lightened by the air contained in their garments.

What a singular cuisine was simmering in that subterranean crucible! What bizarre alloys were forming there! What astonishing transmutations were taking place! Ah, if some alchemist, ancient or modern, had been able to find himself in the place of the two fiancés, with what passion he would have bent down to try to divine the secret of that vat.

Jean Chapuis and Cyprienne had other preoccupations. Having survived was nothing; it as necessary to get out of that devouring Styx, and by their own means, since the tumult prevented them from being heard by Oronius.

In any case, in the present situation, the Master must be impotent to come to their aid. The acrid, nauseating and burning vapors that never ceased to rise opposed an impenetrable curtain to the two young people. They could not take account of the dimensions of the pit. They only knew, by virtue of the duration of their fall, that its depth must be frightful.

Could they get back up? Ay the price of what efforts?

They advanced, groping because it was impossible for them to reconnoiter their route.

From time to time, to acquit their conscience, they uttered appeals. They did not hope to be heard, and they counted even less on anyone responding to them.

So they were immeasurably surprised suddenly to hear a familiar voice ringing out joyfully above their heads.

"This way, M'sieur Jean! What! They've let you fall? This way, Mamzelle Cyprienne! You must both be crazy, saving your respect, to be making a meal of this stew! Advance to the left... Stop! Stop! You're not done for; I'll get you out of the mess."

In fact, along the wall that the fiancés had just encountered, in conformity with the indications of their guide, they suddenly saw a strange cable descend, the extremity of which was weighed with an enormous block of stone.

Jean and Cyprienne could not help contemplating that block emotionally.

It was luminous stone—a fragment of the radioactive substance that, a few hours sooner, would have brought them salvation and spared them many cruel ordeals.

Had it come too late? Alas, the Halcyon-Car and the iron men had to be considered lost.

Another question was posed: where did it come from? Who had found it and brought it?

The cable descended. It took possession of the full attention of those to whom it was bringing salvation.

Of what material was that cable made? Now it was contorting, contracting, agitating like a living thing. Certainly, without the weight of the stone that was ballasting it and stretching it, it would have withdrawn and swung in the air, out of Jean's reach.

The fiancés touched it, and immediately recoiled, overtaken by an involuntary repugnance.

The cable that someone was lowering toward them and along which they were about to climb, really as a living thing; it was a sort of hideous reptile as thick as a boa and certainly thirty meters long.

As if it owner had been able to divine their gesture of repulsion, the voice rang out again, to encourage them.

"Good, eh! It's a bush-eel! It would make a famous bracelet... and a belt, no? I captured it with your intention. What do you expect? One doesn't have a choice; rope is rare in these parts. But this brother will hold and will be good, in view of the fact that one has taken one's precautions and secured it solidly. Given that it has the resistance of wire, you can be tranquil. It could support a good half-dozen of your weight. So, go! Both of you install yourselves on the stone and hold tight to the boa's feathers. Necessary not to put it round your neck, Mamzelle, whatever fashion says! Are you there? It's a funny elevator, but it's the best thing I had to hand."

It was evidently not the moment to make difficulties. Overcoming their disgust, the two your people followed the indications of the voice and installed themselves solidly on the block of stone.

"Are we ready? Ho! Haul away! Don't spare the arm-oil, lads! It's the boss and his bride that you're hauling!"

Those to whom that singular admonition as addressed must have had choice muscles at their service, for, pulling on the boa, they lifted up the block and the fiancés like a feather. In no time, Jean and Cyprienne reached the rim of the fissure.

When they set foot there, they perceived a spectacle that filed them with joyful amazement.

On his knees on the edge of the gulf, Victor Laridon, still holding in his hand the Cyclopean Eye that had permitted him to discover the fiancés, was addressing signs of welcome to them. And close beside him, the iron automata were finishing winding around the rock that had served to immobilize the head the coils of the enormous snake by means of which they had just accomplished the rescue.

The Cyclopean Eye! The automata freed from the magnetic rock! By what means had the joyful Parisian been able to enter into possession of those precious auxiliaries? And how had he succeeded in getting out of his own adventure in order to find himself there so appositely?

"I'll explain that!" he said, with a satisfied laugh. "For the eye, it's not difficult; I took it from the Halcyon-Car."

"You've also found the Halcyon, then?"

"Of course! To prove it, there it is... and in good condition... thanks to a discovery we made in the company on this friend and his little pupils... for it's necessary to tell you that the fellow has become a schoolteacher!"

Speaking thus, the mechanic indicated the precious aircraft a short distance away, its wings deployed, and Tai, under whose guard a troupe of elephant-moles were placidly digging in the ground with their muzzles.

Cyprienne and Jean marveled.

To discover Laridon, alive, after his extraordinary adventure, was their first subject of astonishment; but to find him, in addition, having a troupe of elephant-moles in his service, along with the automata and the Halcyon-Car—all of them having recuperated all their power—truly surpassed imagination.

And yet it was no illusion or mirage. The two fiancés could see it with their own eyes; the enchanting vision did not vanish.

Laridon smiled. The brave fellow was jubilant and doubtless burning with the desire to recount the stupendous incidents that had brought him there. What exciting minutes he must have lived!

In fact, when he had felt himself carried away, clinging to the fur of the elephant-mole, through the subterranean galleries without the possibility of stopping his robust mount or letting himself slide off, he scarcely suspected himself that he would get out of it so cheaply.

He believed that, at the least, he had lost any chance of rediscovering his companions.

That will teach me to want to play at equitation on such stupid beasts, he thought, sadly. *Need the manner of making use of them. Well, no, I don't have what it needs to be a mahout. I have proof of that now. No, frankly, I'd have more aptitude at fencing or boxing in the ring. Where is this runaway taking me?*

The kilometers of the gallery filed past his gaze, accustomed to the darkness; and behind him, he heard the heavy tread of the herd of elephant-moles shaking the ground.

In certain respects, he could be proud; he had rendered the passage free and expelled the monsters. He had succeeded.

I think they ought to be a little bit pleased up there! he thought. *At the time they must have been flabbergasted to see me lead my* cuadrilla *away with so much promptitude and celerity, as if I had been doing it all my life. Afterwards, though, on not seeing me come back, they must have been disillusioned. My good Laridon, you must have taken a rude rumble in their esteem. As a trick rider, you're not weighing heavily on the back of your beast. That's all right! I'd like to have seen Master Julep's face at the moment of my departure at a run! Probable that he'll never have the opportunity to confide his impressions to me... I'm condemned to solitude now... hello! What's happening? Are we at Ménilmuche station or Granbéta?*[9]

An abrupt halt on the part of his mount had just shaken him rudely.

As the neck and head of the elephant-mole presented a slope inclining naturally toward the ground, the Parisian only had to slide over it in order to get down. He regained the ground with satisfaction.

---

[9] Referring to the Paris subway station of Menilmontant and Gambetta.

The landscape interested him immediately. Compared with the fissures already seen, the one in which the subterranean herd had just stopped had only modest proportions, but its rocky sky, its floor and it walls were shining intensely. On bending down the mechanic recognized the origin of the phenomenon, which was due to the presence of billions of fireflies, glow-worms and photophoric caterpillars. They formed a dense layer covering all the available surfaces.

The elephant-moles had all stopped and were licking the ground avidly; the luminous vermin appeared to be their favorite nourishment. That doubtless explained why they had brought the mechanic to the location in question. For the herd it must be a sort of renowned restaurant, particularly frequented—for latecomers, emerging from all the galleries were gradually joining in.

And perched on one of them, uttering little amicable and joyful cries, Tai appeared in his turn.

Laridon opened wide eyes at that. Then a mad joy took possession of him. He ran to the little subterran, who descended nimbly from his mount, and embraced him effusively.

"Ah! Little brother! Old mate! So you've taken the same branch of the *molopolitain*!" he exclaimed. "You didn't want me to travel alone? Good. You can boast of having flair as a scout, especially if you know the region well enough to facilitate my return from the dead. By the way, my zigoto, this little hole isn't bad. There are a hundred candles to the spadeful. If one had pockets one would only have to bend down to make a provision. And M'sieur Oronius would probably arrive here with pleasure; this must have radioactive properties, as he says. You don't know? You're not in on that game? I'll let you off. In any case, it's a feast that delights the moles."

Since he had been in the company of the mechanic, Tai had begun to understand some of what he said and to be able to respond to him. He shook his head in an intelligent manner, bent down, picked up a handful of glow-worms and, showing a small fragment of radioactive stone that could serve him as a personal candle, he declared in a recently-learned language: "Kif-kif!"

"Ah! You're sure?" exclaimed Laridon, very interested. "Good blood of good blood, why isn't the boss here to hear you? Do you know that this could be the end of our predicament? What tells us that this can't replace solarium, radium and all the geraniums that have left us so dirtily flat? One could give a boost to our Halcyon, and even to the other tomatoes, which wouldn't do too badly on it, I tell you! Do you know how lucky we'd be if the diet suited them? We could paint the town red! We'd be back on the pleasure train and fully loaded in order to go and turn the tables on that swine Hantzen and his filthy *gonzesse.*[10] Can you imagine the warm welcome that I'd get if I could bring back a load of your little radioactive worms? They'll go down better than Dada poetry!"

Sadly, he interrupted himself, awakening from his beautiful dream.

"Little brother, all that is just castles in the air, projects à la Perrette![11] I don't have pockets deep enough, and even if you could enable me to rejoin the kite and the tin men, there's no way to bring them a sufficient load."

Tai's intelligent physiognomy reflected the labor operated by the rather long speech delivered by the mechanic. He had certainly understood the regret that Laridon was expressing. He therefore responded, in an argot that we will spare the reader, while indicating the glowing vermin on which the elephant-moles were continuing to graze: "Yes! We can carry it away."

"You're crazy!" protested Laridon. "Neither of the two of us could carry more than twenty kilos. And we wouldn't get to the end of the route, which must be long and which we'd have to make on foot."

---

[10] Girl (slang).

[11] From the French fable *The Milkmaid and the Pot of Milk* by Jean de La Fontaine.

Tai uttered a joyous little laugh and indicated the monsters occupied in grazing on the radioactive insects. "Put all on them," he explained.

"Really!"

"Up to us!"

"You're joking, little fellow," riposted the mechanic, sarcastically. "You're counting on the complaisance of these ladies to recommence ferrying us, and taking us precisely where we want to go?"

"Yes!" said Tai, affirmatively, with a seriousness that was beginning to impress the Parisian.

"Good! I'd like to see that! Is it you, little fellow, who'll direct the molicade?"

"It's me. Look!"

Turning toward the monsters, Tai uttered a series of shrill cries.

Immediately, amazingly enough, as if they were accustomed to obeying that language, the giant moles interrupted their meal and came to arrange themselves in a circle around Tai.

Then, signaling to Laridon, who was astounded, the subterran made him pass between the moles and showed him singular openings integrated into the fur of their flanks. Each of those openings formed a vast pouch into which a considerable quantity of objects could be loaded for transportation.

Laridon could not get over it. The elephant-moles were domesticated and the subterrans used them like trucks or carts for transporting goods. There were thirty of the pack-moles, the lateral pockets of which could easily take the place of panniers. The mechanic calculated that, thanks to the complaisant herd, they would be able to carry several thousand kilos of precious radioactive mass.

"Hurrah!" he cried, enthusiastically. "We're going to make a famous candle of you and your troop.

The loading of the monsters commenced immediately. Laridon and Tai applied themselves to it with a frenetic ardor.

For their part, the moles gave proof of the most perfect complaisance. Evidently, they were used to that procedure.

Tai had no more difficulty taking them take the direction he desired to follow. To guide the supply caravan, he perched, in company with the mechanic, on the back of the leading mole of the procession. The others followed meekly;

Similarly, for the choice of the route, Laridon had to rely entirely on his companion. He had limited himself to making understood his intention to find Oronius and the Halcyon as quickly as possible.

To begin with, that desire was only partly satisfied, and in a fashion that caused the worthy mechanic the sharpest alarm.

After having reflected and doubtless giving planned the itinerary offering the best chance of success, Tai whistled, giving the signal for departure. His choice led toward the central fire; but it did not enter into his intentions to confront it, and when the herd was in sight of it, the subterran contented himself with going around the furnace, going along a rocky ledge.

It was during that part of their journey that they discovered the Halcyon and the thirteen automata trapped and imprisoned by the magnetic rock, Although the cause of that phenomenon could not be understood by Victor Laridon, the spectacle was sufficient to terrify him.

What had become of Oronius and his associates? What had become of Turlurette? Terrible events must certainly have occurred in order for the Master's apparatus of genius and his extraordinary creatures of iron to be abandoned like wrecks.

In despair, he tore at his hair.

Then, as he was not a man to allow himself to be disheartened by adversity, he slapped his forehead with an Archimedean gesture. That was his fashion of gathering his thoughts.

It appeared o him that the best thing to do was to attempt the reflotation of the Halcyon and the automata, after which he would be in a better position to search for his masters and to be useful to them. However, an initial difficulty presented itself: approaching the terrible rock was not without danger. Snatching its prey from it would not be easy.

Laridon did not know the nature of that danger, but, habituated to living in continual commerce with makers of prodigies, he suspected an unknown force that he could not confront without taking certain precautions.

Which? He did not have Oronius' science. Very perplexed, he could not discover any solution to the problem.

Tai got him out of difficulty.

The cunning fellow knew the traps of his homeland and the means of getting out of them. He had certainly identified the rock; it awoke memories in him and, to a far greater extent than the mechanic, he had an almost exact notion of what had happened. After having examined the rock from a distance and shaking his head suspiciously he headed toward the elephant-moles, which had stopped placidly and appeared to be awaiting his pleasure.

From one of the pouches fitted under the fur, Tai took out handfuls of radioactive insects and crushed them underfoot in the fashion of primitive wine-makers trampling clusters of grapes. With the juice harvested by the primitive press he then composed a kind of coating with which he impregnated his garments, his footwear and his asbestos gloves—for the young guide saved by Cyprienne, as you can imagine, had been obliged to lose the habit of walking around unclothed.

Thus asepticized, Tai invited the mechanic to imitate him as quickly as possible, and prepared another provision of radioactive paste, which he shared with his companion.

Both of them headed then toward the magnetic rock, which they were able to approach with impunity, without the metallic parts of their garments feeling the unfortunate effects of attraction.

Those preliminaries had enlightened the mechanic regarding the fashion of employing the paste, its properties, and Tai's plan. As soon as he arrived in proximity to the Halcyon and the automata he hastened to daub all the non-adherent parts with the coating. Then, cleverly, with the aid of a crude brush made from a few handfuls of fur extracted from the elephant-moles, he rubbed the parts stuck to the magnet with the same varnish.

The result filled him with enthusiasm. Gradually, vanquished by the insulating substance, the magnet relaxed its grip; the automata moved away from it; the aircraft was no longer adhering to it. The fatal rock was no longer to be feared.

"That's good grub, not peanut butter, my prince!" Victor exclaimed, vibrant with hope. Come and help me, kid! We'll fetch a provision of this benzene to detach the men of iron... living radium, so to speak. And we'll fill the reservoirs of the airplane and the automata. Necessary to take the chance."

The experiment was a complete success. Under the action of the "irradium" the automata immediately resumed their activity and, submissive to Laridon's thought—his being the only brain that could activate their organs, for the time being—they set about hauling the Halcyon away from the rock.

In the meantime, the mechanic and Tai, reinstalled aboard the airplane, charged the engines and the various reservoirs with the irradium contained in the pouches of the elephant-moles. The rest of the provision was carefully stowed in the insulated lockers of the Halcyon.

It only remained for the latter to deploy its wings.

Before rising into the subterrestrial sky, Laridon took possession of the Cyclopean Eye in order to see whether he could discover Oronius and his company.

As we know, that inspection permitted him to discover the critical situation that Jean Chapuis and Cyprienne were in, becalmed in the midst of their amorous dream.

What could he attempt in order to get them out of it? In the pit, the semi-solidified gold sheet was agitating two or three hundred meters from the crucible beneath the promontory. But how to get down there? Or how to pull up those who appeared to be amusing themselves on the crust of that dangerous bog of an unknown species. It seemed difficult to have recourse to the metallic cables that the aircraft contained; the heat of the vat would undoubtedly have melted them.

A sudden terror on the part of Tai furnished his professor of French with the solution he sought, in an entirely unexpected fashion. The subterran having drawn away to occupy himself with his beasts of burden suddenly came back at a run, uttering terrified cries that demanded help.

That alarm was caused by the appearance of a reptile of unusual size, which seemed to have the intention of swallowing one of the elephant-moles for breakfast.

"Sapristi! What a finer rope that would make!" exclaimed the illuminated mechanic instantly.

And without further ado, he gave the automata an order to take possession of the subterran boa and fit it out as a cable. Thus the rescue of the fiancés has been able to proceed.

After that story, the effusions and the reciprocal congratulations that followed, Laridon first enquired, out of respect, about Oronius, and then, by virtue of sentiment, about the lovely Turlurette,

When he had been brought up to date with events and the menacing presence in the vicinity of Hantzen's crawling machine, he immediately proposed that they take to the air.

"The fulgurite machine is disenchanted and functional," he explained. "If I find an opportunity, I'll have pleasure in sending Hantzen and his wife a few little electric shocks by way of an invitation to the dance. In any case, it's necessary that we make tracks toward M'sieur Oronius, Julep and the girls; they must be tearing their hair out over you. I'll send the other tomatoes out on patrol, and during our excursion Tai can mind the flock. It might still be useful."

The execution of this very reasonable plan had allowed the passengers of the Halcyon to intervene at the right moment and snatch away from Yogha the prey that she believed she already had in her claws.

Chapter Twenty-Four
DUEL OF MONSTERS

Thrown into disarray by Laridon's electrical discharge, the *Snaky* had run away, perhaps to prepare for battle.

Doubtless, inside the carapace, Hantzen, Yogha and their two acolytes had got up again. Furious at their check, but sheltered behind the reclosed maw of their monster, they were probably calculating their chances of victory. In any case, and in spite of the reestablishment of the situation, they seemed determined to accept the battle against the Halcyon and the automata. In retreating and adjourning their attack they were seeking, at the most, to gain the time necessary to put to work all the means of combat of which they disposed.

For its part, the flying machine was readied for the impact. It had landed momentarily, with a determined objective: to take aboard Oronius, Julep, the two soubrettes and the little dogs.

With everyone reunited, it would have been natural to see, during a well-earned rest, the father and daughter on one hand, and Laridon and Turlurette on the other, delivering themselves to certain effusions; but the situation remained very grave, and a sentimental scene of that sort was not permitted to them. For the moment, at least, it was necessary to finish with the enemy and try to put him out of a condition to do any harm. Afterwards, there would still be no time to rest; they would have to occupy themselves with establishing a barrier against the invasion he had launched to assault the surface.

Postponing their legitimate effusions until later, therefore, our friends, reunited safe and sound after so much anguish, contented themselves with exchanging eloquent glances.

On seeing the Halcyon reentered into full possession of its means, Oronius had had a clear comprehension of the various incidents that must have permitted the mechanic to turn things around and bring it back to him. Only the discovery of a vast quantity of radioactive matter could get them out of the bad situation they were in. Victor Laridon had been its fortunate discoverer. At the opportune moment, the Master would know about it and take account of it.

In a tragic circumstance that we shall have occasion to report in due course, the scientist would indeed remember it and pay the price.

Once aboard the Halcyon, Oronius had Laridon's find explained and was shown a specimen of the marvelous insects. His face cleared immediately.

"You're favored by Destiny," he told the impressed mechanic, solemnly. "The discovery to which your name will be attached, this living radium, the active power of which is far superior to anything we have been able to study or anticipate before today, is destined to change the face of human progress. We'll study it later. For the moment it's sufficient to know that we can go to attack Hantzen with means taken to the maximum power. Your knowledge couldn't allow you to divine all that; in thanking you, I ought to inform you of it."

It was not a time for long speeches. Abandoning the direction cabin to Jean Chapuis, with the mechanic underneath in the engine-room, the Master stationed himself at certain apparatus whose efficacy he was about to put to the test.

The young women and the dappled negro were distributed in the other compartments with orders to remain at Oronius' disposal there.

Concurrently with these arrangements, the latter, resuming the direction of his artificial men, was giving them psychic orders when Jean Chapuis' voice shouted: "Look out!"

That was scarcely necessary; installed in the middle of a circle of levers, each of which controlled a mechanism of defense or attack, Oronius had before his eyes a rectangular glass plate, in which he could follow all exterior events. In fact, a polyperiscope projected thereupon simultaneously images of all the parts of space in which the aircraft was moving. He had, therefore, seen even before his pupil the *Snaky* suddenly light up, as if its walls had become incandescent, and launch itself into the air, deploying six clawed wings, which emerged from its flanks like as many membranous hands.

Thus armed and equipped. It resembled some Lernean Hydra already decapitated six times by Hercules.

And as the Halcyon, by comparison, had an appearance that was no less formidable, a spectator would certainly have had the impression watching an encounter of two monsters of the Primary Epoch, Spitting fire through steel nostrils and whipping the air with its formidable metallic tail, Hantzen's engine hurtled toward its enemy with the visible intention of knocking it to the ground in order to tear it to pieces there.

It was sufficient for Jean Chapuis to imprint his apparatus with a slight sideways movement to avoid the impact at the moment when the clawed serpent reached him. Borne by its impetus, the aggressor only encountered empty air and flashed past like an arrow, grazing the Halcyon.

Oronius had expected that; unleashing as it passed a formidable spectrum of magnetic waves, he suddenly unbalanced his enemy, which, caught by the artificial whirlwind, was projected upwards in a spiral.

Launched like a projectile, it crashed into the rocky ceiling, impacting it with a thunderous din, and fell back, pirouetting on its axis.

Was it about to smash into the ground, defeated at the first pass?

No—Hantzen was alert. In spite of the frightful shock that had just been inflicted on it, he had kept control of his apparatus. So, opening wide his generators of elastic vapors, he succeeded in emitting a sufficiently thick layer to form a shock-absorber and prevent him from touching the ground. The Serpent-Griffin rebounded from that layer five or six times, regained its equilibrium reared up and drew away, describing a great circle.

Already, the Halcyon was giving chase; it was important not to let the malevolent beast escape.

For several minutes the two winged monsters pursued one another like gigantic birds, one of which was fleeing hectically before the other, sometimes diving and sometimes rising again. But the flight of the first was only a feint. Profiting from a moment when the Halcyon, which it was trying to evade, was flying less than ten meters away, it made a vertical leap, and its two anterior ailerons succeeded in gripping the prow of the aircraft. It was assuredly only the beginning of a maneuver that it expected to continue to its advantage, but it could only sketch it, and its audacity received a merited punishment without delay.

"Change axis and stabilize!" Jean Chapuis had ordered. "We're going to loop!"

Immediately executing that familiar order, the efficacy of which we have already seen during the rotatory descent of the Halcyon-Tank in the bosom of the ball of clay—Victor immobilized the central cabins in a horizontal plane, while the rest of the apparatus, liberated, begin to spin around them with a vertiginous speed.

Hanging by the shoulders to the prow of the Halcyon, the *Snaky* naturally found itself drawn into that movement, all the effects of which it suffered. That new phase of the dogged, mortal combat, was increasingly analogous to a wrestling match in mid-air between two fabulous raptors.

One might have thought that one of them—the more powerful—was rotating on its axis, shaking the other, which was clutching its throat, with rage.

In truth, that purely visual impression could only give an imperfect idea of what was happening. In that phase of the duel, in fact, all the advantages were on the side of the Halcyon, which was directing it at will, while the Serpent had to suffer passively, to the point of exhaustion, the terrible effects of the inexorable top-like rotation, a mortal "girella," according to the Neapolitan expression.

The positions of the adversaries were not the same; there was a great difference.

Having taken refuge, as we have indicated, in the cabins immobilized by a combination of radiomagnetic forces, the passengers of the Halcyon did not have to fear any malaise due to the movement. They simply saw their apparatus spinning around them at a velocity almost equal to that of a helical propeller; in consequence, they could support that exercise for as long as might be necessary. Not for a second did they lose control of their aircraft

Hantzen and Yogha, by contrast, were deprived of that resource. Surprised by Jean Chapuis' tactic, they and their companions were subjected to the reaction of all the involuntary movements of their apparatus. Stunned by impacts against the walls or asphyxiated by the speed of rotation, they were quite incapable of continuing the struggle. All that they could do was to roll themselves up in the greatest possible number of covers in order to deaden the impacts, and then abandon themselves to their destiny.

The drama was brief. The membranous wings whose imprudent claws had been implanted in the carapace of the aircraft suddenly gave way at the point of conjunction with the body of the apparatus. Torn away by the frightful shocks imprinted on the *Snaky*, they broke off and remained fixed to the Halcyon, while the Serpent-Griffin, liberated but continuing its trajectory, spun three or four times and finally crashed into the ground.

It arrived there in a pitiful state; that last impact, very rude, had just reduced to smithereens two of the four wings that remained to it, and had crippled the other two.

Henceforth incapable of resuming its flight, a bird without plumage, a broken-backed reptile, the disabled monster no longer had any possibility of renewing its attack against the Halcyon. It had no desire to do so, in any case. To begin with, it lay extended on the rock, as motionless as a submarine sunk to the bottom, which would serve as a common coffin for its entire crew, immured in its hull.

Was that the case? Or, at least, were Yogha, Hantzen, Wiwar and Jarrousse so badly injured as to be unable any longer even to think of defending their citadel, which was about to be attacked in its turn, by the redoubtable automata, already set in motion?

While the Halcyon reposed on its prowess above those new assault troops, describing great circles, the men of iron approached, surrounding the Serpent.

Oronius directed that final part of the battle from the height of the subterran sky. His plan was simple. When the encirclement was complete, his automata had only to apprehend the numbed monster. If they succeeded getting hold of it, nothing could any longer save Hantzen; his *Snaky* would not escape the grip of those robust precision instruments, whose untiring hammering would end up breaking its flanks.

How, in any case, could it escape? It could no longer fly, and it was surrounded.

It still did not budge.

Around it, the circle was about to tighten; the automata were only a short distance apart and all close to the recumbent monster. A few more steps and they would be able to seize it.

Suddenly, the bronze serpent reared up, as a true reptile might have done; it rose up vertically, the entire weight of it body reposing in equilibrium, on the last vertebrae of its tail.

Hissing and groaning, it oscillated, getting ready to fall back on to its adversaries in order to crush them with its weight.

It did not do so, however. This is why: in the interior, Hantzen, the animator of that maneuver, must have reflected that it presented a few inconveniences, His huge bronze flail could only crush one automaton at a time, and those combative manikins numbered thirteen.

Would he have time to repeat and succeeded in his maneuver thirteen times? That was at least doubtful. As soon as his first attack, it seemed probable that the other twelve uncompromised automata would leap on to the rump of his serpent, and it would be difficult to dislodge them before they had done irreparable damage.

Changing tactics, he let the bronze reptile fall back and started swiveling on itself rapidly, like a turntable. At each turn the reptile spat out flaming jets of burning liquid.

Humans would have been reduced to ashes, but the automata were unconcerned by those whiplashes, little to fear for brave individuals who had already passed through the central fire. They continued to advance, therefore, and launched themselves forward all together. Twenty-six metal arms with fists as powerful as pile-drivers, with fingers as powerful as pincers, reached for Hantzen's machine. It would have been all over for its annular carapace if articulated legs like those of crane-flies had not emerged from its inferior part and the serpent had not raised itself up to a height that took it out of reach.

Not for long! Wrapping their iron arms around those legs, the automata began to hoist themselves up.

Would it be taken by assault this time? No again! At the moment when those bold gymnasts reached the carapace, a crack was heard, and automata and legs alike all fell to the ground. Using the heroic tactic of certain crustaceans caught in a trap, the serpent had just amputated its inferior limbs. It swung above the iron men and fled, unfurling its coils.

From the Halcyon, the mechanic had followed that scene with a very comprehensible interest; he could not help uttering an oath.

"The swine! They're getting away! Let's get to it!"

Impelled by the will of Oronius, the iron men were already on their feet and launching themselves in pursuit of the fugitive. More rapid still, the Halcyon, "getting to it," in accordance with the Parisian's expression, had just overtaken the runaway in order to cut off its retreat.

An order from Oronius interrupted that maneuver.

"Not like that, Jean! Describe concentric circles around it and try to fly at the lowest possible altitude without touching the ground. Maintain six or seven meters."

Cyprienne's father was demanding a veritable *tour de force*, but he knew the pilot and the apparatus, and he knew that nothing was impossible for them.

In fact, the engineer descended immediately, without hesitation, and commenced his circular course, maintaining the height demanded.

Opening a little trap-door, the Master immediately threw out and unfurled two wires whose extremities trailed in the ground. Having done that, he turned the glass wheel of a machine linked to several accumulators of magnetic energy, and then sent down along the wires a luminous fluid, which, spreading over the ground, marked the circle that the aircraft was describing.

That circle was not yet completely formed when the serpent had already reached it and touched the luminous line.

Immediately, a dazzling flame sprang forth, and Hantzen's apparatus turned an involuntary somersault and fell backwards.

"Caught!" said Oronius, serenely. "I've closed it in the uncrossable circle, No matter in what direction it tries to get out of it, the same magnetic wall will repel it. He's ours.

But Hantzen did not renew his attempt; he must have understood its futility. Taking his apparatus back to the center of the circle he made it execute two or three turns on its axis, digging into the ground with the anterior part of its head. Then, plunging abruptly into the opening of the funnel that its invisible drill had just hollowed out, the *Snaky* plunged into the ground and disappeared.

Chapter Twenty-Five
THE TOMB CLOSES AGAIN

That unexpected disappearing act had caused cries of disappointment to emerge from all breasts. Simultaneously, the automata launched forward by the will of Oronius, and the Halcyon, which swooped down to the ground like an eagle on a prey, arrived at the exact spot where Hantzen and his apparatus had just slipped away from his adversary.

There was no longer anything there but a circular mount enclosing a few square meters of pulverized rock . The ground, having become movable, seemed to be excavated and turned over as if by a plowshare. There was no trace of a hole.

After the passage of the digging instrument, the soil had automatically closed up again and filled in by means of the debris of rock and dust.

Was the *Snaky*, and those it contained, going to escape once again? That would give Hantzen the opportunity to repair his apparatus. The threat would continue to hang over Oronius and his protégés.

Frowning, the Master meditated silently for a few moments,

"The Cyclopean Eye!" he finally demanded.

No one had yet thought of it; they all hastened to obey Oronius. Soon, the powerful apparatus permitted the observers to follow through the ground the trace of the serpent's flight. It was a spiral descent, which plunged into the terrestrial mass a kind of screw-thread. And that did not finish. Contrary to what Oronius had imagined, the *Snaky* did not cease to descend, always further forward.

Given the designs that it could be supposed to have, however, it was extraordinary that it did not change direction after a lateral movement in the ground and return upwards in order to surge forth, away from the gaze of its conquerors; for its task and its unique hope of revenge now summoned it to return to the surface in order to receive and guide the subterran multitudes that it had launched forward.

Were those multitudes not en route for the conquest of the superficial heaven?

Losing himself in conjectures, Oronius continued to follow the descending track with his gaze. He descended with it, always descending, to such an extent that he ended up encountering a vast circular well of a diameter that could not be inferior to several hundred meters, and of immeasurable depth.

At the bottom of that well and against its walls, reduced by distance to the proportions of a moon, the serpent described spirals.

Further below, a black train similar to that made on the ground by a migration of ants, was perceptible.

"The Subterrans!" Oronius exclaimed. "They're marching downwards! What can it mean? Why is that entire crowd following a direction opposite to that of the surface?"

Jean Chapuis, Cyprienne and Laridon shared that amazement. Hantzen's tactic seemed incomprehensible to them.

Holding his sides, however, Oronius let out noisy and spasmodic laughter.

"Simpleton!" he scoffed. "How were you to able to pronounce such stupidities? It's sufficient to reflect to understand. Look! Look at that distant light… at the very bottom of the well. Yes, of course, at the very bottom!"

He laughed again, while the members of his entourage, the Cyclopean Eye against the orbit, leaned over instinctively.

"Its daylight!" cried the Master. "Double idiot! Triple fool! They've passed the center of the Earth, so they're no longer descending, they're ascending. It's only in relation to us that they still seem to be descending."

Then, becoming more grave, he added: "The invasion of the surface has already commenced. The first bands have undoubtedly reached it, and the scenes of horror will doubtless soon unfold; bloody collisions will take place. At all costs, it's necessary to catch up with them and prevent Hantzen from setting himself at their head."

"How can we follow that route?" said Jean Chapuis, anxiously. The mass that separates us from it represents such a depth to pierce!"

"The straight line isn't always the shortest route between two points, Monsieur Engineer," riposted the Master. "It will be sufficient for us, by taking as a radius the distance that separates the point where we are from the center of the Earth, to describe the arc of a circle cutting the vertical of this well. I'll calculate our position and determine the direction to follow. Note that in relation to the center of the globe, we'll remain constantly in the horizontal plane. Thus, we'll have neither descents nor ascents to confront."

He interrupted himself and sighed. "That's not to say that we won't encounter obstacles. How long will it take? If only we had Hantzen's perforator..."

"We have something better, Boss!" cried the mechanic. "Yes, we have something better, since I have a good thirty perforators at your disposal, and famous ones! For it's delightful that I can be generous today: I can offer you a counterstrike into the bargain."

Oronius looked at him askance. He thought that it was a joke.

"I'm not joking, Boss. It's an opportunity."

Cyprienne had understood. She hastened to explain.

"Victor's right, Father. He's talking about the elephant-moles, which you've only glimpsed, and which are in reality domesticated. Tai can serve as their mahout and make them obey him. We can, therefore, utilize their prodigious faculty of excavation."

Oronius could only applaud that luminous idea. It would get him out of the embarrassment, or at least dispense him of imagining and constructing the indispensable material. Reassembling the metal men, who were remarked aboard the Halcyon, they went to the place where Jean Cyprienne and Laridon had left Tai and his flock.

Informed of the labor that was expected of his pupils, the little subterran immediately gathered them and departed in the direction indicated by Oronius. Sometimes using existing galleries and sometimes using tunnels hollowed out by the elephant-moles with an amazing rapidity, the Halcyon-Automobile rolled behind its advance guard of laborers. In a straight line it headed toward the goal. In front of it, the crew of automata swept the terrain at a run. It was a frenzy.

A few hours later. a final hole dug by the animal excavators encountered nothing but emptiness. They had reached the large well, into which the Halcyon would be able to launch itself; but before then, the automata were collected, as well as Tai, who had merited being brought. The herd of elephant-moles had to be abandoned. For a long time thereafter, Oronius was unconsolable for not having been able to bring back a specimen of those bizarre animals from his expedition. But that was a very superfluous regret, for, admitting that the aircraft had been able to take aboard such a burden, no zoological garden could have succeeded in conserving that inmate. Evidently, it would have been child's play for the burrowing monster to escape and regain its subterranean homeland.

When the Halcyon began to rise up in the well, the *Snaky* was no longer in sight, and everything encouraged the belief that it had already attained the surface.

"We'll find them again up there," Oronius predicted. "Fortunately, he won't have had time to repair his wings. We'll therefore continue to dominate the situation,

"Unless he's contrived some trap," Jean Chapuis could not help suggesting.

With a disdainful gesture of his shoulders, Victor Laridon dismissed that supposition. "The fellow's out for the count," he riposted. "That Hantzen has more girth than height."

The Halcyon rose up. Its passengers could now contemplate at their ease the strange spiral route that the *Snaky* had traced along the walls in order to permit the subterrans to reach the surface. Multitudes of the sad beings encumbered that route. As the Halcyon passed, they uttered clamors and waved their fists at it.

"Poor creatures!" said Cyprienne, compassionately. "We can only feel sorry for them. What welcome will they find up there?"

"Alas, they'll be condemned to perish in all fashions," replied Oronius. "The surface-dwellers won't allow themselves to weaken before that invasion. For them, it's a question of life or death. The adventure has no issue. Hantzen is very culpable for having engaged them in it."

Flying with a vertiginous rapidity, the airplane reached the orifice of the well in very little time and rose into bright light.

Dazzled, those who had just accomplished the somber voyage uttered ecstatic cries. They experienced almost the same delight as the subterrans who were emerging from the well at the same time, and camping on the slopes.

The Halcyon was floating under a blue sky in which a dazzling sun was blazing. It landed at the foot of a high mountain, which terminated in a cone with a resplendent cap of snow.

That snow was reflected in the waters of a lake, and the whole area that extended between the waters of the lake and the mountain was a verdant garden. With the foliage of oaks, birches, elms and plane-trees, a tropical vegetation was mingled: magnolias and aralias next to camphor-trees, majestic cedars and pines. Creepers enlaced the trunks and the branches were garlanded with flowers.

The landscape was familiar to Oronius, who had traveled all over the world, and he informed his companions.

This is Fuji-Yama and Lake Biva," he said designating successively the celebrated volcano and the lake that extended at its foot. "We're in the heart of Japan, and there's no Nipponese artist who hasn't drawn this landscape on silk, paper, pottery or wood. On these sacred slopes, thousands of pilgrims meet every year, visiting the sanctuaries that you can see. But the old and placid Fuji-Yama only has the appearance of a volcano now. Its last eruption was in 1707.

He interrupted those geographical considerations to scan the visible area with his eyes.

"Where has the *Snaky* gone?" he exclaimed. "I can't discover it anywhere."

Taking up the Cyclopean Eye again, he made his gaze accomplish a kind of circular tour within a radius far superior to what Hantzen's apparatus could have traveled. The examination gave no result.

Has he rendered himself invisible again, then?" he muttered "Impossible! He'll be obliged to show himself to these poor creatures, whom he'll certainly launch like a devastating torrent on Yokohama. For the moment, the dazzled subterrans can't yet support the sight of so many marvels, above all that of the star. Their eyes need to adapt to our light. Look! They're throwing themselves to the ground and it's necessary for them to protect their heads with their folded arms. Neither Hantzen nor Yogha is among them. Nor can I discover Wiwar or that wretch Jarrousse. Ought I to suppose that they're still climbing under the ground? Is it on the flanks of that volcano that I'll discover them, or lower down?"

While pronouncing those last words, he had directed the Cyclopean Eye toward the ground that he intended to search; but scarcely had he arrested his gaze than an exclamation of terror escaped him. He went pale and with an anguished gesture he recalled Jean and Cyprienne, who were strolling in the slope.

"All aboard!" he cried, in a strangled voice. "Quickly! Quickly! Let's get away immediately!"

They tried to question him. He did not give them the time. His agitation was so great that it infected all of them.

Understanding that a terrible threat was hanging over them, Jean Chapuis dragged Cyprienne; Laridon took possession of the bewildered Turlurette; Julep and Tai framed Mandarinette, who was carrying Pipigg and Kukuss in her arms, and they all ran after Oronius to the airplane, in which they installed themselves.

An instant later, the Halcyon rose into the sky, flying away at top speed from the cheerful place that had just inspired such a sudden and inexplicable horror in the Master.

When they were at a great height, Cyprienne thought that she would finally be able to obtain an explanation of the alarm from her father.

"What is it? Why have we been obliged to that rapid flight?" she asked.

For all response, the Master, who had not ceased to keep his gaze attached to the point that he had just quit, extended his hand. He was very pale.

"Look!" he murmured, in a tremulous voice.

A series of rumbles comparable to those of thunder rose from the ground; then formidable detonations shook the atmosphere, reverberating to infinity. From the dormant crater of Fuji-Yama sprang a thick column of molten matter. Around the cone the ground cracked, rose up, and burst. Ten, twenty, fifty craters opened under the pressure of lava and gases, suddenly liberated and projected toward the surface by a cause that was still mysterious. An eruption of such violence that human memory had never yet recorded anything similar dislocated the flanks of the volcano, reawakened after more than three hundred years of slumber.

All around, shaken by a furious convulsion, the earth opened up. Everything was engulfed in that immense fissure: the waters of the lake, the mountain, the forest… everything!

In the midst of a tempest of fire and smoke, the spectators, gripped by horror, saw Fuji-Yama collapse like a house of cards and disappear into the gaping earth, along with the unfortunates who had emerged from the infernal gulf.

"If that extraordinary manifestation isn't the result of a fissure extending to the central fire," Oronius thought aloud, "perhaps it was caused by my little reserve of nitrocolle drowned under the ruins of the Villa."

The eruption seemed to be calming down. The detonations ceased; the columns of flames, smoke and igneous matter were no longer rising into the sky; the furious waves that had lifted up the terrestrial crust were appeased. Everything became still and silent again.

When the airplane, commanded by Oronius, returned to fly over the devastated region, its passengers no longer discovered anything but a frightfully leveled soil, in the middle of which shone the resplendent patch of a lake of liquid gold.

Over the subterranean world, the tomb opened by Hantzen had closed again, sealing in its horror the millions of unfortunates who had only glimpsed the sky. The invasion with which the surface world had been threatened had been dammed.

Chapter Twenty-Six
THE MORTAL SHEATH

And that was Hantzen's work!

As sly and as cowardly against his recognized adversaries as he was basely treacherous in regard to those he had pushed and directed on the road toward the open air, he had just annihilated a part of his future allies and buried the rest in their tomb.

What motive could he invoke to have that last infamy pardoned?

Had he, at the last moment, taken pity on the race of surface-dwellers and renounced his abominable project of having them annihilated by the subterrans?

Not at all!

In truth, he had not expected that result. By provoking the devastating eruption, he only wanted to attain his superior in science, whom he believed to be still in the bosom of the terrestrial mass.

However, even if he had been able to foresee the terrible result of his action, he would not have hesitated.

The destruction of thousands of subterrans and the eternal despair to which the rest of the race would be condemned, could not, in the eyes of Yogha's ally, seem to be paying too dearly for the crushing of Oronius. It was that goal that, before anything else, and no matter at what price, it was important for him to attain.

Yogha and Hantzen felt themselves under the domination of a superior power. It was necessary for them to liberate themselves from it. What did the ruination of innocent masses matter if, in their estimation, the fatal blow was good?

They had declared to one another at the moment when they were seeking a refuge in the entrails of the Earth: "Oronius has let us escape! Woe betide Oronius and all his companions!"

"But in what manner can we attain him?" the Hindu, always positive, had demanded.

"He must not quit this empire reserved for the dead," replied Hantzen, grimly. "It's necessary that he finds his tomb there."

Unsatisfied by that vague response, Yogha solicited explanations. Her accomplice decided then to specify a plan of which he was proud of being the author.

Do we not know the location," he said, "of the ruins of Oronius' Magical Villa, buried in the utmost depths of the soil? Under its debris, an appreciable quantity of harmful products and explosives must be buried, including the nitrocolle, unknown to me, which was so fatal to Jarrousse. Oronius can't have failed to manufacture more. Now, it wasn't able to save all that. His instruments were much more precious; he must have given them preference."

"Undoubtedly," said Yogha. "But what does that matter to us? We can't think of going to search for that nitrocolle."

"Search for it?" sniggered Hantzen. "That's quite unnecessary. I can attain him from here, along with all the members of his company." He explained then: "I've discovered a liquid fire...liquid, you understand! Thrown into any part of the ground, the product sinks into it and descends all the way to the central nucleus. No species of terrain or rock is impermeable to it, and naturally, it doesn't fail to ignite in passing all the inflammable substances and cause all explosive substances to detonate. If, therefore, I pour outside the *Snaky* the contents of this bottle, which I brought on the off chance, it will certainly reach Oronius' compound and everything that his laboratory might have contained of destructive substances."

"What will the result be?" asked Yogha, serenely.

"A naïve question, my dear. It will provoke in the interior of this immense closed ball a little chaos, of which I dare not venture to estimate the damage. At the least, the deflagration of gases will dislocate all the caverns that exist around the center and the superior layers heaped above them. I won't hide from you that the repercussions might be felt all the way to the surface, and that there will probably be an epidemic of earthquakes up above, for which humans won't be grateful to us. Bah! One can't make an omelet without breaking eggs. The important thing for us is to know that Oronius will be caught in the cataclysm caused by his own invention, crushed with his Halcyon and his entire family. Could you ask for anything more?"

"No, that's very good. One point of information, though. Are you certain that we'll have the time to put ourselves in a safe place?"

"Here, we're quite safe, my dear friend. The danger will only exist in the crevasse—which is to say, where the Halcyon is. For us, who will have the wisdom to surround ourselves with a thick and solid layer of clay, an elastic zone, and therefore neutral to shock, we'll have nothing to fear. After the event, we won't have any difficulty in disengaging ourselves. Our *Snaky*, as you know, is in its element in the bosom of the Earth. It can move about there with as much ease as moles, water rats, pangolins and earthworms."

"Try it, then," approved the Hindu. "If we can get rid of the father of that impertinent Cyprienne, it will be worth the trouble."

"So be it!" sad Hantzen, pouring his provision of liquid fire through the open trap-door.

After which, continuing his route, he had emerged into the well, pretending to climb toward the surface. Before having reached it, however, he had plunged into the interior of the terrestrial mass in order to await the moment of the explosion in security.

That had not exactly produced the effects anticipated by its author, Hantzen.

Nitrocolle, let us remember, is displaced vertically, creating a void. All solid, liquid or gaseous materials that happen to be beneath it are precipitated into that void, and all of that rises up at a velocity figured in thousands of kilometers a second.

Now, attained by the liquid fire, after a time by which, contrary to the hopes of Oronius' enemies, the Halcyon was already out of the well, the provision of nitrocolle remaining in the laboratory had traversed the layer of the eternal fire in a straight line and also the crucible that had nearly been fatal to Jean Chapuis and Cyprienne.

It was thus that the mass of molten metal, following the path traced for it by the passage of the nitrocolle, had aliment-ed the terrible eruption of Fuji-Yama. By the same route—an even more unexpected result—the sea of molten gold had been projected into the air before falling back into Lake Biva to form a lake of gold there.

As he had foreseen, the fall of such a mass of molten metal had instantly volatilized the waters, and the vapors thus formed, crushed under the considerable weight of that sheet had been driven forcefully into the fissures in the ground. The explosion that had blown up the volcano had had no other cause.

The inhabitants of the *Snaky*, sheltered at a great distance under their protective layer, had only felt those various effects in a very vague fashion. By means of the seismograph they knew that important shocks had convulsed their planet. By means of the recording microphone they perceived the muffled rumbles, and the faint echo of the detonations reached their ears. But they were unable to divine where all that had happened, what the extent of the cataclysm was, or what damage it caused.

The impatience with which Hantzen and Yogha waited for the appeasement is easily imaginable. Without that, they could not risk themselves outside in all security and go to verify the results.

Certainly, those hardened individuals would find a certain enjoyment in the contemplation of the ruins and in the thought that it was their work, but the prolonged wait deprived them of being able to ascertain that their principal goal had been attained: knowing that the Halcyon and its passengers were counted among the number of victims.

The last rumbles finally appeared to diminish in intensity and gradually died away; at the same time the seismograph ceased to register shocks. Then, conducted by its inventor, the bronze serpent set forth again.

Hantzen imagined that he was directing it toward the well, from which he could regain the surface comfortably and emerge at the exact point chosen by a long-studied orientation.

He was mistaken, and quickly took account of the fact that the catastrophe that he had unleashed had modified the topography of his itinerary singularly.

Of the well no trace remained; it had been filed in completely by cubic kilometers of blacks of basalt. In which the accomplices would have had great difficulty in recognizing Fuji-Yama.

After having wandered for some time in the recently immured galleries that the serpent hollowed out again less and less rapidly, because its perforator was somewhat worn down, Oronius' rival had to recognize that there was no longer an orifice. He was therefore forced, if he wanted to regain the surface, to do so at random, by going up vertically. When they had emerged, they would get their bearings.

Having decided that, he launched forth through the chaotic collapse, fraying a passage with increasing difficulty.

In ordinary circumstances, no species of terrain resisted the action of the gigantic drill that armed the spear-head of the apparatus. At present, it was quite different; the erosion of the device diminished the ease of the progress; they went up slowly and with difficulty.

Suddenly, Yogha and the three men contained within the carapace had the impression of a new and victorious resistance, as if the apparatus had just become stuck in a thick layer of mud. At the same time, an atrocious heat invaded the compartments.

Wiwar immediately activated the ventilators—without any result! And, a frightful observation, they seemed to see… and then they *really* saw… the metallic plates of the envelope quivering, stretching and going red...

What was happening?

That was the moment when the Halcyon-Car arrived above the lake of gold, the metal of which, partly cooled and subject to the influence of the external air, was already beginning to *hold*.

One might have thought that it was filled with a golden mud, the surface of which gradually losing its heat, formed a semi-solid crust, while the interior paste was thickening from one moment to the next.

It was therefore foreseeable that, after a number of days, when the cooling was complete and had even reached the interior layers, the molten metal would be transformed into a prodigious block of solid gold.

For the moment, it was still a thick and sticky mud, very difficult to shift.

Now—an incomprehensible spectacle, well designed to strike the imagination—before the eyes of the passengers of the Halcyon, which was circling above the lake, its heavy liquid was suddenly agitated. Internally stirred by a living being, which appeared to be struggling desperately, the precious paste swelled and rose up, and a sort of dazzling monster entirely covered in the sticky golden mud, which was streaming over its flanks and from which it did not seem able to free itself, tried to emerge from the surface.

A cry of amazement emerged from all mouths.

"The *Snaky*!"

It was, in fact Hantzen's reptator. His unlucky star had caused it to surge from one of the fissures open beneath the lake of burning gold and it had become trapped there.

Unable to liberate itself from that shirt of Nessus clinging to its flanks, which was rendering its carapace white hot—bogged down, weighed down and less alive every time it fell back—the bronze Serpent knew the horror of a doubly cruel entanglement. Its movements became convulsive; the flexibility that it owed to its annular armature diminished in the grip of the golden robe. Every somersault made that robe heavier and thicker, adding a metal flounce to it.

The reptile, charged like a reliquary, reared up, fell back exhausted and plunged, to reemerge weighed down by a further layer of gold.

That burning paste, that accursed paste, the joy and woe of humans, penetrated into all the interstices of the armature and cooled there, gradually transforming the supple reptile into a long rigid skeleton that could only move all of a piece and could no longer unfurl its coils, imprisoned as they were in a golden sheath.

One last time, a desperate effort of its conductors agonizing within its carapace brought it upright, streaming with yellow liquid. It fell back on the shore of the lake—too late. Around its body the gold had cooled and hardened, molding the form of the *Snaky*, definitively paralyzed and imprisoned. A golden cadaver, it now lay on the shore, contemplated from above by the passengers of the Halcyon, victorious but also petrified by horror.

Chapter Twenty-Seven
THE DISAPPEARANCE OF THE *SNAKY*

In order to contemplate at closer range that spindle of extravagant value, which was presently no more than a phenomenal coffin, they all quit the interior of the victorious apparatus.

Surrounding it were all the people whom the demons now sealed within the monster had sworn to destroy: Cyprienne and Jean, tenderly leaning on one another; Laridon and Turlurette, the joyful lovers inclined to take life cheerfully—which did not prevent them from loving one another in the utmost depths of their hearts—Master Julep, whose polychromatic face was peeping with a marked complaisance in the direction of the yellow Mandarinette; and Tai; and Pipigg and Kukuss! And finally Oronius, the Immortal Master, calm and simple in his triumph.

He had returned to the sunlight, after having accomplished the most terrifying excursion of which a human imagination can dream. Rid of his enemy, he already had but one thought: to resume his work.

Why should he preoccupy himself with destroying his enemies or punishing them? Destiny had taken charge of that.

Completely sealed inside the block of precious metal, deprived of air, with no possibility of piercing the solidified envelope, they were condemned to perish, asphyxiated. Perhaps their destiny had already been accomplished.

The passengers of the Halcyon-Car thus had no more to do than turn their backs on the monster transformed into a sarcophagus and return to Paris.

Lost in a profound reverie, Oronius did not appear to be able to make that decision. He remained in contemplation before the monster lying at his feet, and his gaze went from that broken instrument to the lake of gold glittering in the sunlight.

"Who knows?" he murmured "It can't remain thus. The scourge that we wanted to prevent, which Hantzen's action has driven back and destroyed, was perhaps less to be feared than this one. There's the wherewithal here to make the misfortune of humankind."

Doubtless he was taking about the colossal deposit of gold. Once it became known, that El Dorado could not fail to attract crowds and give rise to horrible competitions. There would surely be no limit to the misdeeds caused by the rivalries and struggles that would ensue.

The customary clairvoyance of Oronius enabled him to divine lamentable ruinations and abominable massacres in the future. Such a mine of billions suddenly offered to so-called sentient beings would hurl them against one another and unbalance even the most civilized social organization. A frightful cataclysm might follow. The history of the previous centuries furnished dire examples. Of all orgies, gold fever is the one that troubles brains most gravely and drives them to the worst follies.

Such were the scientist's reflections; his philanthropic soul revolted at the thought of so many imminent woes; and that is why he repeated, in a low voice: "That must not be."

But could he prevent it? Did a means exist of dissimulating the gold, of changing its composition or preventing its renown making the incalculable riches known?

Could he not replace the waters of Lake Biva? It now extended in a plain that would become a place of pilgrimage for all Japan. Consternated crowds would not fail to flock to contemplate the place where the venerated Fuji-Yama had previously risen.

They would come to mourn there...

Curiosity, for want of piety, would furnish its contingent of visitors; and those visitors would go to spread the news of the miracle everywhere: the transmutation of the waters of the lake into pure gold,

For a long time, Oronius meditated, anxious to spare humankind the evils by which it was menaced. His science found itself impotent for the first time; he could not imagine a practical means of making such a formidable quantity of gold disappear.

Te eruption and the earthquake that had be its consequence, could not fail to have been observed in Yokohama. Probably, missions must already have set forth to come and survey the effects and take account of the causes of the double cataclysm.

"Let destiny be accomplished," murmured Cyprienne's father. "The responsibility can't be incumbent on me. One man can't oppose the mysterious forces that regulate the course of humankind. But at least I can avoid the tomb that the *Snaky* has become being violated."

That part of the problem was less arduous to resolve. The Master had no difficulty in finding, among the resources at his disposal, the ingredients necessary for a coating of a leaden hue. By means of the thirteen automata he had the glittering block of the reptator entirely covered with it; and on the edge of the lake of gold there was no longer anything but a kind of dull rock. It affected the form, to be sure, of a divinized monster, but it could only be disdained by eyes dazzled by the nearby treasure.

Tranquilized, Oronius was then able to give the signal for the departure, and the Halcyon, a winged arrow, returned to its preferred element.

Two days later, Paris acclaimed the great scientist whom it had mourned so much. The resurrection of Oronius was one of those marvelous events that strike the imagination of a people. The twenty-first century owed so much to his inventions that he could not fail to be seen as a kind of demigod.

In the person of the Master people rediscovered a protector. His power, proven many a time, was such a guarantee of security in itself that it was sufficient to invoke it to feel reassured.

Oronius was not to disappoint that confidence. The role that he played in the Great Gold War, which burst forth in accordance with his previsions, further reinforced his prestige. Let us limit ourselves to recalling its conclusion: gold, having become too common, soon lost its commercial value and had to be replaced by Oronium, That rare and precious metal, the most recent chemical composition of the Master, arrived exactly at its hour; its opportune appearance permitted governments to exchange over time the metal money of stored gold with an equal quantity of coins struck in Oronium. Thus was solved one of the gravest crises that humankind had traversed.

Peace reigned again on Earth, and, with transactions facilitated and assured, work could go on, fruitful and remunerative, for the greater good of all.

In the vicinity of the gold-field of Japan, those who had nearly killed one another for its possession went away disappointed. The rarity of the metal had made its glory, especially in the previous century, when many competing nations had been bloodied for substituting paper for it; its abundance having caused its fall, and the Master's discovery having delivered the knock-out blow, nothing remained to it but its industrial uses.

The reign of Gold was over. The proud metal that, in the form of jewelry, had ornamented so many beauties, was no longer used for anything but fabricating the most vulgar and the most commonplace utensils.

What did the debasement of the ex-sovereign metal matter to the happy Cyprienne? Jean Chapuis put Oronium jewelry in her wedding-basket. Young brides, like all young women, have never detested new fashions—quite the contrary!

However, the engineer had wanted to offer his fiancée a souvenir made of the dethroned metal. That souvenir, perhaps slightly cumbersome, was nothing other than the Golden Serpent coated by Oronius and abandoned on the shore of Lake Biva.

A symbol of happiness of an unprecedented kind, difficult to wear around the neck like a little ingot or a four-leafed clover, that trophy now contained the remains of their implacable enemies. Jean had thought of transporting it in order to place it in the gardens of the new abode that Cyprienne's father was having built. Evocative of their terrible ordeals, the original hypogeum ought, in the mind of the young man, to render their present happiness even sweeter.

He had confided his plan to his future father-in-law; the latter had approved it, but for quite different reasons. Without admitting it, Oronius would not be sorry to have the golden monster that contained Yogha and Hantzen perpetually before his eyes and under his surveillance. He would feel more tranquil.

But the future father-in-law and son-in-law were to be disappointed.

When Jean Chapuis tried to execute his project, and charged Victor Laridon with supervising the transportation of the subterranean meteorite, troubling news reached him. The surroundings of Lake Biva, initially devastated by the battles that had taken place along its shores, were presently completely transformed by the installation of industrial townships and a large number of gold foundries, so the Parisian had not been able to rediscover the location of the *Snaky*. The engineers, entrepreneurs and workmen whom he had interrogated adroitly had been amazed by his questions, asked partly in Parisian argot, a language not widespread in Japan. He had been taken for a madman.

A block of rock, no matter how bizarre its form might be, is scarcely noticed. The *Snaky* only appeared to be a block of rock. It had therefore been destroyed by the builders of towns or the collectors of gold.

When it reached him, that news darkened Oronius' expression considerably. Jean Chapuis took it more lightly and attempted to joke about it.

"Evidently," he said, "given the dimensions of the object, it didn't seem to be destined to go astray so easily. Console yourself, Master; the incident is of no importance. It's hollow, so be it, but given its weight, who would have taken into his head or the trouble to open it? And then, what would have been the result? Nothing could have been discovered within but cadavers. After all, it was nothing but a coffin."

"Who knows?" said Oronius, dubiously. "My little Jean, I'd be more tranquil knowing that they were in my home. We'll hear more about that golden coffin and what it contains—I have a presentiment of that."

By an effort of will, he extracted himself from that obsession, and, sensing that his future son-in-law might judge such dreads unreasonable, he added: "You're right. I'm yielding to collectors' mania. Let's not give it any more thought. There ought only to be subjects of joy for you. You've had the pain, you ought to have the happiness. If no new event raises an obstacle to that, you can marry in a month, my children."

Approved by the joyous barking of Pipigg and Kukuss, he hugged Cyprienne and her fiancé in a single embrace.

They were not reassured; the scientist's words had left a doubt weighing upon them.

Would their marriage be celebrated?

www.ingramcontent.com/pod-product-compliance
Lightning Source LLC
La Vergne TN
LVHW041925090826
845145LV00015B/694

* 9 7 8 1 6 1 2 2 7 9 4 8 0 *